REMOTE ACCESS

An International Political Thriller

Barry Finlay

REMOTE ACCESS
An International Political Thriller

Published by Keep On Climbing Publishing

Copyright ©Barry Finlay 2018

(613) 240-6953
info@barry-finlay.com
www.barry-finlay.com

Cataloguing data available at Library and Archives Canada.

ISBN: 978-0-9959379-2-5

ACCLAIM FOR AWARD-WINNING AUTHOR BARRY FINLAY

A PERILOUS QUESTION

"Written with a compassionate, knowledgeable voice, the book is an excellent story of mystery and intrigue." — RECOMMENDED by the US Review

"A high octane thriller laced with insightful social commentary, A Perilous Question hits all the right notes and leaves you wanting for more. It is highly recommended." — Book Viral

THE VANISHING WIFE

"I had a hard time not just giving up the rest of my life and reading this in one sitting." — Vaughan Hopkins, Amazon reviewer

"I never knew where the plot was taking me, and I was swept along for this roller coaster read." — Kare, Amazon reviewer

KILIMANJARO AND BEYOND: A LIFE-CHANGING JOURNEY

"If you're the kind of person who can usually find any excuse to talk yourself out of a great idea this book is the inspiration you need to get out of your comfort zone and make things happen." — Helen Osler, Author, *Cameras of Kilimanjaro*, Australia

". . . at once so inspirational and courageous, so human and humane, and so deeply personal that the reader feels they are climbing right along with this small and highly determined group." — Reverend Dr. Linda De Coff, Author, *Bridge of the Gods*

I GUESS WE MISSED THE BOAT: A TRAVEL MEMOIR

"This is an exhilarating read." — Grady Harp, Amazon Hall of Fame reviewer

"*I Guess We Missed the Boat* is a fresh, ironic and jovial travel adventure novel in which each traveler can recognize himself or herself. It is a travel book that is amusing and practical at the same time." — Reader Views

ACKNOWLEDGEMENTS

First and foremost, I would like to thank all those who have supported me in my writing journey. To all the people who have read my books, thank you for choosing mine among the many options available. I'm humbled and very appreciative.

A book wouldn't get into the hands of the readers without a number of wonderful people being involved and this one is no different.

Thanks to Robin Chu for some insight into the concept of "Face" in the Chinese culture.

Super Editor Kip Kirby was amazing once again as she spent hours ensuring the manuscript was just right and it became a better book as a result. John Seal provided an extra set of eyes on the nearly finished manuscript. Thanks to you both.

I'm grateful to Magdalene Carson at New Leaf Publication Design for formatting the book, Tom Nickerson at ShokVox Productions for brainstorming ideas for the cover with me and Damonza for the final cover design.

Thank you to Wid Bastien and his team at Genius Media Inc. for promoting my thrillers.

Special thanks to my wife, Evelyn, who is my biggest fan and the only one to see multiple versions of the manuscript with all the warts. Her comments, ongoing encouragement and unwavering support are invaluable in bringing the book to fruition.

Finally, rest assured that *Remote Access* is a work of fiction. However, some of the references to hacking situations are real so any errors in fact or detail fall directly on me.

REMOTE ACCESS

CHAPTER 1

The man sat hunched over his desk in the cramped space, his attention consumed by the task in front of him. He was a solitary figure in a room devoid of most of the trappings one would normally expect in an apartment, except for some heavy drapes that ensured no natural light or prying eyes could peek in. Even though his workspace was on the 8th floor, he didn't need someone with a telescope or drone observing him. He considered himself to be a very careful man and the best at his job. That's what had kept him alive until now.

Only a flickering blue light illuminated the work Yang Lee was doing. There were no pictures on the cracked and peeling walls that silently begged for some plaster and a can of paint. There was nothing except a single chair and a long desk covered in computer monitors and wireless keyboards. The room hummed with the sound of massive capacity hard drives working on shelves beside the desk. Unlike many rooms in Shanghai, this one was cooled by adequate air conditioning, more to cool the machines than for anything else. An automatic spray air freshener worked to keep pollution from seeping into the room or at least did its best to mask it when it did. The man sat on the only chair, comforted by the knowledge that the computers were doing their job, gathering data from around the world.

This was his space, the one in which he felt the most complete. His living quarters were on the other side of the city in an affluent part of Shanghai, but he spent most of his time here. He would enjoy his penthouse when he no longer relished his work.

The dancing pixels on his computer monitors illuminated Lee's raven-colored hair and handsome long, narrow face. The blue light emitted from the screens accentuated his sunken cheeks, giving him the appearance of one of the characters in *The Blair Witch Project*.

But it wasn't the computer screens that occupied Lee's attention right now. His other skill had been requested, paid for and put into play. The lower half of his face was obscured by a surgical mask and his dark eyes focused on some fine dust in the bottom of the small white bowl in front of him. His lips pursed behind the mask and his eyes narrowed as he concentrated on his task. His gloved hand vigorously worked the pestle, ensuring there was nothing left of the powder he had started with except specks. The last thing he wanted to do was ingest or touch any of the dust particles he was creating. That was for someone else to do.

The powder was called aconite and it suited Lee's purposes very well. He had used it a few times because of its colorless and odorless characteristics. It was virtually untraceable.

After processing, it was often used in Chinese medicines.

Unprocessed, it was deadly.

He stopped working and leaned back in his chair to examine his handiwork. He pushed down the top of the glove on his left hand so he could see his watch.

It was time to package up his gift and present it to his next victim.

CHAPTER 2

Eric Hartman couldn't wait to fly back home tomorrow. Even though the flight was ridiculously long, clocking in at a travel time of around 17 hours from Shanghai to Washington, he was ready. He'd had enough of this godforsaken place. Really, who could live in a country that censors social media? No Facebook. No Twitter. Now he had just read that the government was confiscating millions of passports and severing mobile phone service! God, what a place.

He stepped out of the taxi into a wall of humidity. His white cotton shirt clung to him as if an octopus had attached its suction cups. His wife had admonished him many times about the gut that hung over his belt, and he had to admit he did carry an extra 100 pounds or so, but still . . . The few strands of hair he had lay unmoving, plastered to his head.

He started across Zhongshan Road when an older man riding an electric bicycle silently whizzed by, missing him by inches. That's another thing he hated about this place. The damn electric bikes were silent killers and they all seemed to be out to get him. Experience told him that when there was one, there were always more, and sure enough, this was no exception. The key was to keep walking once you stepped out onto the road. Stopping would only confuse the cyclists. He felt like a matador sidestepping a charging herd of enraged bulls. I can't blame them, he thought. *Who in their right mind would be walking around in this damn heat?*

Hartman somehow managed to reach the other side of the road unharmed, but wheezing from the exertion and the weather that was draped over him like the lead cloak the dental hygienist put on him when she was taking an X-ray. He'd requested the taxi driver drop him off two blocks from his destination, even though he knew he would be soaking wet by the time he got there. He had told his contact he wanted to meet in a public place, and this certainly qualified. There were thousands of people wandering along the waterfront tourist attraction and each wanted his space as well as their own. *How many people were there in Shanghai? 24 million?* That's about as many as there are in the entire freakin' state of Texas, he thought, as he tried to avoid people on the sidewalk. They were young and old, male and female, pointing, taking pictures, laughing . . . He bumped into a few unapologetically. They didn't seem to mind. He surmised they were used to being jostled.

This was the world-famous Bund, the waterfront along the Huangpu River. Hartman sidestepped a group of giggling young women overly made up for a night on the town. They accessorized their outfits with white pollution masks. Some of them would probably even be cute *if* you could see their damn faces, he thought. *Let me see. Today, I think I'll wear my sexy black lace bra and panty set with my pale blue pollution mask.* He smiled inwardly but he thought, it's no wonder they wear those things since the entire friggin' city is usually covered in smog so thick you could chew it.

He nearly walked over an amateur photographer taking pictures of the distinctive Oriental Pearl Radio and TV Tower. It was a landmark in Shanghai, and Hartman grudgingly admitted the tower dominating the skyline was pretty spectacular when it was lit up like this at night. The colonial architecture of the other buildings was also impressive when you could see it through the throngs of people.

Hartman focused on a bench straight ahead where a tall, impeccably dressed Chinese man sat. He observed the man wearing gray dress slacks with a white shirt open at the neck. In spite of the heat, he wore a navy sports jacket and a lightweight fedora in a striking shade of blue that matched his jacket perfectly. The man was in his mid-thirties and humorless, with a shadow in his face that made him downright scary. This was Hartman's contact. He had never learned the guy's full name. Supposedly it was Ted. *Yeah, right. Ted.* Like Hartman believed that the dude's name was "Ted" for a New York minute. But it didn't matter. The guy had bought him drinks in their previous meetings and promised to pay him a hefty sum for the photocopies he carried in the envelope under his arm. Hartman calculated that the amount he was being paid would buy him a boat that he never could have afforded otherwise. "Ted" could call himself Muhammad Ali for all Hartman cared.

Eric Hartman even knew what his new boat would be called. *E's Revenge*. Because that's what this was. He had toiled in the federal government for 29 years at a ridiculously low salary, accomplishing nothing. Sure, he'd been sent around the world to coordinate trade missions and preliminarily discuss trade deals, but in the overall scheme of things, he felt unappreciated and only minimally rewarded. He was an insignificant player in a cast of hundreds of thousands. He was cheated out of making real decisions that meant anything. His job merely required him to gather data and report. Now his asshole boss was helping the president of the United States put through new trade-restrictive legislation that, in his humble opinion, would seriously hurt the U.S. economy if it actually became law. He had fought against it but he might as well talk to the clouds. Nobody listened. This was something the new president wanted, and it was Hartman's job to help make it happen. All he would receive for his efforts was a pat on the back. Oh yes, and the pittance at year's end they laughingly referred to as a bonus. Hell, he'd be lucky to get a watch when he retired. *Well, to hell with them all.* Thanks to the well-dressed Chinaman sitting stoically 30 feet in front of him, *E's Revenge* would be sailing out of the showroom to a marina near Eric Hartman very soon.

Hartman greeted the guy and sat down beside him. "Hello, Ted," he growled. "Let's get this over with." Yang Lee hid his disdain. "Ah, Mr. Hartman, so good of you to be so punctual."

"Yeah, well, I had to fight my way through about a million of your countrymen to get here. What's in the bag?" He gestured to a brown paper bag sitting beside his contact. According to their unwritten agreement, his payment would be wired to a bank account number he had provided the man earlier. Hartman didn't expect the money to be in the bag. He couldn't lug around a wad of cash and he surely wouldn't be able to take it on the airplane.

"Something very special, my American friend. In the bag you will find a treat. I saw how much you liked our steamed dough buns, baozi, the last time we met so I bought some for you as a token of my appreciation. You have been a gentleman in our dealings and I wanted to wish you well." Lee swallowed hard to hide his disdain for this fat, arrogant pig of an American beside him.

Hartman slapped Lee on the back so hard it caused him to lurch forward. "Well, it's nice to work with someone so appreciative, Ted. I don't see that much where I'm from. Here's your envelope. Enjoy whatever it is you do with these things. Now let's see the money."

People drifted by on either side of the bench, some bumping into it and continuing on as if nothing had happened. An old woman in a flowered shirt that hung loose over blue slacks, her gray hair surrounded by a white visor, slowed and eyed a corner of the bench. Lee said something harshly to her in a language Hartman presumed to be Chinese and she grunted something back in a guttural tone, shuffling off into the sea of humanity. Lee silently took the envelope and checked its contents. Satisfied, he removed an electronic tablet from a brown leather case at his feet and with a press of the power button, it whirred into life. He handed the device to Hartman who did a quick search for his bank and entered his login information. A rush of excitement coursed through Hartman's body when the staggering balance in his bank account appeared on the screen. He nearly gasped.

He had set the account up specifically for this purpose, and no one other than him and the Chinaman knew about it. He would transfer the money to a different account as soon as he got home. Not even his wife would know of its existence. He looked up at Lee with a smile that creased his eyes as he handed the tablet back. A vision of his shiny new boat sailed through Hartman's thoughts.

Lee offered the paper bag to Hartman. The American opened the bag, checked inside and removed one of the Chinese delicacies. Some of the juicy pork landed on Hartman's shirt, leaving a large stain as he hungrily bit into the bun.

Hartman ignored the spill on his shirt, wiped his mouth with the back of his hand and shoved the rest of the bun into his mouth. He murmured through the mouthful of food as he rose from the bench, "Well, see you around, Teddy boy." He enunciated the name with dripping sarcasm. He added to himself, "Not," and wandered back into the crowd, dipping his hand into the bag for his second baozi. Bumping tourists and locals alike out of the way with extended elbows, he made his way to a taxi stand. He didn't care what anyone thought. He was King of the World right now. He brushed the crumbs from the last baozi off his mouth, screwed up the empty bag into a ball and tossed it in the general direction of a garbage can as he waited for a taxi to show up.

Six taxis drove past until one finally stopped. His head swam as he waited, and he swayed as he willed a driver to stop. *Must be the heat.* Waves of nausea shook his body. Half an hour had passed since Hartman finished the last of the baozis. The first cramp hit him in the cab on the way back to the hotel, quickly followed by another and yet another. At first he thought they would pass, but when they arrived at the hotel, Hartman clenched his stomach muscles as he leaned over and threw money at the driver. He barely made it to his room before the contents of his stomach emptied into the bathroom toilet bowl. His condition continued to worsen over the next several minutes. His sight blurred and as he peered through the slits of his eyes, everything took on a yellowish-green hue. He didn't have the strength to drag himself to the phone to call for help as creeping paralysis sapped any energy he might have had. His stomach burned with the intensity of hot coals. His mouth tingled and then became completely numb. It was only a matter of minutes before he lost consciousness.

Within three hours of meeting Yang Lee, Eric Hartman was dead.

The money disappeared from Hartman's account before Lee ever left the bench.

CHAPTER 3

"Would you mind pouring some coffee for me?" Linda Mitchell asked, her eyes twinkling as she held her cup in the air.

"Of course not." Marcie Kane picked up the carafe in her left hand and tilted it with her arm extended and her ring finger pointing outward. She had been presented with the ring a few months earlier and the ladies in the room had seen it many times. Still, the sun glistening through the open drapes reflected sparkles of white from the center and surface of the diamond. Marcie's friends shaded their eyes or opened their mouths in awe as if they were completely bedazzled by the brilliance of the stone on her hand.

The five friends sitting around the coffee table in Samantha Seaforth's sunroom in Gulfport, Florida shared a hearty laugh. The heat of the Florida sunshine had driven them into the house from the manicured back yard. There was some good-natured grumbling about leaving behind the intensely fragrant scent of the blooming pale-yellow gardenias in the garden. However, after hearing the forecast that morning, Samantha had anticipated the move so the women were welcomed into the house by streamers crisscrossing the ceiling. Balloons tied to the lamps wafted in the breeze as the women moved to the chairs.

A pile of discarded colored paper surrounded Marcie's chair. The gifts festively wrapped only moments before now sat on the table in front of her. Most of the presents were sentimental, a few were useful, and others more appropriately fell into the "gag" category. The party was a wonderful surprise for Marcie, but she was even happier to be surrounded by these wonderful women. They had just finished enjoying wine and playing party games, and were settling in for coffee and finger food. The last game left Marcie feeling clumsy, as she had been required to use oven mitts to open a box that had been sealed with layers of tape. After watching Marcie fumble with the tape for a few minutes amidst rounds of laughter, one of the women handed her a pair of scissors. Marcie attacked the tape and unwrapped a frame with a favorite picture of herself with her betrothed.

Linda volunteered with a grin, "Oh, by the way, you can keep the oven mitts."

Samantha Seaforth, or Sami as she was known to her friends, wandered into the room from the kitchen, carrying a tray of hors d' oeuvres. She had arranged the get together to celebrate Marcie's upcoming nuptials.

"So, tell us how does it really feel to have finally met your match?" Sami asked with a straight face. The room rang with more laughter. Every woman in the room knew of Marcie's penchant for finding trouble. No one was more aware of that fact than Sami, since Marcie had helped her husband save her from certain death two years earlier after being kidnapped by criminals. They also knew that Marcie was a strong-willed divorcee who had always said it would take a very special man to change her lifestyle. Marcie still referred to her basketball-playing ex-husband as He Who Shall Not Be Named, and she enjoyed being on her own after their divorce. The financial settlement had left Marcie with plenty of money, and frankly, her friends had all expected her to stay single. They were truly surprised that she had found someone able to convince Marcie to marry him.

Everyone waited for Marcie to answer Sami's question, but she was spared as a tune jangled from somewhere around their feet. Four women simultaneously reached for their purses, but it was Annie Logan who mumbled an apology and retrieved her phone to check the screen. She was the only one of the group who wasn't going to be in Marcie's wedding party. "Sorry," she said again in a barely audible whisper as she rose from the couch and hurried into the living room for some privacy.

It was as if the air had been sucked from the room. The sound of the ringing phone had broken the moment. Finally, Linda sighed knowingly, "Where would we be without cell phones? I'm not sure how we ever lived without them. They've certainly changed things, and not always for the better."

Carole Brouse agreed. She was a tall woman in jeans and a pink shirt. She had never met a conversation she didn't like—or have an opinion on. "Yes, I think we're all dumber because of it. Just watch people as they wander around bumping into things while they text. Or worse yet, crashing into some poor innocent victim on the highway. I love my phone like everyone else, but it's scary sometimes. Did you read about that situation a while back? I can't remember where it was, but a complete stranger was speaking through a child's baby monitor during the night! Can you imagine? I think the poor child was three years old and the man was saying things in a spooky voice, like 'Daddy's looking for you.' The kid could have nightmares forever because of that! I think the man could look through some kind of wireless night vision camera the parents had installed in the room, so he could see when one of them was coming in."

Claire Hanright was sitting on the couch beside Carole. She had to lean back to look at her friend. She was wide-eyed, coffee cup poised halfway to her lips. "Oh my God, Carole, are you serious? Can someone even *do* that? It's horrible! How did they find out about it?"

"As I recall, the parents got suspicious because their son kept saying in the mornings that someone had talked to him over the phone during the night. Then one night, the mom walked in as the voice came from the baby monitor. She freaked out and called the police."

The room was quiet as each of the women reflected on what they had just been told. Carole added, "It seems like hackers can do anything. They always seem to be one step ahead of the police. A follow-up article said that the baby monitor manufacturers are building more safeguards into the design now to make them more hacker-proof."

Marcie, who had been sitting quietly thumbing through a recipe book she had been given, looked up. "I read that you should cover the camera on your computer with a piece of paper or tape or something. I do it when I remember. Then I use Skype and forget to cover up the camera afterwards. Apparently, your camera can be turned on remotely and you won't even know." Then, hoping to lighten the mood, she added, "I don't need anyone checking out this gorgeous body without my say so!"

Sami leaned forward to pick up a mini crab cake garnished with a sliced cherry tomato and a fresh basil leaf. With a wink at the others, she said, "Well, we all know who's going to be checking out that gorgeous body *now*."

Carole innocently picked up on the theme and gazed at Marcie, her eyelids bouncing up and down." Just make sure you buy a hacker-proof baby monitor when the time comes."

Marcie smiled distractedly as Annie walked from the living room into the kitchen with one hand pressing the phone to her ear and the other holding her glass. She had noticed Annie drinking her wine faster and refilling her glass far more often than anyone else. "I'm too old for that," Marcie said over her shoulder as she stood up and started after Annie. "Those days are long gone."

Carole called after her, "Well, at least you aren't too old to practice."

Marcie Kane was a beautiful African American woman. Her almond-shaped eyes, shoulder-length hair and full lips caused men to cast second glances everywhere she went. At 45, she enjoyed working out to maintain her trim figure. She had been born in North Carolina and moved to Florida to follow her first husband, but when their marriage disintegrated, Marcie had become extremely independent and studied for a career as a youth development professional. Her life had been busy and exciting since her divorce, but now she was looking forward to an even more exciting future with her soon-to-be husband Nathan.

Annie had finished her phone call and was refilling her wine glass with her back turned when Marcie approached.

"Is everything all right, Annie?"

Annie visibly jumped, startled by the sound of Marcie's voice, and quickly whirled around. "Yes, everything's fine." She picked up her glass and immediately changed the subject. "What were you ladies talking about after I so rudely walked out?" Her words ran together and "so" became "sho."

"Oh, nothing much. Just idle chit chat. Coming back to join us?"

Annie said nothing but picked up her glass and followed Marcie back into the room. As they sat down, Carole was the first to speak as usual. "So, where were we in our discussion about you having a baby?"

Marcie groaned. "Time to change the subject, ladies."

The conversation was punctuated by laughing fits as it circled around various topics for another hour or so until the women decided it was time to leave. Carole poked Marcie gently on her way to the front door and with an exaggerated wink said, "Make sure you make good use of one of my gifts. You know which one." Marcie grimaced and with a laugh, pushed Carole towards the door.

Annie was finishing yet another glass of wine and was the last to get up. Of all the women in the room, Marcie knew her least, but the fact that Annie seemed to be having difficulty walking and was slurring her words concerned her. Annie lived just down the block from Sami, so she decided to hang back and walk with her. Marcie followed Annie out the door and said to Sami as she was leaving, "I'll be right back."

Annie was about 50, but she carried herself like someone older. Marcie thought they were about the same height, but Annie's slightly rounded shoulders combined with a losing battle against middle age weight gain made her appear shorter. Although she was expensively dressed, her face was flushed and strands of her dark hair hung limply.

Marcie walked up to Annie and said, "Mind if I walk with you? I wanted to thank you so much for coming today."

"No, of course not. It was a lovely party. I really appreciate the invitation from Sami. You have some very nice friends, Marcie." Annie's words were still slurred.

It was noticeably light jacket weather now. Clouds had shoved their way into the area while they had been in the house. Annie rubbed her arms as she walked. "I'm sorry that I had to run out to answer the phone. It was my husband calling from Washington."

Marcie said, "Is he in Washington on a business trip?"

Annie's lips curled up in a half-hearted smile. "I suppose you could say that. He's there all the time. He works there now. I hardly ever get to see him anymore."

Marcie thought she may have just been given a reason for the extra glasses of wine Annie had consumed. "Couldn't you move to Washington, at least for the time being? Or maybe go up for some long weekends? It's none of my business, but it does seem like a good solution."

Annie stopped at a white gate in front of a modest stucco bunga-low surrounded by a lawn in need of mowing. The long grass barely registered as Marcie's eye was caught by splashes of color from a stunning rose garden running along the front and down the side of the house. Annie followed Marcie's gaze and shrugged sadly. "No, I don't think that's a possibility. He works pretty much night and day in his new position. He has a pretty high-powered job there." She shifted her dejected eyes towards Marcie. "We decided it was best if I just stay here and look after the house. This is where we plan to retire, eventually. Listen, it's really been a pleasure meeting you today, Marcie. I'm so happy Sami invited me. Thanks for walking home with me. Maybe we can go for coffee sometime. I could use another friend."

Marcie never missed a beat. "I'd be happy to, Annie. That would be fun! It was nice to meet you. Let's get together soon."

Annie smiled briefly. "Do you want to come in?"

"No thanks, I should be getting home. Nathan will be wondering where I am." She paused and laughed, "Or maybe he knows exactly where I am. I can't help but notice your garden, though. It's gorgeous."

Annie agreed without emotion. "It's a hobby. It keeps me out of trouble."

They exchanged phone numbers and Marcie raised her hand to wave, but Annie had already turned toward her front door. Marcie walked quickly back to Sami's house.

Sami met Marcie at the front door. "Would you like more coffee or another glass of wine?"

"No thanks, I should be getting back," Marcie replied thoughtfully. "I'll just pack up the gifts and go." She playfully chastised Sami for putting the surprise gathering together before thanking her profusely with a hug. They collected the treasures she had been given, and walked out to Marcie's BMW Cabriolet convertible together. As she took some of the gifts from Sami and deposited them in the back seat, Marcie said, "Annie seems kind of sad. Did you think that? She certainly had more than her share to drink."

"Yes, I did notice. I don't really know her that well. They moved onto the street a few months ago, but I never see her with anyone so I thought it might be nice to invite her. She's very pleasant, but she does seem to enjoy her wine a little more than most."

"She said her husband works in Washington all the time, so she never gets to see him. That might make some people happy, but it might cause others to drink."

Sami laughed. "Yes, I suppose it could. Especially when the job is in high-powered politics." She glanced over at Marcie. "You don't know who her husband is, do you?"

"Should I?"

"Well, a lot of people know who he is," Sami smiled. "Does the name Craig Logan mean anything to you?"

Marcie thought for a minute, but couldn't come up with anything. She flipped her palms upwards and shrugged. "Nope, I don't think so."

"Marcie, Craig Logan is the Chief of Staff for the President of the United States. He's probably the second most powerful man in Washington."

CHAPTER 4

Nathan Harris met Marcie at the door of the condo with a bemused look on his face and relieved her of the packages she was carrying. "Wow, have you been shopping?" He leaned forward to give her a kiss, but his lips met air as she brushed by him.

Marcie somehow managed to contain a blossoming smile and forced a scowl to her face. "I was at a party, as I suspect you know very well. It was a lot of fun, but first I have a question for you, Nathan Harris. Did you know about this party?"

Nathan turned with a show of putting the packages on the couch while hiding a grin. He was handsome in a rugged way, and his eyes crinkled when he smiled. The dark t-shirt he wore stretched over his broad shoulders. He had, in fact, played an integral role in planning the deception needed to get Marcie to the party, but he didn't want her to know. When one of the bags fell over, spilling its contents, he seized on the opportunity. He held a plastic object in his hand by a certain extended part of its anatomy. "What is *that*?"

"Well, all I really need to say is that it's one of Carole's contributions to the gifts. You know her mind dwells in or near the gutter most of the time. My guess is that you're supposed to hang your keys on it or something, but I don't think it comes with instructions. All I know is that I don't want to die and have someone find *that* in my underwear drawer when they're going through my belongings. The rest of the gifts are more reasonable."

Nathan shook his head and tossed the anatomically correct, but highly embellished likeness of Michelangelo's David back on the couch. "It could pass for a Roman fertility god." Nathan looked at Marcie, raising his eyebrows up and down repeatedly. "We could keep it next to the bed."

Marcie smiled. "There will be no fertility gods in this house. It will probably find its rightful place in the garbage, but I'm pretty sure I asked you a question. Nice attempt at deflecting. Do you have an answer, sir?"

Nathan threw his arms around her, pulled her close and whispered in her ear. "I'm afraid I have to take the Fifth Amendment to protect myself against self-incrimination." He kissed her emphatically.

Marcie playfully pushed Nathan away. "You're sounding too much like an FBI agent. I don't know what I've gotten myself into."

Nathan chuckled. He *was* a former FBI agent. He had met Marcie in Africa, of all places, when she had stumbled across a human trafficking ring during a visit to a dormitory she had helped fund. Nathan had been assigned to work the case. When they crossed paths, he knew immediately that meeting Marcie Kane was the best thing that had ever happened to him. Until that moment, his job had been his world, but that all changed the minute Marcie entered his life. He quickly discovered that he loved this woman who seemed to be so strong on the outside, yet who was fragile and gentle and maybe just a little reckless, all at the same time. She needed him, and he needed her. In coming together with Marcie, Nathan discovered there was more to life than work.

It had taken Nathan a lot of persuading to convince Marcie that he should give up his job with the FBI and move to Florida to be with her. She had to be sure he really wanted to move, and that he would be leaving his job for the right reasons. Eventually, he broke down her defenses and moved to St. Petersburg to be with her. There, Nathan started a private investigation firm and loved the fact he could pick and choose which assignments he took. His first was back with the FBI in Tampa, working on a project that the division had recently focused on—the protection of children from on-line exploitation and abuse. It was satisfying work, and he quickly discovered there was more than enough to keep him busy.

Nathan learned that many letters of the alphabet were involved in obtaining a private investigator license. Unlike television P.I.'s, who can do pretty much anything, actual private investigators are governed by a state handbook and restricted as to what they can do. In Florida, a Class "C" license is required to work for someone else, and to manage his own firm, Nathan had to apply for a Class "MA" (agency manager) license. To carry a firearm, he needed a Class "G" statewide firearms license. His years of working with the FBI gave him the qualifications to obtain any necessary licenses easily, but he still joked with Marcie that maybe he didn't have everything he needed because there were still a few unused letters of the alphabet.

There were certain restrictions involved. For example, private investigators were not allowed to check on a person's bank account, obtain cellular phone information without authorization, or make an arrest other than that allowed for any other citizen. Frustrating as it could be at times, Nathan understood the reasoning. Being a professional FBI consultant gave him more leverage to undertake certain activities that wouldn't normally be allowed.

Marcie had gone into the bathroom and when she returned, she began to remove the rest of her bridal shower gifts from the bags and tidy up the mess on the couch. She set the David figurine on the counter facing the wall. She thought to herself that she would probably "accidentally" knock it into the garbage the next day. The smell of freshly brewed coffee hovered in the air. Marcie picked up Nathan's empty cup and poured some for both of them. She mixed French vanilla creamer into hers, a guilty pleasure she loved. She set the cups on the table and sat down.

Nathan sat as well. "So you had a good time?"

"It was a lot of fun. It's a great way for me to start my two weeks' vacation, that's for sure. Sami's so nice to put it all together, and the women are great. There was only one you haven't met. They're all in my wedding party except her. Her name is Annie Logan, and she happens to be the wife of the president's chief of staff, Craig Logan. I guess she had a few too many glasses of wine, so I walked her home. She said her husband is in Washington all the time, so she never sees him. But he called her about halfway through the party."

"Well, if I was the wife of the chief of staff working for the current president, I'd be drinking, too."

Marcie ignored the comment. "Sami told me something interesting, Nathan. She said the chief of staff is the second most powerful man in Washington. Do you think that's true?"

Nathan shrugged. "I think it depends on the government in power. The president can decide who to listen to, and I gather our current man in office puts a lot of faith in Logan. A lot seems to depend on how the president likes to run things. To me, though, there are others who are pretty powerful, too. Look at the chair of the Federal Reserve. He can have an effect on the economy by raising or lowering interest rates." He paused in thought. "Then there's the Speaker of the House who can shut down the government. The senate majority leader has the power to start and stop legislation. Take your pick. But the chief of staff always has the president's ear, and that seems to mean a lot to this president. As I understand it, normally no one can get time with the president without going through the chief of staff. Although according to the media, President Hughes seems to have a bunch of people that just walk in and out. That must make Logan's job even more challenging."

Their knees touched and the familiar electrical shocks traced a path through Marcie's body. They switched topics to the party until they finished their coffee. She was thoughtful as she picked up the cups and put them in the dishwasher. Turning around, she said, "It sounds like Logan's kind of a gatekeeper. I wonder what he did to get that job. It seems to be all consuming. I would consider it to be punishment if I had to do it."

"I think it probably *is* all consuming." Nathan wiped the table top with a damp cloth. "I guess it depends on how much you're driven by power and influence—and some people are. The job might appeal to someone who thinks they can change the world. Or maybe he sees himself as a king maker. I'm not sure. All I know is, I sure wouldn't want to deal with it myself. Just working for a government agency with all its bureaucracy was enough."

Marcie stifled a yawn. "Man, I hate politics," but she continued. "Isn't President Hughes running everything himself, anyway, by signing all those executive orders? How does he get to do that? I thought we elected a *bunch* of people to run the country!"

Nathan laughed as he tossed the cloth in to the sink and leaned against the counter with his arms crossed. "That *bunch of people* you refer to is called Congress, but as I understand it, the Constitution grants the position of president the power to sign executive orders that only require judicial review. At least there's that control. It's a pretty powerful tool presidents have, and they've all used it when they think they can't get anything done any other way. Now listen. I'm about to make an executive decision. I think we should forget about politics for the time being. How about you?" He grabbed Marcie's hand playfully and guided her down the hall to the bedroom, flicking off the light switch on the way.

Marcie teasingly chastised Nathan as she leaned against him. "You know I could've dressed nicer if I'd known there was going to be a party."

Nathan smiled inwardly. He had never known his future wife to dress in any way other than stylish. On her most relaxed casual days, Marcie dressed better than most people when they wore their best. He pulled her close, lifted up her tucked-in white shirt, and slid his hand down into the back of her designer jeans. He whispered, "Maybe I can make it up to you. I don't match up to the magnificent David statue you brought home, but I'm still not bad."

Marcie brushed his lips with hers, reached down and replied, "It's okay, I'm not planning on hanging my keys on it, anyway."

CHAPTER 5

Craig Logan, the president's chief of staff, stared out the window of the White House, only steps from the Oval Office and the most powerful man in the free world. Now in his fifties, a softness had formed around his middle after years of sitting at a desk and too many fried meals. His mostly bald scalp was highlighted by a fringe of hair that traversed from ear to ear. He wore the business suit and narrow dark tie that had become his daily costume. His black shoes shone with a mirror-like finish.

His corner office offered a great view of Washington. It was long and narrow featuring a fireplace at one end. Logan anticipated entertaining guests in front of a crackling fire in the winter while sitting in one of the four leather chairs surrounding a low oak table. A large matching oak desk was the centerpiece of the room and a credenza, apparently cut from the same tree, sat off to the side. This is where Logan constructed President Jeffrey Hughes's daily agenda and determined who would meet with him and who would not have that privilege, although a certain few had an open invitation. A leather sofa sat along the side of the room.

The walls were adorned with pictures in frames manufactured in Vienna and inspired by Austrian architecture. Past presidents, including Abraham Lincoln, were featured in some. Others had photos of Logan with President Hughes at various milestone events since his inauguration.

His eyes lingered on a picture of his wife, Annie, that sat on his desk. He missed her dearly. She was so far away in Florida and, among other things, he missed coming home to her after work to talk about his day and hear about hers. The decision to have her stay in Florida, at least until he figured out this job, was a mutual one, but he was finding it difficult. A few slurred late-night phone calls told him that she was finding it difficult as well. She was trying to escape from her loneliness by drinking too much. A sudden heaviness fell over him as he thought about it. It was something he needed to help her with, but the geographical distance between them made that challenging as well. He had been relieved when she told him she had been invited to a party. Maybe she would make some friends. Nevertheless, he decided he would consider bringing her to Washington to be with him at the first opportunity.

Logan tried to push the thought from his mind so he could concentrate on his work. There was nothing he could do about it right now. His eyes shifted to a framed item that he often used as a distraction. It was an excerpt from a *New York Times* article written and published on Sunday, June 5, 1910. The article referred to the secretary to the president, a position that had evolved to become the chief of staff. The excerpt spoke volumes in Logan's opinion.

"If he has a world of tact, or a skin like that of a rhinoceros, or can lie like a thief and can grin with good nature when he is found out in his lies, then he will probably enjoy the job."

Logan considered himself to be more ethical than the quote suggested one needed to be, but he conceded that politics, by its very nature, could lead someone in his position in a different direction. He had found out lately that the president could be difficult as well. He hid a smile behind his hand as he reread the quote. *No one ever lies in politics anyway. It's called spin.*

He often swirled his chair around and stared out the window to contemplate the president's agenda in his mind's eye, but as birds soared on the air currents high above Washington until they disappeared into the brightness of the sun, he thought about the circumstances that had brought him here. Craig Logan knew the president very well. They had gone to school together in Texas. Then they had both studied law at Yale. They had gone their separate ways to start their respective careers, but they had stayed in touch. Logan was enjoying his position as a partner in a corporate law firm and couldn't believe it when his friend had been tapped on the shoulder to become the leader of the party. Hughes had no previous political experience. Running on a platform of creating jobs offered nothing new, so Logan thought that his friend's run would be short-lived. Besides, his opponent was an established political veteran. But it was the way his platform was presented and the fact that Americans were crying out for change that seemed to resonate with the public when it came time to vote, and suddenly Craig Logan's good friend Jeffrey Hughes sat in the Oval Office.

Not long after, Logan's phone rang with a proposal from the president to be his chief of staff. Logan thought about it and talked to Annie. His salary would drop from roughly one million dollars per year to $175,000, but he and Annie had put away enough to live well for their lifetime and they had a modest house in Gulfport, Florida. He thought it would be an interesting challenge and that he would meet potential clients in his new job. He took a leave of absence from his firm with the understanding that he would return in four years or eight years, depending upon his boss' term, with new well-heeled clients in tow. He could go back to earning a seven-figure salary, and he and Annie could eventually retire and live however and wherever they wanted.

The birds were gone now, and the people bustling to and fro through his field of vision barely registered as the president's agenda clicked into place, as it always did, like the final pieces of a puzzle. He turned around in his chair and entered the items into his computer. He struck the final key stroke with a flourish, like a conductor emphasizing the top note of the crescendo of one of Richard Wagner's pieces.

A tap on his door startled him.

"Now there's a man who's obviously satisfied with his work. Or so bored he has to amuse himself somehow."

Logan's face colored as he looked up to see a laughing Jim Prentice, the chair of the Subcommittee on International Trade and Global Competitiveness. Logan had been expecting Prentice, but had put the visit out of his mind while he concentrated on his work. One item in Logan's job description required that he negotiate with Congress and others to implement the president's agenda. Hughes had only been in office a few weeks but already he was shaking things up. Jim Prentice's subcommittee was one of 20 standing committees covering public policy on trade, and he was someone Logan would have to mollify when he found out what the president was about to do.

"Is this a good time, Craig?"

Logan got up and greeted Prentice with a handshake. "Sure, come on in, Jim. I just finished the president's agenda. I think that gesture you saw was more one of relief that it's done for another day. Have a seat." He gestured to one of the four leather chairs around the table.

"I won't keep you long, Craig, but I wanted to talk about the Chinese tariffs report we did. Before we get into that, though, I just wanted to say what a terrible thing it was about Eric Hartman. I understand he was in China when it happened."

"Yes, it was a shock. He was in Shanghai doing a bit of research for me. He had finished his work and was preparing to come home. He even had his suitcase packed. He just dropped dead from a heart attack in his hotel room."

A questioning look flashed across Prentice's face. "Well, it's a shame. And so far from home. That must be even more difficult for his wife."

"Yes, we're making the arrangements to bring back the body. We'll help her as much as we can."

Then the reason for Prentice's face change became apparent. "Look, Craig, I know you don't have a lot of time, so I'll get right to the point. Since President Hughes asked my subcommittee for a report on Chinese imports and tariffs, which we've provided, I've heard nothing but rumors. I've heard that the president's senior advisers are putting together an executive order to force crippling tariffs on China. That makes me wonder what Hartman was doing in China exactly. If it had something to do with trade, shouldn't I have been informed since I'm the subcommittee chair?"

A breath of air escaped Logan's lips. He realized he needed to tread delicately. "Hughes ordered me to keep it quiet, Jim. The Chinese didn't know the real reason for Hartman's visit. Obviously, you had a right to know. The Ways and Means Committee doesn't even know. I almost picked up the phone to tell you as a friend, but if the president ever found out, my ass would be in a sling. It was a risk I couldn't take. I'm sure you can understand the position I was in."

"Well, that's just great. Craig, I know you're new at this, but you do know that by definition, it's the Ways and Means Committee's job to find the *ways and means* to increase revenue, right? That means they're responsible for proposing increased tariffs." Prentice's face took on a crimson hue and his voice rose with every syllable. "I may be jumping to conclusions here, but I hope the president isn't going to increase tariffs on China without going through the proper channels. He needs to listen to people who've been doing this for years and are familiar with how our relationship with China works. Any increase to tariffs should be initiated by Congress and studied by the Ways and Means Committee with input from my subcommittee. Am I guessing wrong about what's going on here?"

"You know, Jim, I've known Hughes a long time and I've always found him to be fair." Logan chuckled, hoping to lighten the tenseness of the mood in the room. "I honestly don't think he thought he would ever get this job. Now that he has it, he's going to be unconventional, to say the least. He thinks that's what got him to where he is. He strongly believes that's what the voters want and what the American public wants. He's feeling his way, of course, but I believe it's going to be his way or the highway."

Prentice looked at Logan and narrowed his eyes. "When the president asked for a report on imports, Craig, I knew something was coming but I thought he would ask for advice as well. I've heard nothing and neither have my colleagues. As I said, I just hear rumors and I don't like what I'm hearing. He's surrounded by neophytes when it comes to foreign relations, yourself included if you don't mind me saying so. I have a lot of concerns as an economist. If this is about electronics, the Chinese are going to retaliate. It's a multibillion dollar industry for them. Most of the smart phones, TVs, appliances and music players in the U.S. come from there. Hell, just about everything comes from there! It seems to me, we'd be better off negotiating a trade deal with the Chinese and keeping them fully in the loop. There are going to be problems on two fronts from what I can see. The Chinese are going to be furious if we impose a tariff, let alone doing it surreptitiously, and the increased cost of their products will put them completely out of reach for American consumers."

Logan took a deep breath. "I'm not saying that President Hughes is doing anything, Jim, but he promised jobs and he thinks the way to do that is to stop people from buying items made abroad so that they'll buy locally-made products."

"Oh, come on, Craig, you aren't that naive! I'm not sure tariffs have EVER worked. They're just another form of tax. A lot of respected economists have argued—and I happen to fall into this camp as well—that when tariffs are imposed, domestic suppliers increase their own costs to match the imports. So in the end, consumers can't afford them no matter where they're made! It accomplishes nothing. And don't forget there are a lot of American companies manufacturing goods in China. What happens when they have to increase the cost of their products coming into the U.S. as a result? That's not going to help anyone."

"Well, *if* the president does something, and I am saying if, we should be better off financially since there will be increased revenue on the electronics imported from China."

Prentice leaned forward in his chair and raised his hands to emphasize his position. His voice raised slightly again. "That's the point, Craig. There probably won't be any increased revenue because people will just stop buying. They won't have a choice."

Logan shrugged. He thought Prentice made good points, but his job was to stay silent on what was happening and help the president with his agenda. After all, that is what Hughes wanted. He leaned towards Prentice with his elbows on his knees and spread his hands. "Theoretically speaking, I think people will buy electronics, and especially phones, no matter how much they cost. Look, I know you should be involved in anything that's going on related to trade and so should the Ways and Means Committee, but the president has a bee in his bonnet about China. He wants to be seen to be standing up to them and he wants to help the U.S. economy at the same time. If tariffs are an option, why not look at it?"

Prentice shrugged, apparently resigned to the situation, but willing to give it one last shot. "Well, it may be an option, but he needs to talk to the experts he has at his disposal about tariffs, not just sign an executive order based on what his inexperienced advisors say. I think the 'why not' is that the Chinese are going to be royally pissed and ultimately so will the American people. I'm not in love with the idea and I just wanted to plead my case to someone. The voters decided this guy should be our leader, so we have to support his thinking, at least for now. I don't suppose there would be any point in talking to him about it before he does something hasty."

Logan leaned back in his chair. "There is one thing for certain. The president wants to do things differently because he feels the old ways haven't worked. So, whether you and I agree or disagree on what he's doing, he's determined to do things his way and let the chips fall where they may, even if he might be a one-term president. No, I don't think there's any point in talking to him. He frankly doesn't want to hear it. I can't either confirm or deny your suppositions and I can't even suggest to him that your sub-committee would recommend against increased tariffs without negotiating with the Chinese, because he would assume I told you something I shouldn't have."

Prentice solemnly pursed his lips and got up to leave. He shook his head. "I think we've got a big problem, Craig, but thanks for your time. I appreciate it. We'll see where it goes. If the president ever decides to use the experience of people besides his so-called senior advisers, my colleagues and I would be more than happy to offer advice. We're a phone call away. Anyway, it is too bad about Hartman. I didn't mean to go off like that. We just never know, do we? I know he was overweight and he seemed to be a hyper guy, but still . . . You never like to see that happen, especially at that age. My condolences go out to his family."

"Thanks, Jim. I'll be attending the funeral, so I'll pass along your condolences."

As Prentice started towards the door, Logan walked beside him with his hand on his shoulder. "We're in for some interesting times ahead, Jim."

As the door closed, Logan walked back and sat down in his chair facing the window with his hands clasped behind his head. His eyes were unfocused as he stared out through the glass, but his mind swirled. *One thing's for certain. It's going to be a hell of a surprise to the Chinese.*

CHAPTER 6

In Shanghai, Ji Cheung threw a document on the desk, causing loose papers to flutter to the floor. Red blotches emerged from his collar until his face became fully flushed. "How can the Americans be so arrogant?"

His visitor understood it to be a rhetorical question and remained silent.

The document lay among papers that had managed to cling to his desk under the onslaught. A few distinguishing features separated it from the others. All the documents that were not the subject of Cheung's wrath were written in Chinese, each character representing one syllable of the spoken language. But the document that had Cheung so upset had the words "SECRET" and "LIMDIS" in large bold English lettering splashed diagonally across the page. The Great Seal of the United States was in the corner of the document. "Secret" in the American federal government lexicon meant that if someone who wasn't supposed to see it, like Cheung, got their hands on the document, there could be serious damage to national security. "LIMDIS" was intended to further limit distribution. Written in a smaller font horizontally across the face of the front page beneath the classification designations, also in English, were the words, "DRAFT CHINESE TARIFF EXECUTIVE ORDER."

Cheung and his visitor were meeting in a quiet boardroom in one of the many lavish government buildings the Chinese constructed a few years earlier in the hopes of attracting investment. This crescent-shaped building featured enormous columns rising three-quarters of the way up the front. A reflecting pool dissected the promenade.

They sat across from each other at the long, narrow boardroom table. The Chinese flag hung from a pole at the head of the table. Cheung had chosen this room for the meeting because it was regularly swept for listening devices and was out of earshot of anyone who might have an inappropriate interest in the subject to be discussed.

Ji Cheung was the 4th Vice Premier of the People's Republic of China. He was in his sixties and wore a gray suit with a white shirt and red tie, a symbol of good luck. He had a full head of black hair without a single strand of gray. He had just returned from a meeting of the Politburo where the presidential draft executive order had been the topic of discussion. He was the oldest of the Politburo members and his way of dealing with things was at least a decade behind. While his colleagues favored diplomacy, he was anything but moderate. His favored approach to encouraging people to come around to his way of thinking was a good beating.

Since he was the fourth-ranked vice premier, industry fell under his purview and he had just been instructed to deal with this important item. It rankled him that the first three vice premiers were responsible for agriculture, finance and land. Even sport ranked ahead of trade.

However, the subject had caught the attention of the Politburo and they wanted it dealt with expeditiously and quietly. They had assigned the responsibility to Cheung who assumed that meant it should be handled in his usual way. He turned to his visitor and peered over his thick glasses. He spoke in English.

"Are you absolutely sure the Americans do not know that we have seen this document?"

Yang Lee's face betrayed no emotion. "I can assure you that the source of the document cannot tell anyone that he passed it to us. You are the only ones that know we have it."

Cheung held up his hand. His English pronunciation was close to perfect. "I don't want to know what that means, Lee, but I will take your word for it. You are here because we must prevent this order from being signed. It was a long discussion at the Politburo. Some thought the new U.S. president just likes to float outrageous ideas and use them as bargaining chips to negotiate a better deal. But since you produced the actual document, they concluded the president is serious this time. The Americans did not have the good grace to negotiate with us. Their arrogance is beyond belief. This focuses on electronics. Last year alone we exported almost $400 billion more than we imported from the U.S. and electronics was the number one export. Our economy has grown about 10 percent a year for the last 30 years, but it has started to slow recently. We cannot let that continue to happen."

Lee's eyes glazed over and he stifled a yawn. Statistics didn't interest him, and most economics certainly didn't impress him. The only economics that did impress him was the dollar value that would be attached to his assignment. It didn't matter to him what the background of a job entailed. Once assigned, he would do the job as requested. He could still hear Cheung prattling on about the impact this would have on the Chinese economy.

His mind wandered.

He had come across the secret American plans when he was sitting in his room mining data from their supposedly-secure network. He thought about how simple it had been, even though the Americans were improving their security techniques. He had started digging into their network by sending an email that he knew would bounce back. Once it did, he had the computer's address. He then inserted some malware into the system, creating an opening that bypassed the normal security systems. The bot or piece of stand-alone self-propagating software immediately started collecting keystroke information and gathering up passwords from the Washington computers and sending them back to his computer through various servers around the world. It took time, but it eventually led to his discovery.

The malware cleverly erased its own trail so that it would never be discovered. The motto that kept him anonymous was "Get In, Get Out." He was paid handsomely by the Chinese government and others to poke into their adversaries' networks and keep officials apprised of anything he discovered. He was quite sure the Americans were playing the exact same high-stakes game in the Chinese network.

The words "Shanghai trip" had jumped out at Lee one day when he had been going through some of the data from the system belonging to the administrative assistant to the chief of staff. Upon further digging, he discovered that an employee by the name of Eric Hartman would soon be in Shanghai to discuss trade initiatives. When he hacked into Hartman's emails, however, two things became suddenly apparent: Hartman was a very disgruntled employee who thought the U.S. Government didn't utilize his talents and abilities, and there was a secret initiative to impose heavy tariffs on Chinese imports into the U.S.

Lee took it further than he normally would because he knew there would be a very lucrative payday at the end. Normally, he would have just reported his findings to key officials within the Chinese government, but this time he took it upon himself to investigate the tariff proposal referred to in the emails. After seeing Hartman's picture on the government website and checking his itinerary, Lee tracked him down at his hotel in Shanghai and caught up to him at the bar. Lee could be charming when he had to be. He started up a conversation, plied Hartman with Tsingtao beer and Chinese food and discovered that the American had a liking for the delicacy, baozi. After getting together over a few nights, buying Hartman many drinks while assessing his character, Lee made his offer: 250,000 U.S dollars in exchange for a copy of the documentation with the tariff plans. Simple as that. Lee could tell that his new friend was practically salivating to get his hands on the money in exchange for the documentation. Hartman did one better. He produced a copy of the actual draft executive order.

Lee knew higher-ups in the American government would be furious if they found out Hartman was carrying the draft document around in his briefcase. It became apparent that Hartman could not be trusted to keep his mouth shut, so Lee had prepared the poisoned baozi. He had seen the overweight American devour baozi, and he knew the entire delicacy would be eaten before Hartman ever got in the cab. The result would be suffocation or a heart attack that would never be investigated. Poor Hartman would not live to use the money he thought he was getting.

Lee realized the lecture about the economy was winding down, so he tuned in again. He knew Cheung was old school in his tactics. Where others would use diplomatic means to an end, Cheung was more likely to take a harsher direct approach. That's why Lee had chosen him to see the document.

Cheung was saying, "One thing you can't do is hack into the American system to stop what they're doing. Because of the clumsiness of the Russians with their hacking, the Americans are much more careful and aware now. I'm sure they have installed additional layers of firewalls and set traps for anyone trying to hack in."

Lee was insulted. "Please," he said, waving a hand dismissively. "You are not dealing with an amateur. I'm better than that, I can assure you. The Russians were careless. They left footprints everywhere. I would be out before anyone ever knew I was in."

"Well, I'm telling you not to do it. If you got caught, we would disavow ever knowing you or we would turn you over to the Americans. Find another way. We want this stopped quietly. Report back to me the minute you have something. Do you understand? For that, we will pay you this amount." He wrote a dollar figure on a sheet of paper and tossed it across the desk.

Once again, Lee's head moved, almost imperceptibly, and his eyes leveled on those of the vice premier. It was almost like a ventriloquist operated his mouth as he murmured, "Do not worry. I'll take care of it."

As the hacker got up to leave, it occurred to Cheung that even though the man had a brilliant mind and particular skills, there was something about Lee that just wasn't quite right.

‹ ‹ ‹ › › ›

Yang Lee stepped out of the government building into a sauna. A light rain fell and steam from the sidewalk swirled around his legs as he strode along the concrete. Rain drops plopped into the pool, the resulting rings disrupting its reflective qualities. He thought of Hartman's complaints about the number of people in Shanghai. It was amazing how almost all 24 million people in the city could simply disappear when it rained. As he crossed through a park, some diehard Tai Chi Chuan practitioners, oblivious to the dampening weather, practiced their slow-motion sets with a graceful fluidity. As he passed unseen in front of the focused group, he wondered why they were out in the rain and he scowled as he held his briefcase over his head. The drops that dodged the briefcase drew patterns on his pale blue suit.

He had not been totally honest with the vice premier, but he had discovered long ago that dishonesty paid better. His next stop was at Hu Electronics, one of the largest manufacturers of electronic products in all of China. Four nights ago, he had delivered the paper to

Bai Hu, the chairman of the company. Lee enjoyed a private joke at Hu's expense every time he thought of the man's name. The Mandarin language is extremely difficult with 21 consonants, 16 vowels and four tones that change the meanings of a word. Depending on how the chairman's first name "Bai" was pronounced in Mandarin and the tone used, it meant "pure" or "white." With the appropriate combination of tone and pronunciation, Hu's last name meant "barbarian." Lee thought that the man could definitely qualify as a pure barbarian at times. He hadn't amassed such a fortune to become one of the wealthiest men in China by being weak.

He had done work for Hu Electronics before. One of Lee's biggest accomplishments to date was to hack into a Canadian electronics manufacturer, one of Hu's competitors, and for several years he had stolen their passwords and their plans for software designs, which ultimately gave Hu Electronics a competitive edge. It enabled the Chinese company to forge ahead in the field. Bai Hu never forgot Lee's contribution to their growing business, and hired him whenever he needed some work done requiring Lee's talents.

Lee knew Hu would be disturbed by the American plans to implement tariffs on Chinese electronics and the impact the action would have on his company. He expected the electronics giant would offer a large sum of money to take care of the situation. By preventing the U.S. government's executive order from being signed, or at least by making it public, he would be paid handsomely by the Chinese government *and* by Hu Electronics. It was the perfect crime with a perfect payoff.

His suit bore dark splotches of water as he completed the short 10-minute walk and arrived at the glass high-rise where Hu Electronics' head office was located. He easily jogged up the stairs to the entrance, brushing off the drops that hadn't soaked in as he shouldered through the large revolving door. Nodding to the security guard at the front desk, he strode confidently across the marble floor and entered the elevator that would take him directly to the 51st floor. The building's atrium rapidly diminished in size as the elevator whooshed him to his destination. He was mesmerized by the hips of a lithe young secretary swaying under her body-hugging one-piece dress as she escorted him into the chairman's office. Lee could smell the cigar smoke wafting through the air before he entered the office.

He had read in a magazine that 53% of Chinese men smoke, and this man loved his cigars.

The man sitting behind the ornate desk was in his eighties, but looked closer to sixty. Bai Hu was a diminutive man with a round head and glasses. When Hu stood to greet him, Lee thought his dress pants were probably worth fifteen hundred dollars and his open neck white shirt was made of silk. Lee studied his friends as well as he did his enemies and he knew Hu had earned his degree in England and that he had two vices. Hu was very popular at one of the local casinos and liked to spend hours at a time trying his luck. The second vice was that Hu had a fondness for good cigars.

Lee bowed before his elder and the old man gestured for him to take a seat. Lee waited for Hu to speak out of deference to the older man. He knew from past experience that this conversation would be short.

Hu spoke in rapid-fire perfect English, his strong voice belying his years. "Well, Mr. Lee, you have uncovered quite a secret that the Americans wish to bestow upon us."

"I thought you might be interested in their intentions. I fear the impact this could have on your company."

Hu drew deeply on the cigar and blew a cloud of smoke that wafted towards Lee. "And rightly so, Mr. Lee. Rightly so. What can you do to prevent this from happening?"

The strong smell of cigar assaulted Lee's senses and he drew shorter breaths to limit his intake of the unstoppable cloud drifting towards him. He spoke as he exhaled." I would be happy to look into the matter for you. As I understand it, this order is being fine-tuned and will be signed soon. It's something the American president wants, and he seems to be a man who gets what he wants without too much trouble. There don't seem to be a lot of people in their government willing to stand up to him, at least at this early stage in his mandate. I can see if I can arrange some obstacles to change their plans."

"I strongly suggest you do that, Mr. Lee. In fact, I strongly suggest that you take whatever means necessary to stop this absurd plan from happening. The economic results would be catastrophic for us here in China and especially for my company. I assure you that if this madness is stopped, you will never have to work again as long

as you live. I will pay you enough that you will be able to retire anywhere you want. I think there would be many Americans who would
be happy to see this man go before he gets too much further into his
presidency. Take care of it, Mr. Lee."

Lee got up to leave. As he exited the door to the office, Hu's voice
behind him left no doubt as to his intention.

"Do what you have to do, Mr. Lee, and do it quickly."

CHAPTER 7

Yang Lee was a brilliant man. When his mother had him tested at the age of nine, his IQ results came in at over 160. It was a blessing and a curse. He was always placed in grades above where he should have been, and the other kids singled him out because he was different. It didn't help that the teachers always asked him for the answer to a question ahead of the others, because he would always know it. He was teased unmercifully by his classmates. His high IQ already came with the burden of a lack of social skills, and his inability to relate to the other kids made him act out. It got him in trouble at school on multiple occasions, and it only worsened as time went on.

At the age of 16 he left China to study chemical engineering at Cambridge University in Cambridgeshire, about 40 miles north of London. His parents happily shipped him off, hoping that being away from home would help him develop some social skills. But it became even worse. He hunkered down and spent all his time learning about how chemicals react with each other and with other agents. He learned which ones were lethal and how to handle them. He had no time for the other students in his class, who were all older. He had no time for anybody. He preferred his own company. The only women he associated with were paid for. He even fantasized about injecting chemicals into the air conditioning system at the university and killing every single one of his classmates.

He did enjoy studying and once he had his degree, he had no intention of joining the nine-to-five zombies staring straight ahead on the subway day after day. He thought about what he should do next. He was fascinated by the computer modeling he did as part of his chemistry studies. He loved computer games because he could play them alone or take on other faceless, nameless people around the world without actually interacting with them. He had an innate understanding of the inner workings of the machines. His next move was an easy choice. He decided to spend the next few years earning another degree, this time in computer science.

Finally, as he neared the end of his computer studies, it became apparent he had to make some money. The fund his parents had set aside for his education had run out, so it was time to find some kind of employment. He could have done many things, such as medical research, working in pharmaceuticals or becoming a software developer in the space program. With his intelligence and knowledge, his options were limitless. But they all required that he interact with people. Instead, he had chosen to put his skills to use in two other areas where he could work on his own and earn more money than he could ever spend.

He followed his first career path, which earned him respect in a certain milieu and copious amounts of money, where a deadly approach was required. His unique knowledge of lethal chemicals was available for hire to anyone requiring that particular skill set and with the money to pay for it. When someone made the decision usually reserved for God to end another person's life, he was able to do so without leaving a trace. He enjoyed this work. The autopsy report would always determine that the unfortunate victim died of cardiac arrest.

But he was also in demand for his second set of skills, computer hacking. He thought of himself as the best. He had yet to meet his match. The knowledge and understanding of computers he had developed allowed him to sell his services to the highest bidder. The Internet and social media made it possible to assassinate someone's character from thousands of miles away with a few keystrokes. There was no emotion for how his actions would affect the people he was hacking. It was simply a job that paid unbelievably well.

The way Yang Lee understood it, his two employers had pretty much given him the entire spectrum to work with. The Chinese government wanted him to disrupt the executive order quietly while Bai Hu at Hu Electronics didn't care what he did as long as the tariff changes never saw the light of day. Either way, he was about to become a very rich man. It was what the American president liked to refer to as a win-win situation.

Back in his room, Lee sat on the chair in front of his computer. This wouldn't be an easy mission. For one thing, it was time sensitive. The president could sign his executive order at any time and then it would go into full force immediately. And Yang Lee's reputation might be over as well. Saving face was a strong motivational factor in Chinese culture and the response to winning and losing was often emotional and dramatic. Lee knew that if he couldn't accomplish his mission, not only would he lose face but neither Ji Cheung nor Bai Hu would take kindly to failure. Lee knew the impact if that happened could be both disastrous and potentially life-threatening for him.

Hartman had told him in one of their meetings that the president's senior advisers were "tweaking" the document and it might be two weeks before it was officially signed. A few things bothered Lee about that. Was Hartman close enough to President Hughes to know what he was talking about or was he just pumping himself up to look important? The president had proven himself to be volatile and unpredictable. He was known for saying one thing but doing something else entirely without any warning. Would he just one day grow impatient with the delay and tell his senior advisers that he had seen enough and decide to sign the executive order into effect? Lee knew he had to move quickly.

He needed to do some research before he could settle on a strategy and in China that was not always easy. Cheung didn't want him hacking into the American government computers any more than he already had. He shook his head and thought how they changed their minds depending on whatever was most convenient at the time. The Americans thought their leader was unpredictable, but he had nothing on this government. Nevertheless, he would heed Cheung's advice—for now. He would search for another approach and if that didn't work, *he* and only he would decide how the situation should be handled next.

He knew that the people he worked for would try to do their own spying on what he was doing. He laughed inwardly, knowing that their attempts would fail miserably because of the series of firewalls he had installed. His system had all the attributes of an automated version of one of China's underground bunkers.

The light shining from the lamp over the sparse working area on Lee's desk reflected shadow puppets on the walls as his hands hovered over the keyboard. He wasn't entirely sure yet how he would approach the assignment, but he knew he could do it. He could do anything. He jostled the mouse and Google jumped onto the screen. He decided the U.S. Government's directory was the first place to go and he jotted down names of President Hughes's senior advisers—people who might be associated with the executive order. His fingers danced over the keyboard and among the names he found were Craig Logan, who was the chief of staff he'd come across before and Jim Prentice, who was the chair of something called the Subcommittee on International Trade and Global Competitiveness. He found the late Eric Hartman's name in the government directory. He became momentarily sidetracked and a quick search of the obituaries told him that the man had "died suddenly" and that he would be greatly missed by family members. In lieu of flowers, donations were to be made to the American Heart Association. The corners of Lee's mouth lifted in a grim smile.

He studied the organizational flow chart to get a feel of where the power resided in Washington. He knew that power shifted, depending on the man in office, so he researched the archives of newspapers like the *Washington Post* and the *New York Times*, among others, to see what they had to say. He was particularly interested in op-ed pieces in the newspapers that were generally published opposite the editorial pages. These helped him understand the opinions of the so-called experts. He scanned network television footage archives to fill in some blanks. Before he knew it, he had scribbled on a few pages in his notepad.

Lee glanced at his watch. It surprised him to see that he had been working for nearly five hours. He scanned his lined pad and sifted through his notes. The sound of his pen tapping on the edge of the desk filled the room as he flipped the pages with his left hand. His handwriting was barely legible even to him as he had scrawled the words quickly. There were two items highlighted. Beside the name of President Hughes, he had double-underlined a single word in bold strokes. *Polarizing.* It confirmed in his own mind that the U.S. was pretty much evenly divided on the merits of the president. There were people who thought he would be the best president ever and there were those who were fighting him every step of the way. This could be valuable information for later.

There was also a bold circle around a single name. Lee was surprised to see that his pen had nearly perforated the paper when he erratically circled the name of the person over and over while he concentrated on the computer screen in front of him. The name he had so enthusiastically circled appeared to Lee to be the power broker in Washington, chief of staff Craig Logan.

His next step was social media.

Most people in China were severely restricted from using social networks except for the one developed by the People's Republic. Even the Chinese version of Skype was coded in such a way that it would intercept and record conversations when key banned words were used. Lee didn't have to worry about any of that. Because of his status with the Chinese government, he had full access to the same social media used by westerners.

Lee searched for Craig Logan on Facebook but couldn't find an account. Logan was smart to stay off Facebook since he was a public figure, thought Lee. He went back to Google and entered the name "Logan" as his search criteria. Many people with that first and last name came up, but there were far too many to analyze. He reduced the search criteria. By backtracking and searching for "Craig Logan family," he was still rewarded with over 11 million results in .58 seconds. But this time, the third item referred to chief of staff Craig Logan's wife, Annie Logan, who maintained the family home in Gulfport, Florida. A family photo showed her smiling back at the photographer. Now I'm getting somewhere, he thought.

He scoured the Internet, scraping together every piece of information he could find about Annie Logan. By looking at photos she had posted on Twitter and Instagram, he was able to piece together a list of family members. He knew the type of car she drove, where she liked to go on holidays and the names of people who followed and liked her activities on social media. He built a profile on Annie Logan that just might come in handy.

Once again, he opened Facebook but this time he entered the name Annie Logan. Surprisingly, only three Annie Logans popped up. One was a young blond woman of about 19 with her head thrown back and her ample breasts straining at her tight sweater. Another was about 14, smiling widely with a mouth full of braces. The third was a woman who appeared to be in her fifties posing in a rose garden. It was Annie Logan, wife of Craig Logan, who appeared on the screen. When he clicked on her profile picture, he discovered that the security setting was "friends only" so there wasn't much information readily available. He noted she had joined some community groups that were open to the public. Most were related to the growth and cultivation of roses.

Lee scanned the community groups and it astonished him to see that some had over a million members. Even though he had been to the West many times and was very familiar with London, it was still incredible to someone living in cramped space in a city of 24 million where the simple act of breathing was nearly impossible, that there would be such interest in growing flowers in a personal area. He decided there were too many groups to scan through. He had to find one with fewer members. He scrolled until he found one called "Roses and the People Who Love Them." It had about 1,100 members so it was more manageable. He began clicking the names of the members in the group and checking their friend lists. He looked for one in particular. There. Someone named Robert Short from Vancouver, Canada had Annie Logan on his list. They had been friends for 3 weeks. Too recent. He continued his search.

It took another 45 minutes until Lee found one that might work. Someone named Mateo Gomez from Columbia had friended Annie Logan two years before. Lee saw no evidence of any recent contact between the two on Facebook. He checked the other social media accounts on Twitter, Instagram, LinkedIn and Pinterest. They had very similar interests about roses. Gomez's Facebook account security settings were open to the public, so anyone anywhere could see his posts. He posted gorgeous photos of roses and jokes about flowers on his various accounts. Lee doubted that Annie would remember becoming friends with Gomez. However, she had decided to become friends with him once, so she probably would be willing to do so again.

He had decided on an initial plan of action to stop the President of the United States from signing the executive order. He would try a subtle approach first. If that didn't work, he would resort to a sledge hammer. This could be fun, too.

Yang Lee found a stock photo of a handsome Latino man and created a fake profile, complete with pictures of roses, with most of

Gomez' information. He built a piece of software that would serve his purpose. He joined several flower-growing groups and a couple of groups dedicated to the joys of roses, and he was ready to go.

He was about to become Annie Logan's newest friend, Mateo Gomez.

CHAPTER 8

Annie Logan was suffering through another lonely evening. She thought the only things preventing her from going crazy were social media and a bottle of wine. The wine usually came first, starting before dinner. The brand didn't matter and neither did she care if it was red or white. She laughed to herself. *I don't discriminate.*

She had sent Craig a text earlier to see if he could chat online but he texted back that he had a late-night meeting scheduled with the president. *The President.* That guy was a piece of work, and yet Craig had more time for him than he did for her. She had showered and changed into her most comfortable evening attire—men's boxers and a t-shirt with no bra. For most people, it would be a treat to be casually dressed and relaxing with a glass of wine before bed. But for Annie, it had become a nightly ritual with no end in sight. And for her, it usually became much more than one glass. She walked from the bedroom to her office carrying her wine glass and feeling fuzzy-headed. She decided it was too early to retire for the evening. Besides, she didn't like trying to sleep when the room spun, although it had been happening more and more recently.

She had converted a spare bedroom in their home in Gulfport, Florida into an office even though she didn't need one. She didn't work. It was a place to put the computer and "office" seemed to be a good name for it. It had a small computer desk and shelving with a variety of books on roses. A sofa bed sat against the wall and a blind on the window closed off the outside world. An exercise mat lay on the floor beside the computer desk and a large blue exercise ball had rolled to the doorway. I guess I could call it an exercise room, she thought, as she nudged the ball back towards the wall. She sat down in front of the computer and frowned as the ball rolled back to its spot blocking the doorway.

She sipped her wine with one hand and pressed the space bar on the keyboard with the other, awakening the computer from its slumber. The glare from the screen reflected off the glass as she set it precariously close to the edge of the desk. She stared at the screen. A number of tabs were open across the top, and she clicked on the one for Facebook. Craig had told her many times to stay off social media but what was she supposed to do in the evenings? She squinted as she noticed she had a new friend request. She already had over 600 from around the world on her friend list. Her list had grown since she had started joining groups related to roses. She could probably actually claim to know only about 50 people on the list, and most of those she had just met casually somewhere. But it was fun having friends, even if they were friends she'd never met. They all shared a passion for flowers and a special love for roses, which gave them a common interest to connect. Social media was a way for her to pass the time while her husband helped to save the world in Washington.

Most of her online friends were women, although there were a few men in the group. Judging by the profile pic, the new request came from a particularly handsome gentleman in Columbia by the name of Mateo Gomez. The name was vaguely familiar but the face wasn't, and she would have remembered that face. His picture displayed a dark-haired man with a touch of bearded growth. His eyes were like dark pools. He stood in a garden and wore an open neck untucked white shirt over dark jeans. His large forearms were crossed in a confident manner. His profile revealed he was single, an author from Bogota, that his interests included martial arts and fast cars, and that he relaxed in his free time growing roses. Nothing like a strong man who likes flowers, she thought. Annie scanned the groups he belonged to and noted he had joined many of the same ones as her. Now here was someone she could enjoy being online friends with. She caught herself smiling and saying, "hmm" out loud as heat rushed through her face when she accepted his friend request.

She continued scanning his profile before moving on to view the day's posts from her other Facebook friends. She couldn't possibly view them all, but she liked some and shared others. She clicked on her Twitter account and scanned the news feed. Because she had so many followers on Twitter, mostly with the same interests as her, the feed raced by like a fishing line unraveling as a great white shark hooked on the other end fought for freedom. She thought she should post something. *What am I going to post? That I'm sitting here alone in a pair of men's underwear drinking myself into oblivion and following strange but incredibly handsome men on Facebook?*

She sipped her wine as she clicked through her other social media accounts. She was just about to shut down her computer for the night when she picked up her glass to drain the contents. A wet ring glistened back at her from the surface of the desk where she had spilled some of the liquid. She got up, punted the ball out of the way and walked to the bathroom for a tissue to clean up the spill. She repeated the process with the ball when she returned, but when she sat down, a notification blinked at her letting her know that a private message waited.

She wiped up the ring and clicked on the message. To her surprise, it was Mr. Handsome from Bogota, Columbia. The message read, "I see you are a lover of roses as I am. Kindly accept this photo of a beautiful bouquet as a thank you for accepting my friend request."

Her breath caught in her throat. *Wow, I wonder if all the men in Columbia are like this.* The picture was a thumbnail so small she could barely see it. She re-read the message and her eyes narrowed as she tried to make out the details in the photo, her face inches from the screen. It was impossible. *The wine probably isn't helping my vision.* She wanted to see the image before she responded to her new friend, Mateo. *Mateo.* She whispered it out loud. The name rolled off her tongue. She knew she was being ridiculous, like some impressionable teenager with raging hormones, and yet the wine she had consumed nudged her to reply.

She wanted to see the photo. It looked beautiful. So her next action was the same thing that millions of other people around the world do every hour of every day. But for Annie, it would turn out to be the biggest mistake of her life.

She clicked on the picture.

‹ ‹ ‹ › ›

The photo sprang to full size. It was a close-up of an elegant bouquet of delicate red roses so vivid that the aroma nearly lifted into the air from the computer screen. She quickly sent a message back to Mateo, thanking him for the lovely picture and for the online friendship. She hurried to the kitchen to refill her glass only to discover the bottle was empty. She inserted a corkscrew into the cork of another bottle and with some difficulty, pried it out. *I really must start buying screw tops or a get a better wine opener.* Annie carried the bottle and her glass back to the office. The ball was wedged between the sofa bed and the wall.

This time, she was surprised to see an email from Mateo. She remembered that her email address was on her Facebook account, so it was easy enough to find. She read the email with anticipation. The message described how he had been working on a desktop photo book of roses and he was asking acquaintances on social media to provide comments. He had taken the liberty to attach an extract in a zipped file and he wondered if she would mind providing some input. She was momentarily concerned about how quickly he had drafted the email. But then she realized that he probably had a standard request ready that he sent out to all his acquaintances. Besides, Annie could feel excitement welling up inside her.

Someone is actually looking for my input. This could be fun! Finally I can do something useful.

She took a deep gulp from her glass and clicked on the attachment, but it didn't open as expected. She tried again, unsuccessfully. She deleted the file and sent a message to Mateo, telling him that something went wrong with the attachment. She filled in time by clicking on various sites. She opened her online banking information and entered her password, so she could check her bank balances. She scrolled through her photos. She couldn't think of anything more to do. Still she waited, finished her glass of wine and hoped there would be a response from Mateo, but nothing was forthcoming. Her computer system sat idle. After two minutes, swirling bands of color erupted on the screen, indicating that the screen saver had taken over. Nothing else was happening. Or so it seemed. The computer's tiny lights and steady hum betrayed nothing of what was going on inside.

‹ ‹ › ›

The photo had been the first step. Embedded inside the image was a tiny piece of coding that gathered and sent back basic data about Annie's computer, including the operating system and type of browser she used, along with details about her security software. The photo was meant to look innocent enough that a user would open it without hesitation and by opening it, Annie did as most people would do. The email attachment was a customized piece of spyware that was activated the second Annie clicked on it. That action opened a door to her computer. It was a RAT—a remote administration tool that allowed its developer to grab control of her computer. Every keystroke, password, piece of banking information, browsing activity and email became available to the person on the other end who had installed the code.

Annie sat for a few minutes, hoping her new friend Mateo would respond, but her eyes closed and her chin drifted to her chest. Her head lolled to one side, startling her awake. She was too tired now to bother with the bottle and glass or to even shut off the computer. They clinked together as her legs jostled the desk when she got up to go to bed. She knew she would flop into bed the minute she got close. The farthest thing from her mind now was her computer.

The indicator light remained unlit, so she had no way of knowing that the camera had been turned on.

The real Mateo Gomez in Columbia was oblivious to everything that had transpired.

Yang Lee sat in his room in Shanghai 8,000 miles away staring at the screen as Annie disappeared from view.

CHAPTER 9

Marcie Kane finished her toast and headed out the door of the condo she and Nathan Harris shared. Nathan worked at cleaning up the breakfast dishes. They had talked about their respective days ahead over a leisurely breakfast, and now Marcie was in danger of being late for her dentist appointment. She recalled that the gas tank was getting low the last time she drove her car, but she hoped she had enough to reach her dentist's office.

Striding with long purposeful steps through the parking garage at the condo, she carried her travel mug in one hand while brushing the crumbs off her white blouse and blue skirt. She wondered why anyone in their right mind would book a dentist appointment during their vacation, but she had been really busy with her job at a state-run agency for children and families. She had decided to take some of her annual vacation to make final preparations for the wedding and the rest for their honeymoon. It just seemed like a convenient time to get the appointment over with. Besides, the weather channel had announced a high of 82 degrees Fahrenheit and sunny skies, the kind of day that deserved a top-down ride in her convertible. The dentist appointment gave her an excuse to go somewhere. She loved this time of day before it became too hot and the wind became a factor.

The car was new. Her previous car had been involved in an accident, and so she had decided to upgrade. She set her coffee cup in the center console cup holder and settled into the buttery soft leather seats. The new car smell washed over her like a cloud. A satisfying throaty sound erupted from the exhaust when she turned the key, but a tiny, urgently flashing gas pump indicator on the dash reminded her that the car's tank needed a fill-up. She pressed the button to fold the top down and turned on the radio. A newscaster talked about protesters around the U.S. who were upset at the president for something they considered to be his latest transgression. Ugh. She was a skeptic when it came to politics. She voted for the candidate she thought would do the best job at the time. She sure hadn't voted for this guy. How could anyone think this man was the best person for running the country?!

Her world view was pretty simple. There wouldn't be half as many wars if it weren't for politicians. People just want to be happy and have enough money to live comfortably and feed their families. That's it. Anything more is a bonus. Then the politicians get involved and decide they should interfere in someone else's business and all hell breaks loose. And then they have the unmitigated gall to say they are speaking on behalf of the people. The thought of it tended to raise Marcie's blood pressure so she tried to let others tie themselves in knots over it. Nathan was more political and followed it all much more closely than she did. He often said it was like watching a train wreck. It was difficult to avert his eyes.

Marcie sighed. That discussion with Nathan the night before about the chief of staff and executive orders had been interesting but I'm just depressing myself, she thought. The car's top clicked into place as she reached into her purse to find her phone. She thumbed through her music and hit the button for the new Rolling Stones blues album. The phone connected itself to the car and the sound of "Just Your Fool" blared from the eight speakers as she wheeled the Melbourne Red vehicle up the ramp and out into the brilliant sunshine.

Marcie decided she probably shouldn't let the gas gauge get any lower, so she headed for an Exxon station on 4th Street North. Nathan often chided her for running close to the bottom of the tank. She hadn't actually ever run out of gas completely yet, but it was probably inevitable if she kept up the practice.

There were three other cars at the four-pump station and she glided up to the empty one. Recently, she had started to pay cash for her gas as her credit card had been compromised at another station. This was one of the few remaining stations trusting people enough to pay *after* they filled their tank. She stared at the numbers rolling by on the pump until they stopped with a thud, indicating the tank was full. She set the nozzle back on its holder, put the gas cap back on and walked into the station to complete the transaction.

Two of the people who had been outside filling their tanks stood in line behind a woman whom she immediately recognized as Annie Logan. Annie was engaged in an animated conversation with the attendant behind the counter. Her voice rose, and the young man's face took on a red hue. He couldn't have been more than 18 years old, and he was obviously uncomfortable with the confrontation taking place in front of everyone in the station. Marcie leaned over so she could hear what was happening.

Annie's voice quivered, "But how can my card be declined? I used this one yesterday and it worked perfectly. It must be your machine."

The young man shrugged and showed her the cash register slip. He looked like he wanted to get rid of this woman as quickly as possible. Alternatively, if a hole were to open up, he would be quite happy to disappear into it. Marcie couldn't see what was printed on the slip, but it was apparently proof that the card had definitely been declined.

The older man and middle-aged woman behind Annie were becoming increasingly impatient. The man turned around and mumbled to Marcie that he felt sorry for Annie, but she had spent enough time arguing. He was sure the card wasn't going to suddenly become valid. Meanwhile, the woman was less sympathetic as she huffed loudly in a thick French Canadian accent to no one in particular, "I guess *some* people have nothing to do all day, but I have a tee time in a few minutes. "Then to Annie, "C'mon, lady, allons-y. Let's go!"

Marcie moved to the front of the line and said to the young man behind the counter, "Maybe I can help. How much is the bill?"

Annie registered her surprise to see Marcie, but she said, "It's $35. For some reason, this station's machine isn't accepting my credit card. I don't think I should have to pay if it's their fault. And even if I thought I should pay, I just used all my cash at the grocery store. I always use my credit card for gas."

Marcie smelled alcohol on Annie's breath and wondered if it was from this morning or last night. She smiled, trying to defuse the tension. "Let me just take care of it for you. It's no problem at all, and these other people can go about their day. You can pay me back when I see you next time." She handed over enough cash to the young attendant to settle both bills, and the two of them went back outside.

Annie was crestfallen. "I'm so embarrassed, Marcie. Thank you for saving me in there. I don't know what happened, but it must be their machines that are the problem. I know my credit card is fine! I always use my credit card. I use the points they give you for car washes. Maybe I should file a complaint."

"We all like to collect those points," Marcie agreed. "But before you file a complaint, Annie, you might want to check with your bank or go online if that's how you do your banking, just to double-check. I had a credit card number stolen at a gas station, and the people that scammed it used it to make purchases. I only found out when the bank called me. It's odd that your bank hasn't called you if there's really a problem, though, but maybe they just couldn't reach you. Anyway, I would just make certain it's the gas station's fault before filing a complaint. Hey, I have to go. I hope you get everything straightened out without too much problem! Take care, Annie."

"Thanks again, Marcie. I'll give you a call so we can meet, and I'll pay you back then."

Marcie drove off without giving it a second thought.

‹ ‹ › ›

As she drove home, Annie replayed in her head what had just taken place. She had been unable to sleep the night before. She had read somewhere that alcohol helps you fall asleep but that it can disrupt sleep later in the night, and sure enough, that's the kind of sleep she often had. Last night was no different. She immediately fell asleep, but got up to go to the bathroom around 3 a.m. and she tossed and turned for several hours after that. She had finally decided to get up, and since it was such a nice day, she had gone out for some groceries and gas.

She was too embarrassed to tell Marcie the whole truth. Annie had first discovered her credit cards didn't work when she went to the grocery store. She had high-limit and low-limit cards from the same financial institution. She used the low-limit card for online purchases and the high-limit card for everything else. She had offered both in the store only to find they were declined. She'd assumed it was the fault of the machines at the grocery store and after paying for her groceries with her remaining cash, she had driven to the gas station to buy gas. She was shocked when her cards still didn't work, especially since she had just used all her cash for groceries.

An increasing queasiness overtook her as she drove home. Frantic thoughts ricocheted in her head. *What's going on? My cards were fine yesterday! There must be some mistake. I shouldn't have been so nasty to that poor young man at the gas station. And that woman getting so agitated behind me . . .* The sound of her phone ringing startled her. Wow, am I ever on edge, she thought. A glance at the screen told her the call was from her bank. *Thank goodness. Just the people I want to talk to.*

It was Leslie Warren from the credit department. Leslie had a perky voice perfectly suited for the job of imparting bad news. Annie conjured up an image of a cute young blonde who wakes up in a good mood every day and in some misguided way, thinks she can brighten everybody else's. She was undoubtedly very efficient and in Annie's mind, completely annoying. Leslie came to the point immediately. Annie heard her say that the bank's system had discovered unusually large purchases on Annie's credit cards. As a service to the customer, the bank had put a temporary hold on the cards until they could speak with her directly.

Annie felt sick. She finally managed to squeak out, "What kind of purchases?" She pulled the car into a convenience store parking lot and let it idle while perky Leslie Warren continued her end of the conversation.

"That's what's so unusual, Ms. Logan. There was an online purchase of furniture in London, England on one card and within a few minutes, there was a purchase of $1,000 worth of electronics, again online, on the other credit card in Singapore. If you made the purchases, we'll unlock the hold that's on the cards, but if you didn't make the purchases, we'll cancel these cards and issue new ones for you. We can have them to you in just a few days. In the meantime, we'll investigate to try to determine where your card was compromised."

Annie's head throbbed like someone was pounding on it from the inside with a hammer. "I can't believe this. I certainly did not make these purchases. But couldn't you have called me earlier? I've been trying to use the cards and was embarrassed when they didn't work."

Leslie's chipper voice seemed to go up an octave as if another jolt of caffeine had just hijacked her nervous system. "I understand, Ms.

Logan, but after we monitored the two purchases, we have reached out to you as quickly as we can."

"Okay, thank you for advising me. I appreciate it."

Leslie chirped, "Have a nice day," as Annie ended the call.

CHAPTER 10

Annie kept herself busy later that day cleaning the house and mowing the small lawn. She had enjoyed a glass of wine with her strawberry and arugula salad lunch. After puttering in her rose garden, she sat in the back yard with an afternoon pitcher of margaritas. She tilted her head toward the untouched canvas of blue sky overhead and savored the scent of the freshly mowed grass. Returning inside, she decided to put off a shower until bedtime, so she put on a ratty white t-shirt and a pair of snug worn blue shorts. She poured the remains of the margarita mixture into her glass and glanced at the mirror on her way out of the bedroom. Her lips tightened in a grimace as she lifted her shirt and noticed some extra flesh around the top of the shorts and the indentations where the white trim bit into her legs. The shorts had been flattering when she bought them, but time and maybe the alcohol had added some extra pounds. Normally she wouldn't be caught dead in the outfit with the extra pounds in plain view, but it really didn't matter now. No one would be seeing her.

She prepared a 30-minute chicken breast and peaches dish from a *Country Living* magazine recipe and ate it in front of the evening news on television with a glass of wine before retreating to her computer room. The exercise ball blocked her way into the office again. She thought of deflating the annoying thing once and for all, but the sight of herself in the mirror was an unwelcome reality check. With a sigh, she set her glass on the desk, leaned onto the ball and struggled through some sit-ups. She didn't keep count, but she estimated it was probably close to 10. She hadn't realized until she nearly lost her balance on the ball how much she'd had to drink. The exercise wasn't enough to work up a sweat, but it was enough to make her thirsty, so she wedged the ball between the sofa bed and the wall and went back to the desk where she lifted her glass.

The computer was still on from the night before, but since it was not in use, it had gone into sleep mode and random patterns lazily drifted around the screen. She sat and looked at the framed adage hanging on the wall directly above the desk. It was something Craig had used as a reminder when he worked at the law firm. It was one of those anonymous words-to-live by quotations that bore the inscription, "Don't Be Too Busy Being a Human Doing to Be a Human Being." She sighed and rolled her eyes. *He should have taken that with him. Maybe it would remind him to think more about his lonely wife than his job in Washington.*

Annie jiggled the mouse and the computer came to life. She called up her browser and clicked on her online bank tab. It accepted her password and she examined her accounts. She confirmed that her credit cards had indeed been canceled. She shook her head with discouragement and leaned back in her chair. The new cards wouldn't be available to her until she received and activated them with a call to the financial institution. She logged out of her bank accounts and checked Facebook, which was also still open from the previous night, to see if there were any new messages. There was nothing new since the night before, so she looked at the news feeds to see what people were up to. She thought it odd that there was nothing from Mateo Gomez since it seemed to be so urgent for her to comment on his book. Oh well, just another social media loser, she thought.

Exhaustion started to overtake her, and she rested her left elbow on her desk as her chin dropped onto her hand. She slowly clicked on various websites. She really wasn't paying attention to what she was doing. It was simply something to do to fill in the time. *I could call Craig, but he'll be too busy to talk to me, anyway.* The thought was fleeting. He'd said he would call when he could.

Annie leaned back again, took a deep breath and flung her arms behind her head in a long, soothing stretch. She arched her back like a cat as the muscles loosened one by one. *I've had enough to drink. I think I'll have a nice long shower and read in bed.* Suddenly she bolted upright, staring fixedly at the computer screen. What was happening? She glanced at her glass. Still half full. She squeezed her eyes shut and opened them again. It was still there. Her breathing accelerated, but it was as if the air had suddenly evaporated from the room. She leaned forward quickly and jerked the mouse.

It had zero effect.

Annie's eyes were open wide and her left hand rested on her chest. She couldn't move. She was frozen in time. She couldn't avert her eyes from the screen in front of her.

The cursor moved by itself.

She managed to move her hand, but no matter how much she jabbed at the mouse and clicked the right and left buttons, nothing stopped the runaway cursor. *Oh my God, it has a mind of its own. What's causing that?*

The cursor on the screen did have a mind of its own and it also had a purpose. It was rapidly closing tabs so that only the browser remained open. Words swiftly appeared in the dialog box of the browser: USA GOVERNMENT WEBSITE. The site opened, and a new dialog appeared: CHIEF OF STAFF. A picture of her husband, Craig Logan, appeared on the screen along with his bio. The cursor drew a large red circle around his name.

A gasp escaped from Annie's lips.

The image was reduced in size so that it was halfway across the width of the screen. The cursor hovered over Annie's word processing program. The application opened, and the runaway cursor called up a blank document. Annie simply stared as the new document slid across the screen until it sat alongside the site featuring Annie's husband's photograph and bio. She wanted to get up and run out of the room, but she was paralyzed by what she saw. Words quickly began appearing on the page in front of her. She couldn't believe what she was reading.

WE HAVE CONTROL OF YOUR COMPUTER. WE WILL DESTROY YOUR LIFE IF YOU DO NOT PAY ATTENTION AND DO AS WE SAY. YOUR CREDIT CARDS WERE ONLY THE BEGINNING. YOUR FAMILY ASSETS ARE UNDER OUR CONTROL AND NEITHER YOU OR YOUR HUSBAND WILL HAVE ANYTHING LEFT UNLESS YOU DO THE FOLLOWING.

WE KNOW YOUR HUSBAND, CRAIG LOGAN, HAS ACCESS TO THE PRESIDENT. THE PRESIDENT IS ABOUT TO SIGN A DOCUMENT THAT WILL HARM CHINESE INTERESTS. YOUR

HUSBAND WILL KNOW WHAT WE ARE REFERRING TO. IT
MUST BE STOPPED. WE ARE COUNTING ON YOU, ANNIE
LOGAN, TO TALK TO YOUR HUSBAND AND GET HIM TO
MAKE SURE THE DOCUMENT IS NOT SIGNED. DO NOT
INVOLVE ANYONE BUT YOUR HUSBAND.
NOD IF YOU UNDERSTAND.

Without realizing the implications, Annie's head slowly bobbed
up and down. The hackers controlling her computer apparently
needed to emphasize. New words appeared on the screen.

BY THE WAY, WE WATCHED YOU EXERCISE. YOU SHOULD
DO IT LONGER FOR IT TO BE OF ANY USE. YOU DRINK TOO
MUCH.
TELL YOUR HUSBAND TO STOP YOUR GOVERNMENT'S
INTRUSION INTO CHINESE INTERESTS.
YOU HAVE 7 DAYS.
WE WILL BE WATCHING.
WE KNOW WHERE YOU LIVE.
TURN ON YOUR COMPUTER AT 10 PM TOMORROW.
WE NEED TO SEE PROGRESS BY THEN.
NOD AGAIN IF YOU UNDERSTAND.

Annie's chest was constricted and her breathing labored. Then she
fully realized what was happening. *Oh my God, whoever is doing
this can actually see me! But how? There's no light. The camera can't
be on.*

NOD AGAIN IF YOU UNDERSTAND.

Annie found a way to move her head. The movement was enough
to force her to act. She knew what she had to do. If this was really
happening, she would print the document as soon as she had control
of her computer again. The idea dissolved as quickly as the words on
the screen did. They were being erased faster than they had appeared.
She couldn't bring herself to touch the mouse. Annie's eyes followed
the disappearing words from right to left across the screen, line by
line, until they were gone. The blank page disappeared, followed by

the word processing program and the government website. The tabs she had open reappeared and her computer screen looked exactly as it had before all this started.

Annie's shaking hand slowly moved towards the mouse and nudged it. The cursor moved under her touch. She tried it again and it moved again. She looked at her glass. She picked it up, downed the remaining liquid and after setting it down, sat with her shoulders hunched and her hands firmly clasped between her legs. She sat unmoving, staring at the screen.

Did that just happen? Am I delusional? I must be having alcohol nightmares! I really have to stop drinking. It didn't happen—did it? Can someone actually see me?

Then she gasped as she realized that whoever it was could well still be watching her.

In one motion, Annie jumped up from the desk and slammed the lid of the laptop shut.

She couldn't stop shaking.

She went to the kitchen and took a bottle of wine from the refrigerator.

CHAPTER 11

Annie's legs wobbled like spaghetti as she stumbled to the bedroom. She set the bottle and glass on the night stand, threw the bed covers back and climbed into bed. She sat up against the pillows with her knees drawn and the covers pulled to her chin. She couldn't stop shaking. She rocked back and forth, and a hundred little drummers beat a tattoo in her head.

She asked herself the same question over and over.

Did that really happen?

It couldn't have. Yet it was there.

I need a drink.

She leaned over, removed the loose cork from the half-empty bottle and with shaking hands poured a generous helping. A few drops splattered on the bed covers as she put the bottle back on the night stand. Her eyes fixed on the wall in front of her, yet nothing registered. Thoughts tumbled end over end in her head like cars of a derailed train flying off the track. She rehashed everything she could remember about what just happened. It was already becoming a blur as her mind refused to consider that someone, somewhere, had control of her computer. It had to be a bad dream. She refilled her glass over and over. She drank and thought, thought and drank. Finally, she stopped shaking. A series of clinks filled the room as she tapped the upside-down bottle against the edge of the glass. Empty. Her body was warm from head to toe now, her headache subsiding. She pushed the covers down and set the bottle and empty glass on the night stand again. She peeled off the shorts and got back under the covers. She had new courage. She had to call Craig and let him know what happened. She wasn't going near that computer tonight to call him on Skype, that's for sure. But she had to tell him. Her cell phone was in her purse in the computer room.

She threw back the covers and ran to the computer room, bouncing off the wall on the way. She didn't even look at her computer, just grabbed her purse and dashed back to her bedroom where she hopped into bed, pulling the covers with her. She dug in her purse until she found the phone and after a series of failed attempts, dialed her husband's number correctly.

A sleepy voice answered.

"Craig, it's me." To Annie, her voice sounded soft and distant, and she thought her words might be slurred.

The voice was wider awake now. "Annie, are you alright?"

"Yes, I'm fine now. I need to talk to you." She grimaced as she knew now that she slurred her words. He wouldn't believe her if he could tell she had been drinking.

"Do you know what time it is? Have you been drinking?" She hadn't fooled him.

"I don't know what time it is and yes, I've had a couple of glasses of wine. Something's happened and I'm scared."

"Annie, it's 2 a.m. I have an early meeting tomorrow. What could be so serious that you're calling me in the middle of the night? It's the damn booze that does this to you. You're obviously drunk. I think you need help. This has to stop."

Annie's voice grew louder. "It's NOT the booze. You're going to want to hear this." Annie's face tightened as her words sounded to her like a jumbled mess. "Something really awful just happened. Do you want to hear it or not?" Anger was overtaking her, and the effects of the alcohol would wear off when it did.

"Well, this isn't the first time you've called drunk in the middle of the night." A frustrated expulsion of air preceded what came next. "All right, what is it this time?"

Annie hesitated. *How is he ever going to believe me?* She plunged ahead, explaining how someone had taken over control of her computer and written a threatening message on the screen. She was forgetting some vital pieces of information that might make Craig believe her. She blurted, "Craig, he could *see* me. He knew I was exercising in the room!"

Craig interrupted with a softer tone. "Are you sure you didn't just imagine it, Annie? How could this person see you through your computer?" Craig wanted to be understanding, but he knew his exasperation would filter through the connection. "How much had you had to drink when all this was happening? You need to get some sleep. I'll send you the number for a private counselor for your drinking problem tomorrow by email. I want you to call them. Do it, please Annie. I'll call you again soon and I'll come and see you as soon as I can get away. In the meantime, I'm sorry, but I have to get some sleep."

"Wait! There's more to this. Yesterday my credit cards didn't work. The bank called and said they had been compromised. Both of them. There were purchases in two different parts of the world that I had nothing to do with. Don't you think it's odd that this happened tonight just after my credit cards were stolen?"

"Well, if the bank called, they have it under control. Cards get compromised all the time, Annie. Now, I'm sorry, but I really must get some sleep. We will get you some help. I shouldn't have let your drinking go on so long without doing something. I really am sorry, but I have to go. We'll talk about this tomorrow. Try to get some rest. Please honey. I love you. Good night!"

"Wait, don't send me an email . . ." But he had already hung up. Annie pulled the phone away from her ear and stared at it in disbelief. *He actually hung up on me.* She threw the phone on the chair beside the bed. It bounced off the cushion and did a swan dive to the floor. *I guess I can't say I blame him for hanging up. The story doesn't sound real. But I'm sure it happened.* She lay back down on the bed, face down in the pillows that were quickly growing damp.

Sleep didn't come until the tears of frustration stopped flowing.

CHAPTER 12

Marcie and Nathan sat on the balcony of the condo with their feet up, enjoying the breeze drifting through the screened-in walls. They had the rest of Marcie's vacation to spend together. Steam rose from the coffee mugs that sat on the low table between them. Nathan was engrossed in a John Sandford book and Marcie flipped the pages of *Brides* magazine. The only sound came from the ocean waves lapping against the shore and the murmur of unintelligible voices from people going about their business below.

Marcie glanced at Nathan who was buried in his book. "So, have you thought more about the guest list? Are you happy with the numbers and where we cut it off?"

Nathan turned the page. "I think it's perfect. We've invited the special people in our lives. Of course, we could've saved all this trouble if we'd just been married on Mars."

Marcie's mouth dropped open before she proclaimed, "Oh, Mars now. When you first talked about a destination wedding, it was Barbados. Now it's Mars?"

Nathan's focus remained firmly on his book. "Well, we did talk about finding a way to keep the numbers down." His mouth creased into a tiny smile.

In response, Marcie dipped her fingers into her coffee and flicked the liquid at Nathan's face.

"Hey, that's hot! And it stains!"

"Oh, you'll live, Wimp. Now that I have your attention, can we have a serious conversation?"

Nathan wiped off the few drops that had landed on his face, closed the book and took Marcie's hand. He laughed before saying, "I'm all ears. Since the date and venue are already booked, I don't think a destination wedding is in the cards anymore. I think the guest list is fine. We had to cut it off somewhere."

Marcie closed the magazine and set it on the table as she turned to face her fiancé. "Yes, I think we did the best we could. I think we're in good shape with our planning. I just have to pick my dress and you need to decide what your entourage is going to wear."

Nathan opened his mouth to respond when Marcie's phone trilled in her purse in the living room. "Hold that thought," she said as she jumped up to answer the call. Nathan admired her figure as she hurried through the patio doors.

She dug the phone out of her purse and was mildly surprised to see Annie Logan's name on the screen. Then she remembered the situation at the gas bar. She answered cheerily. "Hi Annie, it's nice of you to call."

The words tumbled out like a barrier had suddenly been lifted. "Marcie, I'm so sorry to bother you on a Saturday, but I had nowhere else to turn. Something awful has happened. *A foreign country has taken over my computer.* I called my husband to tell him last night, but I had couple of glasses of wine before I dialed and he wouldn't listen. It involves him. I *have* to talk to someone." She deliberately left out the part about her husband hanging up on her, too embarrassed to mention it.

"Okay, Annie, slow down. What happened?" Marcie returned to the balcony and sat.

Annie paused to compose herself. "Remember how my credit cards wouldn't work at the gas station? Well of course you remember, you paid my bill. Anyway, the bank called and told me it looks like my card information has been stolen. It got worse after that. Someone used them to buy stuff in London and Singapore! But then after dinner last night, I got on my computer to do some things and Marcie, someone took control of my cursor! They made my computer start opening a bunch of documents and files and I couldn't stop it. They wrote on my screen that I should tell my husband to stop something he's working on with the president that will affect China or they would destroy our lives. Whoever was hacking in said the credit cards were only the first step. He told me he could see me and he knew where I live. He was writing it all on a blank document on the screen. And then he said I had to do something within seven days or something bad will happen. Marcie, I'm so scared! He could *see* me through the computer. I wouldn't believe it except he said he had seen me exercising just before and he knew that I was drinking wine. He even made fun of the way I exercised."

Marcie's eyes widened as Annie spoke and she glanced at Nathan who was watching intently. The woman was hyperventilating through the phone. She said, "Annie, listen, take a deep breath. Nathan is here, and I want to put you on speaker so he can hear everything you have to say. Nathan is a consultant for the FBI. He'll know what to do. Hang on for a minute so I can tell him what's going on, then I'll put you on speaker, okay?"

No response.

"Annie, are you still there?"

"Yes, I'm here. I'm so scared. They said no one else should know, but okay, put Nathan on. But he can't tell anyone. I think Craig and I are in danger, Marcie."

"Okay, just a minute." She covered the phone. To Nathan, she whispered, "It's Annie Logan. Remember, I told you about her? I don't know if she's been drinking or not, but she sounds terrified. Can you listen to this and tell me what you think? She says it involves her husband, Craig Logan, the president's chief of staff. She called him, but she said he wouldn't listen to her. She sounds frantic."

"Sure, put her on."

"Annie, I have you on speaker. Nathan is sitting right here. Now, tell us everything that happened. Don't leave anything out."

Annie repeated how the unseen person had warned her not to tell anyone but her husband or their lives would be destroyed. She relayed the details again, this time trying hard to remember every single thing that had happened. She admitted her story sounded crazy and that she'd been drinking beforehand. Her voice quavered. "How could this happen?"

In a low, serious voice, Nathan replied, "Computer scams are always evolving and getting more sophisticated all the time, Annie, but I do know something about hacking from working on computer fraud cases with the FBI. It's too bad about your credit cards being compromised. Unfortunately, it's happening too often these days. The bank did the right thing by contacting you and closing those cards. As for your computer's hijacking, well, it's simple enough unfortunately to embed a hidden code in an email or picture. If you were to open them, it gives the hacker access to your computer system. That's why you always see a warning to only open files from familiar sources. It's called phishing and hackers will use it to steal personal information from people. Do you remember opening a strange message from anyone recently?"

Annie couldn't think of anything unusual she had opened, but she did admit to opening pretty much anything that was sent to her. Then: "Oh, wait a minute. I had a friend request on Facebook from a man in Columbia the night before last. After I accepted his friendship, he sent me a photo to open. I did and then he sent a document he wanted me to comment on. I tried but it wouldn't open. Could it be something like that?"

Nathan glanced at Marcie. "That could be it, Annie. Normally, it wouldn't be that suspicious, but under the circumstances, I'd say it could certainly be suspect. Are you sure he was from Columbia? You just told us they said whatever the president is working on will affect China somehow."

Annie's voice seemed calmer now, apparently more relaxed by being able to unburden herself.

"Whoever had control of my computer said it had something to do with China."

"Well, we have to convince your husband somehow that there could be a threat of some kind." Nathan didn't want to panic her again. His voice was even. "It should at least be looked into. Do you still have any trail on your computer from what happened?"

"I haven't looked at my computer since it happened, but everything disappeared within seconds last night. I doubt that there's anything. They said that I should be back on my computer tonight at 10 p.m. They said they know where I live. How would they know that?"

Marcie chimed in. "We don't even know that it isn't some pimple-faced kid in his basement playing tricks on you, Annie. It could be a kid down the street who knows you're alone. But I agree with Nathan, we need to inform your husband, find out if they're working on something that would affect the Chinese and determine if this is a real threat."

Nathan asked, "Would you mind if we come over and look at your computer? Maybe we can find something that would help convince your husband."

Annie's voice rose in panic again. "They can see anyone in my room. They would see you."

"Not if we put tape over the camera, Annie."

Annie's voice was low and resigned. "Okay, can you come this morning?"

Marcie and Nathan agreed in unison that they would be there shortly, reassured Annie again, and ended the call.

Marcie looked evenly at Nathan. "What do you think?"

"I think it might be a cry for attention. Drinking definitely seems to be an issue, and her husband appears to be ignoring her. She might've made this up. There hasn't been anything on the news about the government upsetting the Chinese, but anything's possible, I guess, with this president. Why would they go after the chief of staff and his wife? I guess I could answer that myself by saying a lot of things go on that we don't know about and probably don't even want to know about. Looks like any further talk about the wedding is on hold again."

"She sounded terrified, Nathan. There was genuine fear in her voice like I haven't heard in a long time."

Nathan looked thoughtful. "I want to make a phone call before we go. If this really is legit, it could be a matter of national security. And seven days isn't very long."

"Remember they supposedly said not to involve anyone. Annie was adamant."

Nathan turned to Marcie and said in a tense but level voice, "This can't wait, Marce. If it's not legitimate, there won't be any consequence. If it is legitimate, we have to take this matter extremely seriously."

CHAPTER 13

Nathan's call was to an FBI acquaintance named James Welch. Their paths had crossed a few times, and they'd immediately hit it off. Welch was somewhat of an enigma in the office. He was in his thirties, tall and reed-thin with a mop of long, curly red hair. He favored golf shirts, dress slacks and a baseball hat. His hair generally sprung from the bottom of his hat as if his head was ablaze and flames were licking at his collar. He always attributed the wrinkles around his eyes on his pale freckled face to squinting while following the flight of his monstrous drives on the golf course, much to the amusement of his colleagues.

There was rarely a golf course Welch didn't like, and his clubs rode in the trunk everywhere he took his mid-sized Chevrolet. His physical stature encouraged his workmates to question his claims of being able to crush a ball on the golf course—until they played with him. A gold stud in each ear lobe added to his enigma. Based on his appearance and choice of hobbies, James Welch could have been given any number of nicknames. But his co-workers simply called him "Welchie."

He was known as the wonder kid, although no longer a kid exactly, because he was a cyber-crimes computer expert. He had taken down a number of blue collar criminals, including a recent scheme involving computer attack mechanisms called phishing and bots that targeted mostly elderly people. The scheme was a common one. Many computers were initially infiltrated with a bot or software application that captured the owners' contact lists. The bot then sent emails to everyone on their contact lists letting people know that they owed a small amount of money to the I.R.S. Because the money was overdue, according to the emails, there would be serious consequences unless the debtor contacted a number purportedly belonging to the I.R.S. to provide a credit card number for payment. If they did so, everything would be resolved. But of course, for those innocent enough to be sucked in by the scam, unauthorized charges started showing up on the credit cards within days of the number being provided.

Welch had successfully traced the origin of the scam to a small French island in the Indian Ocean. The scammers used a series of relays, bouncing the signal through computer servers in Iceland, Hawaii and the Maldives before landing in the U.S. Welch determined that after the phishing email was sent, it took on average about 2.5 seconds until the first one was opened by someone. It didn't take much longer for the phone calls to be made to the bogus I.R.S., especially by seniors who are most susceptible to this type of attack. It was a relatively small scam compared to some he had dealt with, but it gave James Welch huge satisfaction to bring down the perpetrators of this one. The case was assigned to the Paris office for final arrests. Unfortunately, new scams popped up nearly as fast as he shut one down.

Nathan was pleased and surprised when Welch picked up on the second ring.

"Hey, Welchie, it's Nathan Harris. Isn't it your tee time yet?"

Nathan always enjoyed Welch's enthusiasm. "Nathan, my man, how are you? Yeah, well, you know scammers never sleep and the FBI's work is never done." He laughed on the other end of the call. "Some of these guys have real jobs so they supplement their income by doing their dirty work on the weekend. Early weekend mornings are a good time to fish for the phishers, if you know what I mean! Besides that, there are too many duffers on the golf courses on weekends." He chuckled and added, "S'up?"

"I have something I need to run by you," Nathan responded. "It's hard to say, but it could turn out to be an issue of national security." Nathan filled Welch in on Annie's frantic phone call, explaining that she was the wife of Craig Logan, the president's chief of staff. Then he added, "I know the story sounds bizarre, Welchie, but it *is* true that Mrs. Logan's credit cards were compromised. My fiancée, Marcie, was at the gas station when Mrs. Logan couldn't use her credit cards. The lady loves her booze, though, so it's possible she just had a weird computer aberration rather than being hacked. Or she could just be looking for attention and made the story up. From what she told us, her husband certainly didn't seem concerned when she tried to explain all this to him. He asked her if she was drunk. But Mrs. Logan insists she saw a message onscreen that she was not to involve the authorities." Nathan paused for a second. "I don't know what to think, but we have to explore it. We told Ms. Logan we would come over and take a look, so at least her husband might take this more seriously. But if her story is true and someone has found a way to watch her through something embedded in her computer, we can't risk waltzing in there and being seen. If someone really is watching her like she says they are, they wouldn't like seeing us there. What do you think?"

He could almost hear James thinking on the other end of the call. "Well, I can tell you that we get hundreds of threats against the president or his staff or the entire government every day of the week. Everything from people saying they've planted a bomb in the president's phone while he was sleeping to having compromising pictures of the first lady they're going to release at midnight to information about the vice president belonging to a secret society involving the worship of a giant centipede. By the way, do we know whether there really is secret legislation going through that would affect the Chinese? Wait, I'll answer that myself. We don't know because it's secret."

Nathan chuckled. "I think I would be checking out the centipede theory myself. If those things are big enough, they can do some serious damage. I saw one named Cynthia at the Marizayra Sanctuary in Barbados that was seven or eight inches long. It ate a mouse."

"Huh, that must've been something to see."

"I don't think the mouse enjoyed it much." Nathan glanced at Marcie who had been sitting forward on her chair listening intently to Nathan's side of the conversation. Her eyebrows knitted closer together and the left side of her mouth bunched up her cheek as she raised her hands in a look of exasperation. With her palms turned upwards, she waggled her fingers as if to say, "C'mon, let's go."

Nathan smiled at his fiancée. "At this stage, we don't have a clue what the government is doing to the Chinese or anyone else or why someone would contact the wife of the chief of staff. All we know is that Annie Logan has a crazy story and she's panicking. If she's making all this up, it's an Oscar-winning performance. James, let me ask you a question. I think I already know the answer, but if someone really wanted to harm a person through their computer, what could they do?"

"The possibilities are endless, my friend. Let's say someone has control of your computer. They could start by transferring all your money to some offshore account. They could run up serious debt in your name, put drug charges on your record, plant child pornography on your computer and provide the authorities with an anonymous tip that it's there . . . Hell, they could even create a file with copies of invoices proving that you sold arms to some terrorist group. You might get your life back, but it would take years and lawyers and money you don't have because it's sitting in someone's bank account in the Cayman Islands. Need I go on?"

"Nope, I get the picture."

"I agree you need to check it out, Nathan. Did they say they were going to contact her again?"

"Yes, at 10 tonight."

"Okay, if you start poking around in Annie Logan's computer and someone really does have control, they're going to know. They can tell by just monitoring your keystrokes that you're not Annie. Different pressure applied, different rhythm. You could disable the camera, but I would suggest against that right now. *If* someone does have control, they need to think they're only dealing with Annie and she's not computer-savvy at all. We don't want to tip them off or make them suspect someone else is involved. Tell you what, after you see her and if you're satisfied there's something to her claim, swing by the office on the way back. And bring your laptop. I'll have a piece of software that we'll install on your computer that'll give you remote access to hers. We need Annie's full cooperation, though. Tell her you'll send her an email with a simple attachment that she is to open. The more normal the email the better, just in case someone really is snooping around in her computer. Once she opens the attachment, you'll be able to monitor the activity on her computer just like the hackers are doing. I'll help you create the attachment when you get here, but think of an email that is totally plausible and be sure to alert Mrs. Logan that it's coming. If it turns out that her story really is true and she's been hacked for national security reasons, I'll get a lot more involved and fast. Sound like a plan?"

"Sure. We can do that, but if someone else is watching, won't they know we're monitoring them through the same computer?"

There was an indignant expulsion of air at the other end of the phone followed by obvious exasperation. "Puh-lease. Nathan. You forget who you're talking to, my good man. See you soon."

‹ ‹ › ›

Nathan's next call was to the special agent in charge of the Tampa field office. His name was Charles Walker. He was a tall, sandy-haired, no-nonsense man with two decades of experience in the FBI, many of them in the Atlanta office where Nathan had worked. They were good friends and mutual admirers of each other's abilities. Nathan imagined Walker in a dark suit, white shirt and blue tie, an outfit he always favored.

Nathan relayed Annie's story in full detail and then added what he had learned from his subsequent phone call to James Welch. He emphasized the hacker's insistence of total secrecy on Annie's part and how they'd said she was in serious danger if she involved others. Then he asked Walker if he wanted to assign someone else to the case rather than him. Walker immediately said other resources were stretched thin and that this case would be added to Nathan's existing contract with the Bureau. Nathan figured the situation was probably going to turn out to be a dead-end street, anyway, and happily accepted.

They took Marcie's car to Annie's place. The sun shone down from a cerulean sky, but neither noticed. Nathan had provided Marcie with a brief rundown of his conversation with Welch as they walked to the car. But now the interior of the car was silent. Even the always-in-play car speakers were quiet, unusual for Marcie who couldn't drive out of the garage without the sound system blasting at top volume. She and Nathan were both lost in their thoughts.

Then Nathan spoke. "I've been thinking. If this really did happen to Annie's computer, there's a way they could pinpoint her location."

Marcie glanced at him. "Yeah? Like look her up in a phone book?"

Nathan glanced at her quizzically. "Do they even make phone books anymore? I'm concerned about her home address but I'm also wondering about something else. It's simple enough to find where she lives. But what if someone also wants to know the places she frequents? If she took pictures somewhere with her smart phone and had the GPS location feature on, the picture would contain data that identifies the latitude and longitude of where it was taken. It's called geotagging. It wouldn't identify her exact location, but it would be close."

Marcie turned the car onto Annie's street as she followed up on Nathan's statement. "And if she shared the pictures on her social media pages, would the data be there?"

"Not necessarily. Social media sites usually strip out location information before a picture becomes public, but if the pictures are just sitting in a folder on Annie's computer, the location information would still be readily available. If the data is there, someone with access to her computer can see it. You just right-click on the photo and then look under Properties. The latitude and longitude could still be there. It doesn't mean it's someone sophisticated snooping around Annie's computer. A kid with some computer smarts, which all of them have, could do that."

They pulled into Annie's driveway and Marcie turned to Nathan as she shut off the car. "Are you going to be able to tell if someone has access to her computer when we start monitoring?"

The voices of excited children playing in the street, accompanied by an equally exuberant dog vying for their attention, drifted through the open window, nearly drowning out his answer. "I will if the attacker accesses her computer again. As I understand it, after Welch installs his software, I'll be able to see everything Annie can see. Eventually, we'll probably need to reach out to the FBI experts for assistance. We'd want Welch and his crew involved. The real experts are in the regional computer forensics labs. The closest ones are in Kansas City or Louisville. Louisville's closer, maybe around 13 hours away. But Annie said she only has a few days to deal with whatever they want, so there may not be time to get the computer analyzed. Anyway, we're here so let's go and talk with her. I'd really like to get a sense of whether this is a pathetic cry for help or if the sky really is falling."

They got out of the car and walked past the manicured lawn with bright red roses rimming the house and rang Annie's doorbell.

When Annie answered, they could see she had made an attempt to comb her hair, but her eyes bore dark shadows. The smell of alcohol lingered on her breath. Her complexion was paler than the last two times Marcie had seen her.

Marcie introduced Nathan as they were led into the house. Annie immediately started walking toward the office. She looked over her shoulder as she walked. "Thank you so much for doing this." Marcie frowned when Annie announced, "I have to make Craig understand, so maybe you can find something on the computer that will help convince him."

Nathan leaned forward and gently placed his hand on Annie's arm as Marcie ran a zipping motion across her lips. He motioned with his finger back to the living room. As they turned in the hall, Marcie poked her head into the office and was disturbed to see an empty wine glass by the computer. She closed the door as she left.

The living room was spacious and brightened by soft minty green walls with white trim. Annie gestured for Nathan and Marcie to sit on one of the sections of a three-piece sofa while she sat facing them. The faint scent of the roses resting in a vase on the coffee table in front of them hung in the air. Magazines and newspapers were strewn across the table, and one of the many plush decorative cushions had tumbled to the floor. An unwashed glass sat on an end table. Marcie glanced at the magazines, which included *American Rose*, *Sunset Magazine* and ironically, *Good Housekeeping*.

Now, as they sat facing each other in the living room, Nathan whispered to Annie, "Is your computer on right now?"

Annie sat with her hands clasped on her lap. Bewildered, she shook her head. "No, but . . . but aren't you going to turn it on to look at it?"

Marcie put a reassuring hand on Annie's. "We can't just yet. The person or persons told you not to involve the authorities, so we have to be very cautious in our approach."

Nathan interrupted softly. "Marcie's right. We don't know how much they can hear through the microphone on your computer. That's why I asked if it was on. Now, Annie, one more time, can you please tell me again everything you can about the words on the computer?"

Annie shuddered and remained quiet for a few minutes. Her eyes glistening with tears, she finally spoke, "I'm sorry. This is just so overwhelming. Please give me a minute to compose myself. She quickly rose from the couch and rushed into the kitchen. Nathan and Marcie exchanged glances as glass tinkled around the corner. Marcie released a sigh as she slowly shook her head and pushed herself off the couch to check on her new friend.

CHAPTER 14

Yang Lee lay propped up on the soft pillows in a room in one of the most luxurious hotels on the Huangpu River in Shanghai. He stared at the large flush-mounted light over the king-size bed. He had been invited here to this opulent room with its calming soft pastel walls and wood highlights by the woman in the bathroom. Lee was naked, covered only by a sheet as the rest of the covers lay in disarray at the foot of the bed. Only sheer drapes covered the view through the floor-to-ceiling window as the city lights dimmed and the rising sun cast its rays over the river. Clothing lay scattered across the chairs and sofa. While he had thoroughly enjoyed the night of unbridled passion, his thoughts never strayed far from the work he had to do. Although he did have to admit his guest had his full attention a few times during the night as she explored his body with her hands and mouth.

His role playing had certainly paid off, and only needed to last a little bit longer. His goal had been to get close to her, as difficult as that was with his distrust and general dislike of people. Normally he paid for his women, but this was different. It was a job that paid extremely well. The 12-hour time difference between Asia and the U.S. gave him the time away from his new assignment for this distraction and the opportunity to complete an obligation.

He had observed her for two weeks to determine her personal habits before making his move. He never expected to end up in bed with her, but a few drinks and knowing from his research how he could manipulate her had paid off better than expected. When she got up to use the bathroom, it gave him the perfect opportunity to complete the task that had been contracted to him. When he finished, he ordered room service. He expected orange juice, tea and breakfast dim sum to arrive at any minute.

The bathroom door opened, and Lee stared appreciatively as the naked woman padded confidently across the marble floor. Her name was Lian Lu and she was a 27-year-old lawyer with a prestigious firm in Hong Kong. She had been in Shanghai for a month on a large expense account, courtesy of a bill her alleged drug lord client was about to receive for her getting all charges against him dropped on a technicality. The young woman's naked pale skin was flawless. She had taken great care to put her hair back up in the loose style she had worn into the hotel. Her almond-shaped eyes and pouty lips gave her an innocent appearance, which Lee now knew was a facade.

Lee recalled the unique ways the Chinese have of describing beauty that is indescribable. He recalled something his father used to say about his mother, that she was so beautiful, flowers closed up in shame when they saw her. Such was the beauty of Lian Lu. Now, as she crossed the room to the bed, her perky breasts and thin waist were silhouetted in the brilliance of the soft morning sun breaking around her through the sheer drapes. He felt himself respond as she climbed onto the bed and ran her fingers up and down the length of his body. Just as she leaned over to kiss him, a knock sounded at the door.

Lu sank back onto the pillows, pulling the sheet up to her neck. Lee slipped on a bath robe and walked to the door to allow the room attendant to roll in the breakfast cart. He tipped the young man and closed the door behind him as Lu climbed out of bed and, ignoring the newly-delivered breakfast tray, ran to the jacuzzi at one side of the room. She climbed in and laid her head back on the side of the tub.

Lee asked, "Aren't you going to be late for work?"

She said nothing. The bubbling water covered her to the top of her breasts until she sank further into the water. She smiled demurely and her slender fingers emerged from the water, gesturing him to join her.

She reached for him as he stepped into the tub. Breakfast would have to wait.

〈〈〉〉

Later, as they sat across the table from one another, Lee reflected on how much he had enjoyed spending time with this intelligent woman. It was such a shame doing what he had been contracted to do. She was the only woman, well, the only person really, with whom he'd made any sort of connection. He was tired after their lovemaking session in the jacuzzi, but Lian Lu seemed fresh and full of life. He was fully clothed in light blue jeans, white shirt open at the neck and an open weave summer jacket that allowed airflow to survive the Shanghai humidity. As he sat across the table from her, he deftly used his chopsticks to pick up some noodles from his plate. In Chinese, Lee murmured, "I'm sorry I must leave so soon, my treasure. I enjoyed the night with you immensely. I'm so happy that our lives intertwined in such a way that we have been able to get to know each other so well."

Even at her young age, Lian Lu was a well-respected defense law-yer and she had earned an enviable reputation. But she had also made some enemies. She was considered a hero by many in Hong Kong but a dissident by others for her refusal to swear allegiance to China. She had been born and raised in Hong Kong and had grown up appreciating the limited democracy enjoyed by the people living in that city. It was to remain a Special Administrative Region for fifty years after British Rule ended in 1997, but the Chinese government was making noises to end the autonomy Hong Kong enjoyed much sooner. More and more in Hong Kong were speaking out against the communist rule of mainland China, and thousands were inspired to march by Lu's television appearances and newspaper interviews where she advocated for the furtherance of democracy.

Lu's law firm turned a blind eye to her free-time activities so they could have plausible deniability, but the partners silently cheered her on for her actions. They had tremendous faith in Lian Lu's abilities and had her earmarked for a partnership in short order.

Lee didn't know where this particular assignment had come from. He had been contacted anonymously and payment had shown up in his bank account. That was good enough for him. He had done his research and knew about her activist leanings. He also became aware of her defense of drug lords. He had hacked into her computer and learned enough about her personal life to know that she was on the rebound from a relationship. Her enemies and his employer could be from within or outside government. It made no difference to Lee.

Lu wore the bath robe provided by the hotel. She had not taken great care in doing it up, affording Lee an ample view of her breasts.

She leaned forward and placed her hand on his. "Thank you. I enjoyed my time with you. I look forward to the next time. I will shower and get dressed." She gestured towards the open laptop facing them on the desk. "I have to be in court this afternoon, so I must prepare before then."

She had looked deeply into his eyes as Lee imagined she would do when cross-examining a witness. He understood how witnesses would wilt under her cross examinations. As he got up to leave, he kissed her passionately and her body pressed against him. For a brief moment, he wished he could stay.

As he strode from the hotel, his forehead glistened from the sheen of sweat that had broken out as soon as he stepped outside. It was going to be a scorcher of a day. He removed his jacket and stuck his hand into one of the pockets to remove a sealed lead-lined bag. The bag contained surgical gloves. He tossed it into the river as he sauntered along the boardwalk. The bag landed with a plop. A weight he had added would ensure its path straight to the bottom.

He had used the gloves to spread a variation of a VX nerve agent over the Enter key and space bar of Lian Lu's laptop. A lethal dose is .00035 ounce. He'd applied a thin coating to the keys, which should be enough to bring down a water buffalo. It was colorless and odorless and would be completely unnoticeable on the keys. Lee expected the young woman would already be in trouble by now. As soon as she touched the keys, the lethal nerve agent would be absorbed into her skin. Within seconds, she would experience twitching, nausea and vomiting. This would be followed by severe shortness of breath and suffocation. Death would be very quick.

As with all his jobs, Lee replayed his actions through his mind as he walked. He always planned every minute detail and ran through every scenario meticulously to satisfy himself there were no mistakes. He didn't have to worry about fingerprints. He didn't have any. When he had determined after graduating what his life work would be, he'd had skin grafted from his feet onto his fingertips so tracking him would never be an issue.

He was confident all of the nerve agent would be absorbed into her skin. Only minute traces would be left, if any. Any DNA Lee might have left behind would be obliterated by the cleaning staff before anyone figured out Lu hadn't died of food poisoning. As an extra precaution to the surgical gloves and lead-lined package he had used to protect himself from the poison, he would inject himself with a two-part antidote when he got back to his work apartment.

Lee smiled to himself contentedly as he pushed through the throngs of people on their way to work. He was superior at his job. He couldn't remember being hired on two jobs so close together before. A few days earlier, he had ended the life of that fat American pig, Eric Hartman's, life and now this. They were two more perfect crimes to add to his resumé.

He thought once more of the beautiful Lian Lu as he picked up his pace along the boardwalk. Such a waste. Then, within minutes, all thought of her was ejected from his mind as if she had never existed.

Now it was time to get back to the subject that had preoccupied part of him all night.

The subject's name was Annie Logan.

CHAPTER 15

Marcie's arm hung around Annie's shoulder as they re-entered the living room. Annie's eyes were red, and her shoulders slumped in defeat. They sat back on the couch. Nathan was relieved to see that Annie was not carrying a glass when they came back. He had expected her to use some liquid fortification, but thankfully, Marcie must have been able to talk her out of it. He didn't know that Marcie had been greeted by unwashed dishes piled in the sink and still scattered around the kitchen table. Two empty wine bottles sat on the counter, along with an empty pizza box. He and Marcie exchanged glances and Marcie gave her fiancé a nearly imperceptible nod.

While he waited, Nathan decided he needed to take a different approach. He had to admit to himself candidly that he didn't totally believe Annie's story. Something didn't add up and yet, watching Annie's reaction when he asked her to repeat what had happened on the computer caused him to lean towards believing her. He wanted to believe it, for Annie's sake, but why would another country choose to attack the wife of a prominent member of government? Why not just go after Logan himself? On the other hand, blackmailing a spouse could be a sinister way of getting what they wanted. The security on a personal computer would be far simpler to hack than a government site.

First things, first. His goal was to study Annie's reaction as she answered his questions. There were certain telltale signs that would help him decide if even she really believed what she was saying.

"Marcie has probably already told you that we're sorry this is happening to you, Annie. We're here to help in any way we can. Did you have something to eat this morning?"

Annie eye's lifted from the carpet where she had been staring. She cleared her throat and then averted her eyes again. "No. I, uh, just got up and had a shower before you came over."

His question should have been easy enough to answer. But Nathan thought her statement wasn't quite truthful. The hesitation, clearing of her throat and averting her eyes all pointed to something else behind her words. He was pretty sure she had just unwittingly confirmed that the hint of alcohol he had noticed on her breath earlier was not from the night before. Nathan suspected that her breakfast had, in fact, been liquid.

"Well, I'm starving," he said, trying to distract Annie so she would let down her guard. "Maybe if you don't mind, Marcie could make us some toast and coffee while we're talking about your computer. Everyone okay with that?"

Annie frowned but nodded slowly and Marcie headed for the kitchen.

Nathan continued. "Annie, I didn't mean to suggest we didn't believe you when I asked you to repeat what you had told us. I just want to make sure we understand exactly what happened. Maybe you'll think of something you forgot when we talked on the phone. Actually, if you don't mind, I'd like to record everything this time to make sure we get it all in detail." He waited until Annie quietly agreed, took his phone out of his pocket and tapped the voice recorder app.

Nathan pushed aside one of the magazines on the table and set the phone down. As he did so, he commented, "You have some beautiful roses outside. I can see by these magazines, roses must be a hobby of yours."

For the first time Annie's face reflected a hint of a smile. "Oh yes. It's a passion, I guess. I'm not sure what I'd do if I didn't have that to occupy my time."

Nathan observed her closely. Her eyes rose to Nathan's and some of the tension seemed to ease from her body as her shoulders visibly relaxed. He said, "I think everyone needs something to take their mind off things at times."

He pressed "record" on the phone. He had noticed Marcie quietly closing the door to the office, so he was comfortable they couldn't be heard even if someone was listening through the microphone on the computer. "Okay, here we go. Please repeat what you told us on the phone when we talked about someone taking over your computer."

Annie tensed again and stared at the phone lying on the table as she talked. Her voice was barely audible and hesitant at first, but she gained confidence as she spoke, and her eyes rose to seek out Nathan's again.

"I was just checking emails and doing the usual stuff I do on the computer when it started." She reiterated each detail about how she had lost control of her mouse as someone on the other end manipulated it across the screen for their own purposes, and then began typing the awful threats in front of her eyes.

Nathan had chosen to record Annie's words so he could observe *how* she said what she said. He would listen for specific details later, but while she spoke, he studied her for any revealing nuances in her delivery. From the way she had responded to his earlier questions, he thought she had probably lied about breakfast, but told the truth about the roses. But now he didn't sense any untruthfulness or deceit. The story didn't appear rehearsed. Twice while she related the story, he interrupted her and asked her to tell him what happened just before that. She easily recalled what had happened. He watched her eyes. She held his gaze while she talked, but not so much as to try to convince him of a lie. Not once did she shift her eyes upward to the right, a dead giveaway that a person is looking to the imaginative part of the brain to concoct a story. Nathan knew from previous experience that people who are knowingly lying wave their hands around much more. Annie's hand gestures matched the story she was telling. They mostly stayed still on her lap. Either Annie Logan was a skillful fabricator or she was telling the truth, bizarre as it sounded.

Just as Annie finished her narrative, Marcie poked her head around the corner and announced. "I have scrambled eggs, toast and a carafe of coffee if anyone is interested." The timing of Marcie's pronouncement indicated she had been listening from the kitchen, not wanting to interrupt until Annie had finished completely.

Nathan switched off the recorder. "I'm certainly interested! How about you, Annie?"

They entered the kitchen. It was spotless other than the pan and bowl Marcie had used to make the scrambled eggs. Annie's face colored. Her eyes flashed to the spot where the empty bottles had been sitting. She mumbled, "Uh, thanks for cleaning up, Marcie."

Marcie shrugged it off. "I didn't do much—just put the dishes in the dishwasher and wiped off the table. Let's eat."

As they sat down to dig into the meal Marcie had prepared, they spoke casually about Annie's rose garden and her time in Florida. That was an opening for Marcie to ask about Craig Logan.

"I guess your husband's pretty busy in Washington, huh?"

Tension again. "He hardly has time to talk to me. But he has an important job, so I understand."

"Well, I *guess* it's important," Marcie tried to deflect the awkwardness of the situation. "Being the chief of staff is not something everyone could handle nor would want to. I can't imagine everything they have to go through. You really need to speak to him about the incident with your computer, though. We're going to help you gather evidence."

Annie poked her eggs around the plate. She picked up her coffee mug, nearly spilling it in her shaking hands. She spoke in a soft tone while focusing on her cup. "How are you going to do that if you can't look at my computer?"

Marcie continued, sensing that Nathan thought it better if she carried this part of the conversation. They had discussed the email Marcie was going to send Annie on the way over. "We have access to a piece of software that will allow us to monitor what's happening on your computer. The person who has control will not know we're doing it. We'll need you to open an attachment in an email I'll send you before the 10 o'clock deadline tonight. The attachment will be a thank you note for attending my engagement party. That's all you have to do. You need to act normally with your computer activity to let the person know you're complying with whatever he says. Then we'll have a way to support you when you talk to your husband." Marcie leaned forward and put her hand on Annie's arm to reassure her. "Does that sound okay to you, Annie?"

It was more than Annie's hands that were shaking now. Her whole body moved. "He . . . he said no authorities. What if he finds out you're watching?"

"He won't be able to. Trust us, Annie. We know what we're doing. It's the only way to confirm what's happening so that we can discuss it with Mr. Logan."

Annie nodded numbly.

Nathan asked if he could borrow her cell phone, which she readily provided. He clicked on the camera feature, then settings and checked the "location tags" application. Sure enough, it was in the "on" position, meaning that the geographical location of every picture or video Annie had taken would be available to anyone with the knowledge and desire to find it.

Nathan explained the problem, turned off the setting and handed the phone back to Annie. He gathered the breakfast dishes, scraped them into the garbage and loaded them into the dishwasher while Marcie continued. "Annie, there's something else. I might be overstepping my bounds here, but I noticed the wine bottles on the counter. If people see them, they might not take your story seriously. Everyone needs a drink once in a while, but too many drinks could weaken your story. Please be careful, okay?"

Annie fidgeted in her chair. "I'm not sure what you're saying, Marcie. I only have the occasional social drink."

Marcie put her hand on the other woman's shoulder. "Okay, Annie, I'm sorry, we're just trying to help you. Look, I'll send the email as soon as I get home. Please open it right away. Remember, that's all you have to do. We'll be right here with you, in effect. Log onto your computer later tonight, just as they told you. If there really is someone on the other end and they take control again, we'll be able to see it. We'll be in touch afterwards to figure out a strategy. We know this is stressful, but you're not alone, we're here to help. We want to get to the bottom of this for the safety of you and your husband."

Annie walked them to the door. She seemed relieved to see them go, but she offered an apology. "I'm sorry about my mood swings. I just feel so strung out. Thank you so much. I really appreciate the help you're giving me. With any luck there won't be anyone on my computer tonight. And this will all turn out to be a crazy dream."

As Marcie started the car, Nathan said chillingly, "I don't think she will be that lucky. I wish it *were* a crazy dream, but I'm convinced now that she'll hear from them again. Whoever *they* are."

CHAPTER 16

Nathan and Marcie rolled the windows down to enjoy the Florida sunshine on the drive until they stopped by James Welch's office to fill him in on the discussion with Annie. The FBI field office in Tampa, established on June 1, 1960, was now housed in a large four-story beige building backing onto a field. A number of windows overlooked a pond and some palm trees in the front, suggesting that it could belong to any affluent member of the Tampa community. There was no mistaking the low sign on the lawn, however, designating it as a field office for the Federal Bureau of Investigation and the large guard house where Nathan and Marcie stopped.

After flashing his credentials from the contract he had with the FBI at the gate, Nathan signed Marcie in at the front desk. His laptop was swabbed as they passed through security and they were lead to an interior office. They arrived as a golf ball rolled across the carpet into a small mechanical putting training aid that clicked and spit the ball back for another shot. Welch sported a white golf shirt and hat, navy slacks and running shoes. Marcie thought that this slender golf-loving computer security expert with the gold earrings and shock of bright red hair falling out of his white baseball cap seemed like an odd mixture. One thing was for certain—James Welch was going to be an interesting man to get to know.

A surprisingly deep voice came from the slender man. "Ah, there they are. C'mon in and grab a chair. I do my best thinking with a golf club in my hand. Relaxes the mind. Gets the creative juices flowing. Helps me stay one step ahead of the bad guys. Well, most of the time." He chuckled as he set the putter in the corner of the office and Nathan and Marcie stepped over the plastic putting tool on the floor to sit in the chairs facing the desk. "Sorry, that thing is kind of blocking your way. I know it's a bit old school. They have a hundred different tools now to help your putting game, but I like this because I don't have to chase the ball. It encourages me to be accurate so it will send the ball back to me. Otherwise I have to walk over and get it." His scrawny shoulders shook as he gave a hearty laugh.

Welch sat with an audible groan on the only piece of furniture behind his desk—a stool. By way of explanation he said, "It's easier for me to use a stool. Not as far for me to bend. Doctors tell me I have early arthritis in my knees. Probably from too much bending down to take the ball out of the hole. They say knee replacement is in my future. No time for that. Too much golf to play."

Marcie and Nathan smiled, and Nathan introduced his fiancée. Marcie noticed Welch's desk was completely clean except for a laptop and she couldn't resist. "So you're able to solve some of the biggest cyber crimes in the world using just a laptop?"

"Sometimes that's all it takes. That and a little ingenuity, of course. The truth is this little laptop is connected to some pretty powerful servers in the basement. That's where the magic happens. It's all encrypted up the wazoo. I also work closely with the forensics people in our computer labs. They have some great toys for solving problems. Now, I take it since you're here, you believe there's something to the lady's claims?"

Nathan responded quickly. "It looks that way. We believe her enough to watch what happens next. The thing that's nagging at me though is why another country would attempt to stop a piece of governmental legislation by coming after the wife of the president's chief of staff. I haven't been involved in this type of investigation, but I'm sure you have. Do you have trouble swallowing that notion?"

Welch shrugged. "Not really, there are malicious threats flying all over the place between countries. You said it might be China involved? Well, let's see, there have been verified attacks by China against embassies, corporations, the United Nations, large and small governments, the media . . . Hell, in 2014, the federal grand jury returned an indictment against five people in a special unit of the Chinese military for stealing information from American corporations and for planting malware on their computers. They had apparently been doing it since 2006! We're not squeaky clean, either. The United States was accused, along with Israel, of sabotaging a nuclear enrichment plant in Iran in 2010. I'm sure you've heard of that one

on the news. That ol' Stuxnet virus made the turbines' speed fluctu-
ate, and they would have eventually blown themselves apart without
intervention. But you know the best part? The virus made it look to
anyone monitoring that the turbines were still operating at normal
speed." His voice rose. He was clearly enjoying talking about the
world of cyber espionage.

"Russia's still being accused of hacking U.S. elections. The thing
is, every industrialized country is doing it, and so are some of the
rogue nations, but now everyone is taking tougher precautions to
make sure it doesn't happen to them. So what better way to try to
accomplish something than through the back door? Why not hack
into the computer of the wife of a senior White House official to try
to get him to influence the president's decision making? It's kind of
low tech meets high tech, but ingenious. Could actually work. Well,
on second thought, maybe not with this president."

Welch's eyes glinted and narrowed, almost as if he were fired up
by the idea and keen to take on the challenge.

Marcie shook her head. She thought that this kind of talk would
scare the pants off computer-literate people, induce paranoia in
those who already had some fear about information sharing on the
Internet and for those who thought technology was the work of the
Devil, it would surely give them a chance to shout from the rooftops,
"I told you so." She simply asked, "Should we all be afraid to turn
our computers on now?"

The room rumbled with Welch's hearty laugh. "Well, if you want
to go back to the dark ages, I suppose you could leave it off. For
the average person who wants to embrace the advantages of what
online technology offers, it's not an issue—and they aren't married
to someone high up in the government, either. Of course, we all need
to take basic precautions—anti-virus software, cover your webcam,
be careful not to open files from sources you don't know, update
your browser regularly and don't go to sites that aren't trustwor-
thy, that kind of thing. But in Annie's case, we're talking here about
cyber espionage, Marcie, and that's quite a different story. So those
of us here in the agency have the challenge of making sure the Internet stays potentially safe and serious cyber crimes get investigated
and shut down."

Marcie: "Mind if I ask a dumb question?"

"I had a prof once who said there was no such thing as a dumb question and then when we asked it, he would nearly choke trying to stifle his laughter. Nice guy. Sure. Ask away."

Marcie hesitated, unsure whether that was encouragement or a suggestion that he was going to laugh at her as soon as she asked it. She asked it, anyway. "Why not just unplug Annie's computer? Whoever it is on the other end already has seized control. Why let him continue watching her with the computer on?"

"That's not a dumb question at all, Marcie. Believe it or not, it's not that simple. They have control of Annie's computer, which means they've already downloaded all her personal information and anything she had stored on her computer that was related to her husband. It means they have control of her passwords and her bank accounts. They know who Craig and Annie's friends are. They've seen her Facebook groups, Annie's birth date, her bank account information, her Social Security number. They've basically stolen her identity by now for their own purposes. They can destroy the Logans' lives right now or even worse, track them down and harm them if they want to."

Marcie's brow furrowed. So, if it's too late, I'll ask again, "Why not unplug Annie's computer?"

Nathan picked up the discussion "Because if the attack is legit, we need to convince them that this part of their plan could be effective. They would obviously have a fallback position if this doesn't work. They seem to be desperate to stop the trade tariffs from being implemented. This is only the first part of the plan. If we can convince them there's still a possibility it could work, they won't go on to Phase Two, which for all we know could be much worse. It buys us time to try to find a way to stop them."

Nathan continued, "Welchie, you're really the one who should be monitoring Annie's computer. You know what to look for."

"That's not a problem, Nathan, you'll know, too. For now, let's just confirm that this threat is real. That's the next step."

"Can you show us how to install this spyware?" said Nathan. "Because I still don't understand how a spy at the other end controlling Annie's computer won't know we're there."

Welch glanced at him. "For one thing, he won't be expecting you in there. For another, I do this for a living. Annie won't be able to tell you're monitoring her computer and neither will these guys who have no right to be watching her. In effect, we'll be creating a mirror image of her computer. You won't be poking around. All you'll be doing is observing to confirm that what she thinks is happening really *is* happening on her computer.

"Now shall we get started? It's really quite simple. Software like this is available commercially to allow parents to monitor their kids' activities on the computer or corporations to monitor their employees. This is more sophisticated, obviously, but it's the same general idea. It's totally stealth and cannot be detected by anyone who is controlling that computer."

With a few keystrokes, Welch installed the monitoring software on Nathan's computer. "Did you discuss an email with Annie?"

Marcie responded, "Yes, Annie attended a surprise party for me in honor of our upcoming wedding. I'm going to send an email with a thank you note attached. Is that good?"

"It's innocuous enough, but it has to be executable. So let's make it an animated thank you card that she has to click on to activate. I'll embed the RAT into the executable file and voila, you will have access."

Marcie looked confused. "I'm sorry, but what's RAT?"

"A RAT means Remote Administration Tool. When Annie clicks on your thank you card to see it, Marcie, the software I'm installing will kick in and become active and give you access to Annie's computer. You'll be able to see everything she's seeing. It's like you'll be sitting in front of her computer watching over her shoulder except you'll be at home. Just give me a minute."

James Welch tapped away on his keyboard. After a few minutes, he swung the computer around so Marcie and Nathan could see it. There was a thank you note he had composed with a "Click" button on the front. He clicked on it and an animated rabbit popped out of a hat holding a sign. The sign read, 'Thank you for attending my surprise party.'

Marcie's eyes were the size of saucers. "You created *that* just now while we were sitting here?"

"Sort of. Sorry, Marcie, but you don't really need to know more. The less you know, the better. Let's just say I adapted an existing card a little. Your job now is to encourage Annie to play dumb. We have to convince the hackers that their plan could still work. We want to see what they try next. Send Annie the email and let me know what happens. That's going to be the next step. And it's going to be critical."

CHAPTER 17

Marcie and Nathan thanked James Welch and walked to their car. As soon as they pulled away from the building, Marcie turned to Nathan. "What did he mean, the less we know the better?"

"Well, I suspect he borrowed the graphic software for the animation from one of those automated greeting card sites." Nathan used air quotes when he referred to the word "borrowed," indicating that his friend may not have been totally above board with his online activity in the office. "The software would be proprietary, so if he did that, it's not exactly legal. I think that's what he didn't want to tell us."

"Oh my God, it's unbelievable. This is a world I know nothing about. I'm beginning to think nothing in the computer world is unattainable if someone with professional know-how and a few tricks up their sleeve really wants it."

Nathan agreed. "Yeah, just remember, we're doing this to help a friend, but we don't know what we're really involved in. We have to be careful." He remained quiet for a few minutes before reaching out and resting his hand on her leg as he drove. Then he added, "Marcie, I have to tell you something. I might have to ask you to step away if this really does become a matter of national security. There's only so much you should see—you don't have security clearance."

Marcie's brow furrowed as they drove on in silence until they arrived at the condo.

Once inside, she plugged in the laptop and turned it on. She clicked on her email app and hit "Send" on the message with the thank you card to Annie's address.

Then they waited.

‹ ‹ ‹ › › ›

Annie walked in and out of her office a few times throughout the day. There would be an email from Marcie waiting for her, but she couldn't bring herself to turn on her computer. Her shoulder muscles tightened every time she stepped into the room.

Around 6 p.m., she decided she had waited long enough. She recalled Marcie's comment about drinking, but she poured herself a glass of wine, anyway. Craig's words wanting her to call a private counselor about her drinking also ricocheted around her brain. He was probably right, but now was not the time. She needed strength to deal with her issues. Alcohol gave her that strength. She would deal with the problem later. She was proud that she had managed to talk herself out of a drink several times that day, but now she absolutely needed it for fortification. She'd only had one glass, and that was before Marcie and Nathan had come over in the morning. She had to do what they had told her to do and she would need the strength to do it. But just like other times lately, one glass led to more. Finally, she'd imbibed enough liquid courage to boot up her computer.

〈 〈 〈 〉 〉 〉

"Where the hell is she?" Marcie ran her fingers through her hair as she checked her email account for what seemed like the hundredth time since they got home. "Didn't she say they told her to turn on her computer at 10 o'clock? It's 9:15 and she still hasn't opened my email. How're we supposed to help her if she won't help herself?"

Nathan shrugged in the chair he sat on beside his fiancée. "I don't know, Marce. Maybe we weren't convincing enough. We can't just let it go. We'll have to talk to her again."

Steam rose from the coffee mugs on the desk in front of them. They had busied themselves throughout the afternoon, running errands. After dinner, Marcie had brewed a fresh pot—mostly to make the time go faster and to keep her busy. Nathan never turned down a freshly brewed coffee. He had become addicted when he worked for the FBI since it was an unwritten rule that a meeting could never be conducted without coffee. Twelve cups a day was not uncommon. He was making a valiant effort to cut back with Marcie's help, but she had determined that what they were about to do could not be done without coffee.

Marcie got up from her chair and was through the door of the office on her way to the bathroom when a faint notification sounded announcing the arrival of an email. She ran back to the chair and there it was. An acknowledgment that her email had been opened had finally arrived. She moved over so Nathan could have a better sightline to the screen.

"I feel guilty looking at someone else's computer," Marcie said uncomfortably. "I feel like a voyeur. This is your field of expertise."

"I presume you don't mean my field of expertise is voyeurism." Nathan opened the remote administration tool's dashboard and with a couple of clicks, they were staring at Annie's computer screen. More specifically, they were staring at an email that Annie's husband Craig had sent her. The email was a combination of straight talk with an underlying current of caring. It essentially begged her to get her life together, stop her drinking, and it ended with a phone number that Craig wanted her to call. Nathan murmured, "Counselor for her drinking, probably" as he read the text and Marcie murmured an agreement. The email sat open on the screen for a long time. Nathan and Marcie couldn't tell if she was still staring at it or had walked away from her computer. Then, at 9:50, Annie clicked on her Facebook page.

Nathan and Marcie watched as Annie scrolled through her timeline updates. She clicked open some group pages, but didn't remain very long on any page. Apparently, Annie was just mindlessly clicking. She was probably also fully cognizant of the fact that she was being watched, possibly by more than just Nathan and Marcie.

Precisely at 10 o'clock, the slow methodical meanderings of Annie's cursor were replaced as if the mouse had been ripped from her hands. It darted around the screen. Nathan and Marcie stared as the cursor raced here and there, shutting down each of the programs Annie had open. Then it clicked open her word processing application. A shiver raced down Marcie's spine. Watching this happen in mere seconds made it seem as if the computer was possessed—as if it had been taken over by an alien life form. She sat forward with her hands buried under her legs. She shivered again. Her eyes were fixated on the screen and her breathing had escalated sharply. It was like she was being chased and the person behind her was gaining with every step.

Nathan's attention was rigidly focused on the screen in front of him. All doubt vanished in an instant. Annie had been telling the truth. Someone was unquestionably controlling her computer.

Words began appearing on the screen in huge block letters.

HELLO ANNIE LOGAN

  WE'RE BACK

  YOU LOOK GOOD IN GREEN

  YOUR CONVERSATION WITH YOUR HUSBAND DID NOT GO WELL

  HE DOES NOT BELIEVE YOU

  YOU HAVE TO TRY HARDER

  THE EXECUTIVE ORDER TO TAX CHINESE IMPORTATIONS TO AMERICA MUST BE STOPPED WITHIN SIX DAYS

  YOU MUST DO BETTER

  IF YOU DON'T WANT YOUR LIFE AND THAT OF YOUR HUSBAND DESTROYED FOREVER

  TALK TO YOUR HUSBAND AND GET HIM TO STOP THE EXECUTIVE ORDER

  TURN ON YOUR COMPUTER AT 5 PM TOMORROW

  WE MUST SEE PROGRESS AT THAT TIME

  TO PROVE WE ARE SERIOUS, SOMEONE WILL BE AT YOUR DOOR IN A FEW MINUTES

Marcie and Nathan sat frozen, but nothing further appeared. Marcie fumbled in her purse to find her phone so she could take a photo of the screen, but she barely pulled it out when the word "MINUTES" disappeared from the screen, rapidly followed by all the other words from right to left until they were all gone.

"Shit," she said as she threw her phone back in her purse. "I should've been ready."

Nathan sprang from his chair. "Let's go! We'll call 911 on the way. We have to get over there *now*. Annie's in danger!"

❮ ❮ ❯ ❯

Annie sat unmoving in her chair, except for the convulsions that were wracking her body from what she had just seen. Terror raced through her unchecked. She was frightened in a way she'd never been before. She shivered, yet sweat trickled down her back and formed in her armpits. *Who was doing this? And why me? Why couldn't they have picked someone else?* She felt violated. They *knew* she was wearing a green blouse. They could *see* her through the camera, but the camera wasn't on. There was no light to indicate it was on. *How can they do this?* She had to talk to Craig and make him understand.

But it was the last sentence that had her shaking uncontrollably. *Someone was coming to the door?* What did *that* mean? Her heart was beating so fast that she couldn't breathe. She wouldn't answer the door. She would hide in the kitchen. There was no gun in the house, but she had knives in the kitchen. She would defend herself somehow if they broke in. She ran to the front door and made sure it was locked. She ran to the back door. Locked. *Should I call 911?*

Then Annie heard a rustling noise outside.

CHAPTER 18

Could she have imagined the sounds of someone outside? A wooden block with slots for 15 knives sat on the counter of Annie's kitchen. There was also space for a pair of kitchen shears and a sharpening steel. By the time she raced from the computer room to her kitchen, she had thought of what she would do. She yanked an 8-inch carving knife from its slot and held it in her hand. This is insane, she thought. Could she really fend someone off with a knife? *What if they had a gun?* Neither Craig nor she believed in having guns in the house. *What choice do I have?*

She couldn't stop shaking. She had to calm herself. A half-full bottle of wine sat on the counter and she wished she had time to pull the cork out and swig two mouthfuls. Just two mouthfuls. She would feel the familiar warmth that would ease some of the tension from her body.

There was no time.

She looked around the room for a convenient hiding place. The only place out of the sightlines of the kitchen windows was the entrance into the living room. She quickly moved there, knife in hand and lowered herself with her back to the wall. She peeked around the corner into the living room. Satisfied that she couldn't be seen from any of the windows in the house, she sat back with her legs under her, balancing on her feet. She took a deep breath and listened as hard as could.

She strained her ears as she crouched. Only eerie silence responded. The wind rustling the trees. *Wait! Was that only the wind? Or was it someone just outside the door? Where were Nathan and Marcie? Hadn't they seen what had happened on her computer? Were they on their way to her?* Maybe the sounds were the police. Her mind swirled, clearly not firing on all cylinders. She thought she should call 911 but her phone was in her purse in the living room where she had tossed it as she left the office earlier. She was shaking uncontrollably. She could only hope that someone would come to rescue her from this nightmare. If only Craig were here . . . She felt the weight of the knife in her hand. *Why wouldn't he listen to her? But how could he?* She was a mess and she knew it. If she survived this ordeal, she vowed to pour all the wine in the house down the sink and never buy another bottle. Ever.

She stole a glance at the back door. It was still securely locked. Should she unlock it and try to leave? Where would she go? There was a 5-foot privacy fence wrapping around her back yard—there was no way she could climb over it. If she left, she would be trapped. *Besides, what if whoever it was came in the back door instead of the front? What if there was more than one and they came to both doors?*

Annie stared at the knife jiggling in her trembling hand. Her whole body shook. A chill swept over her, yet her blouse clung to her as rivulets of sweat trickled down her body. Even the soles of her feet were wet. She switched the knife to her other hand and wiped the sweat from her free hand on her leg. She repeated the motion with the other hand. Then she gripped the handle of the knife with both hands to try to stop the shaking.

Tires screeched as a vehicle slid to a stop on the street. Annie squeezed her eyes shut in terror. She opened them again and inched her head around the corner to look into the living room, but the drapes remained closed. They hadn't been opened since she got the first message on the computer. Something flashed in the corner of her eye. She looked back towards the kitchen window. She was sure she had seen a light bounce off the side of the neighbor's house. *I'm so scared. What is going on?* Suddenly, the front door shook as someone rapped loudly.

The doorbell rang. Once. Twice.

This is it.

Annie leaned her head back against the wall and squeezed her eyes shut again. *Go away.* Annie was frozen with fear except for the trembling that wouldn't stop.

A loud voice on the other side of the door announced, "Police. Open up."

Was that the man at the door pretending to be the police to lure her outside? Could it be the police?

Annie stayed still, frozen in her spot. She gripped the handle of the knife tighter.

The same loud voice: "Annie Logan. Are you in there?"

Her eyes flew open. What should she do? She had to think. Her mind was so cloudy. She couldn't think. She could run to the front door and using the element of surprise, try to run past the man.

What should I do?

She put her head back against the wall and took in three long breaths.

She put the knife in her right hand so that her left was free to unlock the front door.

She took a step around the corner into the living room. She would grab her phone and dial the emergency number. Then she would peek through a crack in the closed drape to see who was there.

She took one full stride towards the entrance when the front door crashed in.

She covered her ears to try to stop the noise.

CHAPTER 19

Nathan and Marcie raced towards Annie's house in Nathan's car, exceeding every speed limit. He hoped he didn't get caught as he burned a red light at one intersection and blasted through a stop sign at another. As he swung the car around the corner onto Annie's street with tires squealing, Marcie gasped. Emergency vehicles blocked the street in front of Annie's house, their red and blue flashing lights bouncing off the sides of neighboring houses.

Nathan slid his car to a stop in front of the yellow police tape, startling an officer standing just inside the perimeter. He commented, "There's an ambulance, that's not good," as he opened the door with one hand and slammed the shift into park with the other. "This is a crime scene, Marcie. You're going to have to stay outside the perimeter." He was relieved he had been working on the exploitation case under contract with the FBI so that he carried the credentials to get in. "I'll let you know as soon as I find out what's happened."

"Okay, I see Sami over there in the crowd. I'll go and talk to her."

Nathan hopped out of the car and ran around the front, leaving the door gaping open. The startled young officer guarding the perimeter had his hand on the handle of his gun as Nathan approached. After a brief stop to flash his credentials in the glow of the street lights, Nathan continued past the young officer, past the police cars, fire trucks, ambulances and first responder vehicles. He was taken aback when he saw Annie sitting forlornly in the back seat of a police car closest to the entrance to her house. Nathan stopped at the closed window to show Annie he was there and shouted that he would be back after he talked to the person in charge. Perplexed, he jogged to the doorstep of Annie's house where he was met by a burly police officer blocking the door. Nathan was shocked to see the door hanging askew from one hinge.

"Can I help you?" Gruff and deadly serious.

Nathan flashed his credentials again. "I'm a consultant with the FBI. We've been working on a case with international implications with Ms. Logan. I saw her in the car. Where's the officer in charge?"

The officer's demeanor softened. "Officer Juanita Suarez is the one in charge. She's right over there."

Nathan stepped aside as first responders exited the house. Over his shoulder, Nathan noted that the young officer was pulling down the police tape, and the various vehicles parked in front started to pull away from the curb, except for the car with Annie in the back. The police officer to whom he'd been directed sat on the same couch where Nathan had taken his notes earlier that day. She looked to be about 5 feet 5 inches with a stocky frame. Her hair was tied back in a pony tail, and her tanned skin highlighted her blue eyes. By contrast, the face he had seen in the back seat of the police car was ashen.

He stepped over pieces of wood from the shattered door and introduced himself to the officer, who told him she was Sergeant Juanita Suarez. Flashing his FBI credentials, Nathan explained that he was working with the bureau on a classified international case. "I'm sure you understand I can't divulge the details," he said as she nodded. "Anyway, Officer, can you tell me what happened here?"

"Of course, Mr. Harris." She consulted her notes. "We got a call just after 10 p.m. that someone was threatening to commit suicide at this address. The caller identified himself as Craig Logan, chief of staff to the president of the United States. The caller sounded frantic to the dispatcher and identified the victim as his wife. When we arrived, no one answered the door, although we identified ourselves and knocked loudly. Based on what we had been told—and the lack of response from the interior of the house—we believed there might be a potential suicide in progress, so we used a ram on the door to break in. Ms. Logan confronted us with a large knife in her hand. She didn't drop the knife when she was requested to do so, so we had to use force to disarm her. She had alcohol on her breath. So far, she has refused to say what she planned to do with the knife. That's why she's in cuffs in the back seat of my car."

Nathan imagined the scene before responding. "We were on our way over and called 911 as well, but our call must've been received after the call from Craig Logan. We didn't know what was going on, so it may've contributed to the confusion. Yes, I saw her in your car. You can release her into my custody. She's not a threat to anyone, and I believe the knife in her hand was merely to protect herself from an unknown assailant. She's had a rough couple of days, trust me."

"Okay. I can do that."

As they approached the car, Annie bit her lower lip and her elbows were pressed into her sides as if she was trying to disappear. When she was released, she leapt up and threw her arms around Nathan.

He gently removed Annie's arms and guided her back into the house.

Suarez followed. "I'll just need you to sign a document turning her over to you."

Annie sat on the couch and stared at the carpet with her hands clasped firmly between her knees. Nathan looked at Suarez. "Sure, no problem. Did you call Ms. Logan's husband back to tell him his wife's okay?"

"I was just about to do that when you walked in."

"I suggest you go ahead and do it, so you can close the case from your end. I'll take it after that. Sound okay to you?"

"Yes, that's fine." Annie's phone now sat on the coffee table. "I'm sure you have your husband's name on speed dial, Ms. Logan. Mind if I use your phone?"

Annie looked up with a start, but Nathan quickly stopped Suarez before she could pick up the phone. "Would you mind using your own phone, Sergeant? We might need to use Ms. Logan's for evidence in the case we're working on."

Suarez frowned as she glanced at Harris, but let it go. "The chief of staff didn't leave a private number when he called. Do you have one I can use, Ms. Logan?"

Annie slowly recited the number as if she was on autopilot.

Suarez dialed.

Nathan listened closely to Suarez' part of the conversation after she introduced herself.

"Mr. Logan, this is Officer Juanita Suarez here in Florida. I'm following up on your 911 call to let you know that your wife, Annie, is fine."

Suarez' face tightened.

"The phone call you made around 10 o'clock, sir, expressing your concern about your wife's health."

Suarez' head jerked back in surprise as she listened.

"So you're telling me you didn't make any phone calls? Can you tell me where you were at that time?"

Suarez's eyes were drifting slowly back and forth between Harris and Annie.

"In a meeting with the president? I see. Thank you for your time. I'm sorry to have bothered you. Would you like to speak to your wife? She'll explain everything."

She nodded as if Logan could see her through the phone line. "Just a second, please." She handed the phone to Annie.

Nathan knew Logan would want to know what was going on, and Annie would certainly want to tell him. But he caught her eye instead and shook his head no. He whispered, "Tell him not to worry, that I'll call him in a few minutes to explain everything." Nathan could hear their conversation through the speaker on Annie's phone, and he could tell Logan was upset about receiving a phone call from a police officer asking him about a call to his wife that he had never made. He would have to make the call soon to explain everything.

Harris heard Annie's soft, halting voice trying to placate her husband. It seemed to make him more upset when she told him he would be getting a call from the FBI. She ended the conversation and slowly and deliberately handed the phone back to Suarez.

Suarez got up to leave. "It looks like you have a case of swatting on your hands, Mr. Harris."

Nathan glanced at Annie whose eyes stared at him questioningly.

He said to Annie that he would explain the term later and then looked back to Suarez. "I take it Mr. Logan said he didn't make the 911 call."

"He said he was in a meeting with the president. I'll leave it to you to sort this out. It seems you have some knowledge about this that you're not at liberty to share. So if you don't need anything further from me, I'll be on my way."

"Thanks very much, Sergeant. One more thing. Could you have an officer stationed outside Ms. Logan's house until this blows over? I'm pretty sure this is more than a prank phone call. In fact, I suspect it's related to the case we're working on. It's possible nothing further will happen now, but just in case . . . Other than that, I think we can take care of it from here."

Suarez started to object. "Mr. Harris, we're short staffed. I don't see how . . ."

"Did I mention this is possibly a case of national security, Officer?"

Suarez' eyes met Nathan's. "You did. I'll have someone sit outside. There will be someone there for as long as necessary."

"Thank you, Officer Suarez. I appreciate that." Nathan signed the necessary documents and watched her leave before turning towards Annie. "You've been a victim of swatting. It seems like the person or persons controlling your computer wanted to reinforce to you the power they have over you. Usually swatting is done as a prank call to bring the whole Swat team down on someone as payback or revenge. There've been many instances like yours where the team has broken down doors and arrested people on the spot until it gets sorted out. It scares the victim half to death, as I'm sure it did to you. We saw everything on your computer, Annie. We saw the threat that someone would soon be at your door so we hurried over. I think we can assume the person who has control of your computer called 911 and told the dispatcher he was your husband and that you were about to commit suicide. Why were you holding the knife? Was it to protect yourself?"

Her voice trembled and she rubbed her wrists. Her words spilled out. "I absolutely hate this. I feel like I'm falling apart. Why are they doing this to me? I—I didn't know who was coming. They just said they were 'sending someone.' That's why I hid in the kitchen with the knife. They said they were the police when they knocked on the door, but I didn't want to take any chances. I didn't know for sure. How could I? I was just going to get my phone to call 911 myself when they crashed through the door. I felt like a deer in the headlights when they burst in. They were yelling and shining lights in my face." She shuddered. "It—it was like the knife was stuck to my hand." Her head sank towards her chest. "I feel so humiliated. What're the neighbors going to think? What about my door?"

Nathan rested his hand on hers. "I understand. Don't worry about the neighbors. You're doing really well, Annie, under the circumstances. I'll call someone to get the door replaced. But first there's something else we need to talk about. The hackers said that your conversation with your husband didn't go well. Were you in front of the computer when you made the phone call to Mr. Logan? Or did you call him on your computer? Did you use Skype or something?"

Annie thought for a minute. "No, I used my cell phone in my bedroom. Oh no . . . !" Her hand shot to her mouth.

Nathan leaned back on the couch looking directly into Annie's eyes. There could be no mistake about what he was about to tell her "Listen, there's something I'd like you to do. I'm going to call your husband to explain everything. When he calls you back, and he will, just go with whatever he says. You'll have to play a role. I'm going to ask him to do the same. Just play along with each other. Do you think you can do that?

"I don't know. I'm such a mess right now. Why do I have to do that?"

"I think you know why, Annie. We have to assume that the people doing this are listening in on your phone calls now, too."

CHAPTER 20

Nathan found Marcie outside talking to her friend Sami among the crowd of anxious onlookers. Much of the crowd had disbursed, but there were still a few hangers-on milling about. Nathan announced in a loud voice that he had just been inside, that Annie Logan was fine, that it had been a misunderstanding and that everyone should go home. Shouted voices asked who he was, but he ignored them. He greeted Sami, who nervously pinched the skin at her throat.

"Is Annie really all right, Nathan?" Sami asked. She added quietly, "Does this have anything to do with, uh, you know—her drinking?"

"Not this time, Sami. I can't divulge what's going on right now, but I can assure you she's fine. She's just going through a difficult time. Marcie and I are going to help her as much as we can. I'm going back in the house in a few minutes to spend some time with her. We're going to have to get that door fixed. Would you mind arranging that for her and maybe staying with her until it's done? I arranged for police protection, but I think she could use more friends right now."

Sami assured them she would call the handyman she and her husband Mason used, and that she would stay with Annie as long as she was needed. After they said their goodbyes, Sami walked back in the direction of her house and Nathan and Marcie headed up the walkway back towards Annie's place. Nathan stopped Marcie before they reached the shattered door at the front step and filled her in on some of the details of the swatting incident. He put his hands on her arms, looking directly into her eyes. "I'm not sure how much you should be involved in this, Marcie. This is clearly becoming a case for the FBI and probably Homeland Security. I could get into a lot of trouble by involving you any further."

"I understand, Nathan. I really do, and it's okay. You know I want to help any way I can, but you're right, I don't need to be involved in national security stuff. That's what you do." Marcie smiled at him affectionately. "I'll go home and make some calls to ensure everything's okay for our wedding reception. Your job, in addition to saving the world, will be to show up. Sound fair?"

"Sounds good to me." Nathan kissed her and watched her walk back to the car. He said as she turned to wave, "I'll be out in a few minutes."

Nathan walked back inside the house to find Annie sitting on the couch. She looked sheepishly at him as he sat down beside her.

"I know what you're thinking. I have to stop drinking so much. I wouldn't have been in so much trouble with the police if they hadn't smelled alcohol on my breath."

For the first time, Nathan noticed a scrape on her chin. Probably where she landed when the police took her down. Her wrists were an angry red from the flex cuffs the police had used to bind her. They would be sore in the morning. "You weren't exactly in trouble, Annie. They just didn't know what you were doing with the knife. Obviously you couldn't tell them the truth, although maybe you could've said you thought you heard an intruder outside your house. Or handed over the knife when they first asked you. Anyway, Annie, your drinking didn't help the situation. You should seriously consider taking your husband's advice and getting some help."

Nathan kept his tone even to make sure his point was taken. "Now, I'm going to take Marcie home and when I get there, I'll call your husband. It's a lot safer to do it there if people are listening on your phone. I'll ask Mr. Logan to call you when we've finished talking. I jotted down the number when you gave it to Sergeant Suarez."

"Thank you so much for your help, Nathan. I don't know what I'd do without you and Marcie."

"You know, Annie," he replied, "Marcie and I thought about asking you if you'd like to come stay with us for a few days. But I thought it might be easier if we arranged for police protection instead. There'll be someone outside until this is over."

"Is that going to be a problem since someone's already watching what's going on through my computer? They said no authorities."

"I'm pretty sure they wouldn't be surprised a police presence has been added. By calling 911, they've already upped the ante. Besides, you're the wife of the chief of staff. No-one should be surprised to see security outside your door."

"Thanks, Nathan. Sami said earlier that she could stay with me as well and I think I'll take her up on it."

"Good idea. You have a good friend there, Annie. Don't worry, we'll get this sorted out. But please, put the wine away. Remember what I said. When your husband calls, go along with whatever he says. We want you to act like everything's normal on the surface for the benefit of whoever's on the other end of your computer. We need to play their game for now. It'll buy us some time. I'm sure you'll hear from your husband soon."

As Nathan turned to leave, Sami came through the door. Good, he thought. Reinforcements for Annie. Leaning over to Sami, he whispered, "See if you can get her to stay away from the wine," and walked out to his car where Marcie was waiting.

‹ ‹ › ›

Nathan and Marcie drove back to the condo and Nathan went into his office to dial Craig Logan's private number on the secure phone line he had installed when he started his consulting business. The connection was made immediately. Nathan introduced himself and Logan was anxious for answers.

"What's going on, Agent Harris? How is Annie? The police officer told me you'd be calling. Why is the FBI involved?"

"Mr. Logan, thank you for taking my call. Annie's fine. I'm actually a former FBI agent, but I'm working now as a contract consultant for the agency. I'm on this case partly because my fiancée Marcie is a friend of Annie's. Just bear with me and everything will become clearer. Your wife has done nothing wrong, sir. I just came back from seeing her a few minutes ago. A friend is staying with her. I wanted to assure you she's okay before saying anything further. What I'm about to tell you should be kept in strictest confidence.

Logan's concern was clear. "I'm so relived Annie's okay. Please go ahead."

Nathan took a deep breath. This is where things would start to get tricky and he needed to be sure Logan didn't get defensive. "I think you're aware, sir, that Annie's credit cards were compromised.

Apparently she's the victim of more than just identity theft with her cards. Someone that we suspect is from another country has managed to infiltrate her computer and possibly her phone as well, and they are now making threats. You probably will know more about this than we do, but whoever it is says there is some secret executive order that's about to be signed by the president. Supposedly this order would gravely affect China trade and they want to stop it before it's signed. We planted our own software into Annie's computer to monitor what's happening and everything she says is true. They apparently can even see her through her laptop camera, and they say that if she doesn't cooperate and get you to stop the law from becoming effective, that there will be dire consequences. They haven't been specific about what those consequences might be, but they have referred to ruining your lives. I believe Annie tried to tell you about this last night. The reason I'm calling you right now, Mr. Logan, is we believe they've hacked her cell phone as well as her computer so it isn't safe for her to speak to you on her own phone."

Nathan stopped and waited for a response.

Logan had been listening intently and after a moment, he responded.

"Oh my God, I can't believe this. I feel terrible. She did call last night talking about people taking over her computer. It sounded like it was straight from Star Wars. I'm afraid I wasn't very patient with her. You're probably already aware that Annie has a drinking problem and I know that can occasionally lead to paranoia. I told her to get help. Why wouldn't they come after me? Why Annie? Cowards!"

"I'm aware that she has an issue with drinking, but right now we need to understand why someone is doing this. If there's any truth to the fact that there is some kind of upcoming secret law that would adversely affect trade relations with China, then this means someone somewhere is prepared to take any steps to stop it. Since you're the president's chief of staff, they must think you have enough influence over him to get him to take a step back from signing the executive order. I'm sure it would be easier to hack into her computer than yours. They're using her as leverage to get to you. It would help to know whether you are working on something with the president that will affect the Chinese."

An audible intake of breath. A definite tell that something other than the complete truth was coming. "I'm afraid it's highly classified. I can't confirm or deny."

Nathan sighed and tried again. "The Chinese have apparently found out about something that's being worked on and they're trying to stop it by using your wife to get to you and ultimately, to the president. Her computer has been hacked and they're threatening to ruin her and you, if you don't take steps to stop it. I understand that you aren't at liberty to say anything to me, sir, but please take a moment to reconsider. I don't have the information to substantiate the reason for their threats, but surely you do." Nathan paused, then added, "I believe they've referred to proposed tariffs on Chinese products coming into the States."

Seconds ticked by without a word being spoken. Nathan could only hear Logan's breathing. Finally, he spoke. "Okay, we're working on something that could have a serious effect on or maybe even destroy their economy when it becomes law, but there's no way they could've found out about it. They referred specifically to tariffs? And an Executive Order? But how? It's highly classified and the only way they could've found out is if there's a leak somewhere. This is unbelievable. What do they mean they'll ruin us?"

"They've warned Annie not to involve anyone other than you because they feel you're the key to stopping the progress of the proposed law," said Nathan. "My fiancée Marcie who's become friends with Annie now, stumbled across this by accident." Now that he had the chief of staff's ear, Nathan filled in all the details for Logan swiftly, including the takeover of Annie's computer that he and Marcie had witnessed. He added, "It's probably best not to involve White House security until we get to the bottom of how the Chinese got their hands on the information they shouldn't have. The FBI can investigate externally. By being able to infiltrate Annie's computer, everything on it is compromised, sir, and anything there that relates to you as well. Let me ask you this: How close is this law to becoming effective?"

"It's being considered by President Hughes's advisers right now. If and when they agree on something and President Hughes also agrees with it, he will sign an executive order to make it happen. It will be effective immediately."

"Then that's why the person said he wants it stopped within seven days—well, less than six days now. We need to buy some time so we can try to determine who is doing this and put a stop to it, Mr. Logan. Is there going to be opposition? How can the process be slowed down? Does it ultimately have to go to the House for debate?"

Logan's tone changed slightly. "I'll be totally honest with you. I know you've got security clearance as a representative of the FBI, so I assume you'll keep this to yourself. President Hughes is going to sign the executive order very soon, and the few people involved know this. It's true there's opposition because some people don't personally like the way this president does things. Many in Congress and the Senate agree that something needs to be done about the trade imbalance. But many members of the House also feel that negotiation and diplomacy are the best way to get things done with the Chinese and wouldn't support suddenly springing surprises on them through enacted executive orders. Add to that the fact that the order was drafted by the Executive Branch instead of by Congress, and they feel it was done behind closed doors without input or debate. When the president signs an executive order, there's no debate. It's a done deal unless judges overturn it and they could care less about trade. The bottom line is, when this goes through, this could cost the Chinese economy billions. Their economy has been slowing. They want to *increase* exports, not diminish them. As I said earlier, it could even set back their economy for years. So, they're not going to be happy. *If* they really know about it, it might be enough to make them react."

Logan stopped for a moment and then asked Nathan the inevitable "what if" question. "So, given that the executive order is likely to happen soon, what's the worst that can happen to my wife and I if it is signed?"

"We don't know the full extent of their plans, but I asked that question of the computer experts at the FBI. Without going into the sordid detail, your lives could become a living hell. Never knowing if you're safe anywhere you go. Your identities stolen, your finances wiped out, your credit destroyed—the possibilities are endless, I'm afraid. And they aren't giving us much time. We only have a few days left according to the hacker. Maybe it's time for you to think about telling the president. He'll listen to you, won't he?"

Logan hesitated but didn't respond to Nathan's question.

After a few telling seconds, Nathan said, "Well, anyway, your wife Annie is waiting for your call. But there's something I'd like you to do. We want to convince the people controlling her computer that their plan could work, but we need you to make a big show of telling your wife you're skeptical. Let's keep them off balance. Use whatever tactic you want. She'll be expecting it. We want them to keep trying so they will hopefully make a mistake. We'll set up a secure call for the two of you afterwards so you can have a proper conversation."

"Oh great. So they can start taking steps to destroy us in public? And then what??"

"It's a gamble since they say they're going to try wipe you out. We're playing a cat and mouse game here. We're trying to flush them out. We can take precautions. It's a calculated risk, but we don't have much time. I'll keep you posted on any developments on our end. In the meantime, I strongly suggest you try to get the president to slow down on this law, whatever it takes. They're threatening you and your wife, but I suspect they have bigger plans. The security and safety of the entire country could be at stake here."

Logan's tone didn't sound optimistic. "I'll talk to him. Thanks very much for bringing me up to date."

Nathan was about to hang up when he barely heard Logan saying something else into the phone. Nathan put the phone to his ear again so he could hear.

Logan must have sensed that Nathan had not heard as he started again. "Something just occurred to me that might somehow be connected. One of my staff visited Shanghai not long ago and died there very suddenly. He was severely overweight, and it happened to be brutally hot and humid in Shanghai the week he was there. Everyone was saddened to hear the news, of course, but nobody thought it could be anything but a heart attack. But I'm wondering now if there was another connection somehow. The truth is, he was actually over there on a trade mission."

"Did his mission have something to do with this particular executive order that the Chinese are concerned about?"

There was hesitation at the other end of the phone. "I'm not able to tell you more, Mr. Harris, other than to say that I would advise you to look into the death more closely."

Just before he hung up, Logan added, "His name was Eric Hartman."

CHAPTER 21

Yang Lee prided himself on the care he took with missions, thinking them through, never making mistakes. Sure, a mission never went exactly as planned, but when you were handed an assignment in China, you completed it. The lovely Lian Lu was barely a distant memory. Her death had been a job for which he was well paid. She was the mission and he'd completed it as required. And that fat pig of an American, Eric Hartman. Getting rid of him was a pleasure. He would have gladly paid back some of the money for that job.

Yang Lee had lost count of the number of people he'd poisoned or destroyed through his computer hacking. But this new assignment wasn't going so well and it troubled him. He'd pored over the information gleaned from Annie Logan's computer and there was a treasure trove of passwords, banking information and other personal data about the Logans. The Americans may think he had it in for the Logans for some reason, but that wasn't the mission. The mission was to stop the executive order from being signed.

The problem that Lee could not have anticipated was the woman's drinking. She wasn't credible even to her own husband. He'd listened to a conversation between the Logans and it had gone badly. Logan was, to say the least, skeptical. Even when she told him about the police incident, he blamed her for overreacting and told her if she hadn't been drinking, none of it would have happened. He dismissed it by telling her it was a bunch of kids that had called the police. He had even used the example of a 16-year-old kid who had faced over 60 charges for prank calls that brought out entire SWAT divisions.

Craig Logan hadn't even completely believed her about Yang Lee's threatening messages on her computer screen. He had told his wife that at any given time, there were various pieces of legislation before Congress that were trade-related and some involved trade with China. Anyone could read about them in the paper, he'd said. He had disavowed any knowledge about the Executive Order. Logan had finally ended the call by insisting that she seek help for her drinking.

Now Lee sat again across the desk from Ji Cheung, the 4th Vice Premier of the People's Republic of China. A muscle was clearly visible in Cheung's clenched jaw and he tapped a finger slowly on his desk as he listened to Lee's update. The Vice Premier leaned forward in his chair. His voice was menacing. "So, as I understand it Lee, your progress report is that there is no progress. It appears we are no closer to resolving this issue than we were a few days ago when we spoke. What am I supposed to say to the Politburo? That we are going to fail? That soon we won't be able to export our electronics to the U.S. because no one will be able to afford our products?" His voice rose and the sharp retort of his hand slapping the desk rebounded around the room. He wasn't finished. "That our economy is going to slow to a crawl because we couldn't stop this idiot president from raising tariffs astronomically? They will want your head, Yang Lee, and possibly mine too if I tell them you failed. I don't think we want that."

Lee seethed inside. His university professors had spoken to him like this, some of whom he respected as experts in their field. He had tolerated that. But this guy was a *politician,* someone who was an expert at nothing, someone who let others do his bidding. He glanced at a pen on the desk and an image flashed through his mind of picking it up and sticking it into Cheung's eye until it penetrated his brain. But he uttered through closed lips, "I understand the importance of this mission. I assure you it won't fail."

With that he rose from the chair and turned towards the door. As he rounded the corner into the hall, Cheung's parting words echoed through the open door. "Make sure it doesn't fail, Mr. Lee. You will not like the consequences if it does."

As he walked outside, his mind swirled. Why did he ever take this job? The time frame was too short, the U.S. president too unpredictable and the people assigning the mission too hung up on saving face. That included the old man, Hu. Especially Hu. It was a perfect storm of potential problems for Lee. But, once he had accepted the assignment, that put his own reputation into play and he was not going to fail.

As he had done a few days earlier, he stopped next at Hu Electronics. The same exotic young beauty escorted him into Hu's office. Lee could have simply floated blindfolded into the office on the faint Jasmine aroma that trailed behind the woman. This conversation would not be an easy one, either, so he enjoyed the assault on his senses from the perfume while he could.

He sat in front of the old man who was as alert as ever. The smell of cigar smoke hung in the air, replacing the lovely perfume scent. He waited for Hu to speak first.

"So, Mr. Lee, you have brought me good news?"

"Unfortunately, sir, I'm afraid I don't have much to report yet." He decided to throw in a proverb to mollify the man. "Be not afraid of going slowly, be afraid only of standing still. I am working on our problem and should have a resolution soon."

Hu was not amused and threw a proverb back. "Coming events cast their shadows before them." He added slowly, "And I see shadows coming, Mr. Lee. Must I remind you that you are doing a job for which you have promised success. You understand you will be well paid? I wish to see you have success. Failure, you see, is not an option."

"I understand your position completely, sir. I will be happy to report back when I have good news to share. Please be patient while my plans take their course."

"Time is very short, Mr. Lee," Hu responded without emotion. "As I said before, you are to do whatever is necessary to stop this American tax on our exports from coming into law." Hu repeated for emphasis, "*Whatever* it takes."

Lee's body was wound tight as he left Hu Electronics. Pain throbbed between his shoulder blades. The sky was leaden, which suited his mood perfectly. It was as if the clouds were dropping to earth. He had just been warned by two very dangerous men. He knew all too well how closely linked the corporate world in China and the Chinese government were. Most major corporations are state-owned and have a member of the Communist party occupying an office in their building. Hu Electronics retained its independence by paying a hefty tax to the state. Lee doubted that Hu and Cheung knew of the other's involvement with him, but he had to be careful. Anything was possible.

Lee crossed through the park, totally ignoring the ever present tai chi practitioners as he walked by, his head down and his mind fully occupied. He thought about next steps. There were any number of things he could do. Of course he would destroy the Logans' reputation no matter what. They were causing him problems and they weren't co-operating. But there were other options as well. He could use Annie Logan's computer to launch any number of terror attacks. It might be possible to cause train collisions by controlling the track switches, shut down power grids, control street lights in a major city, shut down the Internet . . . He could even poison a water supply. His technical capabilities and experience were limitless, but he didn't have time to be creative. If this mission actually did fail, he would consider those things later. He would have to do something to save face. Someone would pay.

He might be able to hack directly into the government's computers again to create well-planned havoc. He could place some child pornography on the computers used by various members of Congress and connect them all to make it look like a coordinated effort. Too risky. Each of the actions would require time to probe weaknesses and develop software to launch an attack. And thanks to the clumsiness of the Russians with their election meddling, he had noticed when he discovered Hartman's travel plans that the Americans had significantly upgraded their security measures and encryption capabilities. Besides, this wasn't about nuisance attacks. It was about stopping a law from coming into effect. It was about stopping a reckless president from doing something that would require years for China to undo.

Yang Lee had heard enough in the phone call between Logan and his wife that he still had some confidence his initial plan would work. He still had a use for Annie Logan. He would use her, or at least her computer, to put pressure on the president through the American public and politicians. Yet, he realized the situation might call for even more immediate and drastic measures. He was always prepared.

He arrived at his building and upon entering his apartment, turned on his computer. He searched for the latest *Washington Post*. He also looked at some of the online sites that spewed anti-president

commentary because they often shed more light on political activities than mainstream media. He sifted through articles about the
president's penchant for meeting with his staunchest supporters. He
leaned back, contemplating what he had just read, sifting through
ideas to ramp up his plan. Quickly Lee made a decision. The people
he was working for would not tolerate failure and his ego would not
let him fail. If his next action with Annie Logan didn't work, it was
time to bring down the hammer.

That was his backup plan.

He picked up the phone and dialed.

A man at the other end answered. "Delta Airlines. How may I
help you?"

CHAPTER 22

President Hughes gestured for Craig Logan to come in and with his index and little fingers pointing to his ear and mouth, gestured to his chief of staff that he should wait until a phone call was finished. In spite of his reason for being there, Logan always held the Oval Office in high esteem and treated it with the reverence it deserved. As he sat on one of the beige couches, Logan could hear one side of the conversation through the partially-open door to the private study on the west side of the office. The president was making his views known to the person at the other end of the call in no uncertain terms.

Logan thought about the news he had received from Nathan Harris. He scanned the office as he went back over their conversation, hoping the history surrounding him would calm his nerves. He never tired of breathing in the historical significance and power of this office. Bursts of reds, whites and yellows caught his eye through the east door that led to the Rose Garden. The garden was perpetually in bloom, thanks to the colorful annuals that had been added to supplement the primary reason for the garden, the roses. He thought how much Annie would love it. As he continued his visual tour of the room, he marveled at the First Lady's decorating skill and attention to the significance of the country's history. Each president had the option of decorating to taste and choosing paintings from a collection maintained by the White House. The First Lady had chosen a portrait of George Washington to hang over the fireplace mantle on the north wall. A bust of Abraham Lincoln sat on a credenza along the side.

Logan's favorite part of the oval office was the choice of desks. Six desks had been used during various presidencies, but the one now utilized by President Hughes was the Resolute Desk. Logan recalled that it was made of the timbers of the HMS Resolute, a British Royal Navy Ship, which had been frozen in the ice in the Arctic and abandoned, but later found and refurbished. He didn't recall the whole story of this desk, but he did know that it had been used by a number of presidents, including John F, Kennedy, whom he admired greatly.

His thoughts were interrupted by the sound of the president ending his conversation. President Hughes strode into the room from his private study and greeted Logan. At 61 years of age, he was not the youngest nor the oldest president at the start of his term. He fell somewhere in the middle as eight of his predecessors were in their forties and one was seventy when they took office. His thin shape and erect stature made his 6-foot 1-inch frame look even taller, and it was topped with a full head of silver white hair. His royal blue suit sported an American flag pin in the left lapel. A recent poll suggested that 68% of the public thought his appearance to be "presidential." On the other hand, an abysmal 38% thought he had done a good job so far. His tanned face was thin and, Logan noticed, bags had recently appeared under his eyes after only a few weeks in power.

Logan dreaded the discussion they were about to have. The two sat on the sofas facing each other with an oval coffee table between them. The president started the conversation. "Before we begin, Craig, would you like some tea?" He lifted the pot sitting on the table and gestured towards the empty cup sitting in front of Logan.

"No thanks, sir. I don't want to take up more of your time than I have to."

Hughes added to his half-full cup that was now probably lukewarm after sitting there during his phone call. "I won't tell my wife you rejected tea from the teapot she designed. She actually designed the whole set of china. It arrived yesterday. Now, let's dispense with the "sir" stuff. You and I have known each other for a long time, Craig. I understand you have some concerns about the Chinese tariff policy."

Logan decided not to tell the president about the intrusion into his wife's computer—at least, not yet. "I'm really sharing the concerns of others, Jeff. There's a feeling among members on both sides of the House that we're poking the bear, so to speak, by not involving China in a trade discussion. There's some concern that imposing trade tariffs will simply encourage them to expand trade with other nations like Japan, New Zealand, Canada . . . As a result, some feel that the new tariffs may not have the desired effect and it will only anger the Chinese. The worst-case scenario is that we would lose our relevance in global markets."

"Craig, I need to send a message, plain and simple. I've heard rumblings that certain members of the House are unhappy. So what? Screw them! What have they done for me lately besides put up roadblocks for everything we've tried to accomplish?"

"With all due respect, Mr. President, there are experienced people you could call in for advice. They've dealt with the Chinese and know how they'll react in certain situations."

"I'm perfectly within my rights to sign this executive order, Craig, and I have some good advisers with strong business backgrounds telling me this will work. As my legal counsel has pointed out, I have three options. It may set your mind at ease to know what they are." He got up, walked to his desk and picked up a notepad.

Consulting his notes, he said, "I could use the *Trading with the Enemy Act* of 1917. It just says we have to be at war with someone—anyone—to impose tariffs as high as we want. We're at war with the terrorists, so that shouldn't be a problem. Then there's the *International Emergency Economic Powers Act* of 1977, which allows me to impose tariffs during a national emergency. I think our trade imbalance is a national emergency, don't you, Craig? Come on, lost jobs?! There's another one called the *Trade Act of 1974*. Section 122 of the act gives me authority to impose across-the-board tariffs if something is causing an adverse effect on our national security. Losing jobs to outsiders could certainly qualify. But under that one, we can only increase tariffs by 15% for a few months and then it has to be extended by Congress. I don't like that idea much.

"No, I'm confident we're on solid ground here, Craig. We've been in an unfair trade situation for a long time—too long! In fact, it's the biggest, unfair trade imbalance of any of our trading partners." The president's voice had risen. Clearly this was a topic that he wasn't in a mood to budge on.

Logan sensed he was facing a losing battle. Still taking the high road, he agreed with the president about the legalities being on his side. Without mentioning names, Logan explained the Chair of the

Subcommittee on International Trade and Global Competitiveness, Jim Prentice's concerns that increasing the cost of Chinese electronics could backfire, resulting in an increased cost of similar products. This argument also fell on deaf ears, as the president shot back, "Economists are always fear mongering. I haven't seen or heard a valid reason yet why we can't and shouldn't do this, Craig. My mind's about made up."

Logan felt a twinge of desperation. Somehow he had to make the president understand there was a lot more at stake than he could possibly know. He hesitated as he leaned forward, clasping his hands together with his elbows on his knees. "May we speak as the friends we were before all this started, sir?"

The president glared at Logan. "Of course, Craig, but if it's more of this talk about stalling the trade initiative, sorry, you're wasting your breath."

"It is in a way, sir, but not in the way you might expect." Logan inhaled sharply and didn't mince his words. "Annie and I are being blackmailed. And there's reason to believe it could be tied to the signing of the executive order."

The president stared at Logan over the tea cup poised at his lips. "Go on."

Logan explained the infiltration of his wife's computer, the dire threats that had been made not to tell anyone, the short time constraint and the clear message that their lives would be destroyed if action wasn't taken to stop the trade policy. He told the president about Nathan Harris' involvement, in spite of the warning not to tell the authorities and the FBI's belief that the threat was real. He was pleased to see the president was listening intently, but his argument was weakened when the president asked if China was behind the hacking. "We don't know yet," Logan said truthfully. "We have no way of knowing for certain at this time that it is actually the Chinese that are doing this. Although it seems very likely it's them."

Logan realized he had barely taken a breath as he explained the situation and now he sat back and waited for his old friend to say something. The president's next words shocked him, but it gave him a better understanding behind the president's motivations. He listened in stunned silence.

"Craig, I'm sorry to hear of your situation. When we're in positions of power, we make ourselves and our families vulnerable to attacks. I think you've done the right thing by including this Harris fellow and the FBI. But there are a few things that should encourage you. There's no way the Chinese could know what we're up to. I trust my advisers completely and they wouldn't leak the information. One of the reasons I didn't want to go to the House for approval is that U.S. Representatives don't even have to be security-cleared. Can you imagine? There are 435 of them there, and any one of them could be leaking details about this if they knew. We've kept this totally confidential."

Logan thought to himself that if this was becoming a matter of national security, a sane and rational approach would be to involve members of the National Security Council. But obviously that wasn't the way the Commander in Chief wanted to do things.

The president continued, "My feeling from what you've told me is that it's just some kid getting his kicks out of terrifying your wife and now you. And even if it isn't, we don't negotiate, Craig. You know that. We want the world to know how strong we are, and we're not going to kowtow to some guy with a computer and a death wish. Just keep doing what you're doing, Craig. Let this FBI guy deal with it and keep doing your job."

"May I remind you, sir, that the person or persons seem to have highly-specific details about your tariff executive order. I'm not sure how they would've received it, but whoever it is certainly knows of the existence of the order. This could signify there's a leak some-where close to you. The FBI is investigating Eric Hartman's death as a possible link since he was in China at the time."

The president volleyed back immediately. "I met Hartman in meetings a couple of times and I can't imagine him being involved. Besides, he was a low-level hack that had no access to anything important. Even if the Chinese found out about it somehow, we can't allow ourselves to appear weak. This may be one of those situa-tions. Stay strong, Craig. Once we have this trade tariff in place, we can focus our attention on the South China Sea. We want that area to remain as international waters in spite of what the Chinese think should happen to it. We have trillions of dollars of trade going through those waters. They'll know we mean business on trade when we hit them over the head with these tariffs."

Then the President of the United States revealed another reason for his insistence on following through with his plans, a reason far more personal and petty.

"Do you know the Chinese wouldn't even take my phone calls when I first took office? They never called to congratulate me, and I couldn't get through to their top leaders once I was elected. They didn't think it was worth their time to have a conversation with me."

Logan tried to keep from showing his shock at the president's words.

With lives on the line and a possible international crisis in the offing, he couldn't believe what he was hearing. The president of the United States wouldn't back down because his feelings were hurt!

So that's what this was about. The president had been insulted and it was payback time. He was throwing his weight around *because he could.*

Logan got up and thanked Hughes for his time.

All that prevented him from slamming the door on the way out was deference to the position and office of the President of the United States.

CHAPTER 23

The silence lay over the interior of the house like a shroud. Only the soft breathing of the three occupants hinted that there was anyone home. Marcie and Nathan sat unmoving, staring at the laptop sitting on the coffee table in Annie's living room. They were certain Annie was doing the same in her office.

It was 4:55 p.m. and they were waiting for the hackers to contact Annie again as they had promised to do in their last message. Nathan had decided they should observe Annie's computer through their laptop at her house, so they could be there for support when it was over.

Marcie sensed rather than saw Nathan roll his shoulders to loosen a knot that had formed. He stared intently at the screen. Marcie knew he was anxious to see what the next move was going to be so that he could plan his counter move. It was a chess game with deadly consequences. Marcie felt badly for Annie, knowing how she must be feeling, alone in her office.

Marcie glanced at the time in the lower right corner of the screen as she had done many times in the last few minutes. 4:57 p.m. It seemed like 10 minutes since it had been 4:56. The palms of her hands were sweaty as she held her cell phone, ready to snap a photo when the words appeared on the screen.

4:58.

Marcie jumped as a car door slammed outside. She glanced at Nathan and sighed heavily. There! The cursor moved! She leaned forward in her seat, but the arrow traced a lazy random path across the screen, not the rapid movement used by the hacker. Nathan whispered that it must have been just Annie testing it to see if someone else had control yet.

4:59.

In one minute, the hackers, who had proved to be extremely punctual the last time, would deliver their next message. Marcie's breathing slowed. Nathan sat perfectly still beside her. Marcie sensed her eyes would explode as she concentrated her entire focus on the flat monitor in front of her and the tiny cursor that she anticipated would be racing across the screen at any second. She realized her hand holding the phone was cramping so she released her grip and flexed her fingers. She held the phone up with the camera facing the screen, ready to capture the scene.

The clock at the bottom of the screen ticked over.

5:00.

The cursor lay still. Marcie noticed Nathan flinch as it suddenly moved, but it started and stopped. It must have been another nudge from Annie.

Seconds ticked by and the cursor continued to lay motionless.

5:10.

Nothing.

The clock moved laboriously forward. Marcie had never seen it move so slowly. But the cursor still sat where it had been since Annie's last nudge.

At 5:20 Annie dragged herself out of her office. Marcie felt so sorry for this woman who had been through so much. Her shoulders sagged, and she looked like she could collapse at any second. Even her clothing seemed to be too large for her. The buildup to this non-event had taken another toll.

Marcie rushed towards Annie, threw her arms around her and led her to the couch where she sat with her head down.

Nathan broke the silence. "I don't know what to say, Annie. Maybe the hackers have decided their plan with you is not going to work so they've moved on. I think you should just shut down your computer and try to get some rest. They've been watching you. They know you aren't in front of your computer now so it's not likely they will try to contact you. Maybe sending the police here was their last threat. Or maybe it is really just kids trying to scare you."

Annie remained quiet for a few seconds. Finally, she lifted her head. "I'm so sick of this." Her voice rose as she spoke. "Whoever the hackers are, I hope they rot in hell." She straightened up, seemingly gaining some resolve after the initial shock of nothing happening wore off. She quickly stood up and stormed into the office. The sound of a stream of screamed expletives directed at the hackers followed by the laptop lid slamming shut drifted down the hall from the room.

Marcie looked at Nathan with a small smile as her shoulders lifted in a shrug. "There's a few days of pent up frustration coming out. Hopefully, the hackers understand enough English to know what she said."

They stayed with Annie for a few hours before driving home. Just before they got to the condo, Marcie turned in the passenger seat to face her fiancé. "You're not saying much. What do you think?"

Nathan had been thoughtful on the drive. The reason why became clear with his response. "This isn't over. I don't know what's coming next, but it won't be good."

CHAPTER 24

Marcie lay supported by her pillow with her laptop resting on the comforter over her stomach. The bedside lamps on both sides of the bed were on. She turned her head to Nathan who leaned back against his pillow with his fingers woven together behind his head. They had both confessed to exhaustion and had gone to bed early.

Nathan's eyes focused on a blank spot on the wall. Marcie spun the laptop towards him so he could see more clearly what she was looking at on the screen, but his head still didn't move.

"How do you like this dress?"

It was like someone had replaced the real Nathan Harris with a wax replica. There was nothing to indicate he had picked up on Marcie's words.

"Naaaathan, can you hear me? Do I need to get the defibrillator?" She waved her hand in front of his eyes to break his concentration.

He turned his head towards her with a reluctant smile, indicating that he had been only half listening. "Did you say defibrillator? I don't think I'm ready for one yet. Besides that, when did you go and buy one? I'm sorry. I was just thinking about Annie. What were you saying?"

"How do you like this dress? Wouldn't I look good in it?"

Nathan recognized the person in the picture as Kim Kardashian on her wedding day. The caption read, *Kim Kardashian's $400,000 Givenchy dress.*

"You would look stunning in that dress, my dear. But unless you intend on marrying someone with the same bank account as Kanye West, you might have to temper your plans just a little."

Marcie laughed, closed the laptop and set it on the nightstand. "It's okay. I've already bought a dress and I guarantee you, it *will* be stunning. And it cost much less than $400,000 to boot."

She leaned over and kissed him, the silk of the satin chemise covering her breasts brushing against his bare chest. He pulled her close and kissed her back before she returned to her spot on the pillow. She smiled, "I think you need to clear your head if you're going to get any sleep tonight."

He leaned forward to look at the clock. It read 9:45. "The only way I can do that is to try to talk to James Welch. I've got a million things running through my head right now. I'm worried about what they might try next with Annie's computer. If, as Welch said, they can ruin the Logans' lives, we have to do everything we can to prevent it. Would you mind if I try calling him now?"

"Of course not, Nathan. I want you to do what you have to do." She lifted her eyebrows a few times in a beguiling look. "I'll be here waiting for you when you get back."

He knew she meant when he got back emotionally because he wasn't going anywhere physically. It didn't matter if she heard his side of the conversation. He trusted her implicitly and anyway, he would bounce anything off her to help clarify his own thoughts. She often raised things he hadn't thought of. Their minds worked very differently, and he loved that about her. He was an analytical thinker. He liked things to fall into place in a straight logical line. He had discovered that Marcie thought well outside the box. When she looked at something, she didn't always see a direct approach. She didn't hesitate to speculate or ask the "what if" questions he didn't always think of. He thought of her way of thinking as "free form." It sometimes led to spontaneous actions that some would consider reckless, but he valued her thought process and believed it to be completely complementary to his. He would never shut her out of his work more than he was required to by law under the oath he had sworn and even then, he bent the rules to get her input.

He leaned to reach his phone from the side table, pulling the covers with him. Marcie tugged them back.

"Don't be such a cover hog," she complained sleepily as she reached to shut off her night light, pulling the covers back with her.

Nathan grinned as he dialed James Welch's number at the office. He wasn't all that surprised when Welch answered on the first ring.

Welch had obviously checked the name on the phone display as he answered. Or maybe, Nathan thought facetiously, he could have programmed his phone to shout out the name of a caller when it rang.

"Nathan, I wondered when I would hear from you. How's Annie doing?"

"You never cease to amaze me, James. I thought I would have to call you at home, but then again, I guess there are no golf courses open at this time of night."

"Only the lighted par threes and they're for amateurs. So how's it going?"

Nathan filled Welch in with more details on the swatting attack at Annie's place. Then he told him about Annie's phone being hacked.

"Well, that's easy enough to do. Smart phones are like miniature computers, so they're easily hacked. You can get instructions on the Internet on how to do it. It would be easy enough to listen to phone calls, intercept messages and so on. I suspect they've hacked into the operating system, so that information from Annie's phone activity can be sent to a third-party computer. People don't realize they need to put security software on their smart phones just like any other device. Nevertheless, I have no doubt we're dealing with some hacking heavyweights here. It's interesting they missed the 5 p.m. deadline. I wonder what that's about."

"I do too. I still think we have a big problem, and it could quite possibly be the Chinese."

"If it's any consolation, which I'm sure it isn't, I read an article in the *New York Times* recently where a cyber security reporter said there are two kinds of companies in the U.S.: those that have been hacked by the Chinese and those that don't know they've been hacked yet. The biggest problem is that if you knock them off one day, they'll be back on the next. They're always stealing intellectual property to give them a competitive advantage Do you know they stole the formula for the color white from a major brand paint manufacturer?"

"Well, this is all very depressing. Could you trace where the hack is coming from if you had access to Annie's computer?"

"I can, but it could take months. I'm sure they're running the attack through servers all over the world. It's a laborious process to track down the source tying up huge resources and quite often, by the time we find out where it's coming from, they've moved on."

Then Nathan brought up Logan's comment about Eric Hartman.

Welch thought for a minute and asked the question that had been bothering Nathan. "Could Hartman be the source of the leak?"

"You know, I think it's quite possible. The timing seems about right. I'm going to look into it more in the morning. Maybe get Homeland Security involved. I've taken up enough of your time. Sorry to bother you this late. Thanks for listening, Welchie."

"Listen, man, it's no problem. This is all pensionable time." Welch laughed. "One good thing about the hacker. He may not be as smart as he thinks he is. By giving Annie a heads-up that he's going to destroy them, he's given us an opportunity to put in some counter-measures. I guess he relied on her not going to the authorities, which technically, she didn't. She went to you and you went to the authorities. Or, you are an authority. I'm not sure which. Anyway, there are some things we can do to try to protect the Logans, but we don't know what their next move might be." He proceeded to outline a plan that could counteract whatever the hackers were planning to do with the Logans' personal lives.

The plan sounded like a good one. Nathan thanked Welch again and hung up before setting his phone back on the nightstand. Marcie had rolled over on her side away from him sometime during the conversation, and he was sure she hadn't heard a word that was said. He was certain she had drifted off to sleep.

Nathan spooned up against her with his arm around her waist. He slid aside the covers that she had pulled up to her chin just enough that he could kiss the back of her neck.

She mumbled into the covers. "Mmm . . . s'curity cams in Shanghai?"

Nathan frowned, wondering what she was getting at. Then came her next statement in a garbled, barely audible voice.

"D'ya think we should get a dog?"

It wasn't something they had ever discussed. Nathan propped himself up on his elbow and leaned over Marcie so he could see her face. Her eyes were closed. She seemed to be in deep repose. He smiled and reached back to turn off the light.

Marcie's breathing deepened and leveled off. She was sound asleep.

He whispered, "I love you, Marcie."

CHAPTER 25

Nathan hadn't fallen asleep quite as quickly as he had hoped after talking to Welch. The computer expert had outlined a plan to give all the financial institutions the Logans dealt with a heads-up that possible hacking was coming. In cooperation with the financial institutions, he planned on setting up mirror sites of the Logans' financial accounts to trick the hackers into thinking that they were ruining the Logans without actually doing so.

Nathan thought this might protect Craig and Annie, but Welch admitted there was a myriad of other actions the hackers could take to destroy their reputations, and they would be far more difficult to combat.

But it was Marcie's last sleepy comment that had really kept Nathan awake. Of course they had cameras in Shanghai. It was a closed society so there would be cameras everywhere. He had already thought of that. But even if all the cameras available to mankind were in Shanghai, they wouldn't be able to find an unknown hacker in a city of 24 million. He finally fell into a fitful sleep, thinking that maybe it was some off-the-wall comment formulated by a dream Marcie had had.

The clock on his bedside table clicked over to 3:20 a.m. as Nathan sat bolt upright in bed.

Hartman.

He wasn't entirely sure what Marcie had been thinking, but perhaps they could use the security cameras to track Eric Hartman's movements in Shanghai. Then they could determine if he had met with someone secretly, someone who just might be interested in gaining access to the executive order. They knew the hotel he was staying in. They would have to follow the trail of Eric Hartman's activities leading up to his supposed heart attack. That must've been what

Marcie was thinking as she fell asleep! Brilliant! Nathan wanted to wake her up and kiss her on the spot, but decided discretion was called for and let her sleep. He lay down, turned on his side with his hands under his pillow and fell into a deep sleep, knowing that he had a lot to do the next day.

In what seemed a very short time, Nathan awoke and waited for the night's cobwebs to clear and his thoughts to coalesce. He reached over to Marcie's side, but the coolness that met his hand from the fabric of the fitted sheet on the bed told him that she was already up. The clatter of dishes from the kitchen confirmed it. He got up, threw on a white terry cloth robe, used the bathroom and croaked a version of his favorite song, "Sweet Caroline" by Neil Diamond. He cleared the night from his throat and tried again. Satisfied that it was as good as it would get, he followed the aroma of the brewing coffee to the kitchen like a hound on the trail of a fox. Even though he had cut back on caffeine since leaving the FBI, he still craved that first cup in the morning to jumpstart his day.

Marcie was standing by the stove, carefully monitoring omelets in the frying pan. She wore a short satin floral dressing gown and to Nathan she looked sweet and sexy, even though it was early in the morning. Nathan wrapped his arms around her waist and kissed her neck. She dexterously flipped the omelets in the pan as she greeted him. "Good morning! I was just about to come and get you out of bed. Since you're here, make yourself useful and put some bread in the toaster. Sorry I couldn't stay awake until you finished your call last night. How did it go?"

Nathan opened a loaf of rye bread and popped four slices in the toaster. "The call was okay, but you gave me an incredible idea as you were falling asleep. It just might work if we can get the cooperation of Chinese law enforcement."

"*Me*? What did *I* say?"

"Well, you did ask if we should get a dog." Nathan laughed. "We can negotiate that one later. Just before you mentioned the dog, though, you mumbled something about security cameras in Shanghai. It took me awhile to figure out what you were getting at. Then it hit me. I assume you meant we should try to track Hartman's movements before he died to see if there was anything unusual about his activities—like maybe he met with someone that he shouldn't have.

He was in China on a trade mission, so who he met and talked with could be valuable information for us."

Marcie looked perplexed as she took the frying pan off the stove and dished the omelets onto a plate. "Huh! I remember thinking about that possibility before we went to bed, but I wanted to wait to talk to you about it this morning so you could get some sleep. I guess that didn't work out too well. I don't remember saying anything out loud or saying anything about a dog." She laughed. "Glad I could be of help, but I'm sure someone at the FBI would've thought of it. Even *you*!" She turned to Nathan, smiled affectionately and threw her arms around his neck to kiss him on the lips before sitting at the table. "Better get the toast before the fire department shows up."

Nathan lunged to the counter, waving at the smoke wafting up from the toaster before removing the darkened slices, buttered them and sat at the table close to Marcie with their knees touching. "Eric Hartman hasn't been a priority in our investigation yet, but there definitely could be some connection. Maybe he did just die of natural causes, but we've got nothing else to go on. Guess I'm going to have to pay closer attention when you talk in your sleep, Marce. You might come up with a cure for cancer or something without even knowing it. I'll keep my phone beside the bed so I can record your every word."

Marcie teased, "Not my every word. You might record something you don't want to hear."

They continued to chat easily through breakfast about everything and nothing—the easy conversation that lovers have. Then Nathan said, "We don't have an FBI office in Shanghai, but we do have an agent in Beijing. His name is Danny Chin. He's Asian and has worked in China for a long time. I've met him a few times. Really capable and likable guy. I'll ask Welch to have someone contact Chin to try to get a look at the security recordings for the time Hartman stayed in Shanghai. I don't know how willing they're going to be to cooperate. We may have to scratch their back to get them to share their video footage, but it's definitely worth a shot."

He looked at his fiancée. "Do you have any free time today?"

Her head tilted as if she was suddenly in deep though. "Hmm-mmm. I don't know. I'm *awfully* busy with the wedding. What did you have in mind?"

"Well, if you do have some time, you could do something for me." He didn't want Marcie to feel left out when he knew he couldn't share all the details of the case with her.

She perked up. "Sure, what can I do?"

"It would be helpful if you could do an online search for Eric Hartman. See if you can find anything in China's English-language papers on-line about his death. Maybe there would be something about an American government official dying in Shanghai. Let's see what they have to say about it. It's a long shot but it's something we need to check out."

Nathan got up to clear the dishes from the table. "I'm going to see Welchie about the security cameras, and I also want to see if he has any other ideas. Oh, you know what, there's something else you can do. Go over to see Annie and ask her for a list of contacts and accounts for every financial institution she and her husband deal with. Once you get the list, we'll go from there."

He walked to the large glass wall overlooking the bay to open the vertical blind. The condo sat on Pinellas Bayway, and the view on most days was worthy of capture in an oil painting. Today, however, the view was one of steel gray skies and rain knocking against the window. To the north, the view of Tampa, which was normally clear and bright, had been stolen away. Bullets of rain battered the surface of the pool below and puddles shimmered on the surrounding deck. Faint spears of sunshine from the front side of the condo provided hope that the storm would be driven out to sea.

He closed the blind. "Not the brightest day out there."

As Marcie walked towards the bedroom, she shot over her shoulder. "I'm jumping in the shower. We both have work to do so it might save some time if you joined me."

Nathan smiled to himself as he followed Marcie, undoing his robe. "Oh yeah. You don't have to ask *me* twice."

<< < > >>

After the enjoyable shower with Nathan, Marcie had dressed in jeans, a striped linen t-shirt and a hoodie with a butterfly on the left breast and driven to Annie's place. She had spent an hour with her friend gathering information on the Logans' financial institutions. There were quite a few and Annie had to dig out old bank statements since she couldn't look them up on the computer. Marcie was relieved not to smell alcohol on Annie's breath, and there was no evidence of wine bottles lying around. Maybe there had been a breakthrough when Nathan had talked to Annie about her drinking, but Marcie didn't bring it up. She had texted the list to Nathan so that he and Welch could start informing the various financial institutions about what might be coming.

Once that was done, as Nathan had suggested, she scanned the Shanghai and China daily online English-language newspapers subsequent to Hartman's death. She didn't really expect to find anything. Apparently Hartman had died of natural causes so the only thing unusual about it was that he was an American in China on government business. And that wasn't that unusual. She was surprised when she did come across two lines buried near the back of the Shanghai daily news about Eric Hartman. The first line stated that he was an American government official in Shanghai to discuss trade and that he'd died unexpectedly in a downtown hotel room. The second line tersely reported that foul play was not expected. End of article.

Marcie scanned the remaining online pages out of curiosity to see what the Chinese English-language writers deemed important. There were articles about health care reform, U.S.–China cultural exchanges, anti-smog campaigns, and the latest activities of the U.S. president. The mention of the president was simply a statement of fact delivered in flat prose. The articles were interesting but, she thought, she had really accomplished nothing. She would tell Nathan about them later.

She clicked on a travel site, and went back to honeymoon planning.

CHAPTER 26

Nathan and Marcie were on their way to the Sup Tot Restaurant. The restaurant was one of their favorites in Tampa, and they always enjoyed spending time there. When Nathan had arrived home earlier, they decided they deserved a break from everything, although they both knew conversation would inevitably swing to the Logan's situation. A quick call to the restaurant reserved their favorite private spot in the back corner.

They rode in Nathan's car so the music remained at normal levels, allowing for casual conversation. Nathan's taste leaned towards classic rock. Bruce Springsteen was telling the world about girls and cars and that he was born to run, but it fell on deaf ears as the vehicle's occupants chatted quietly about inconsequential things while Springsteen sang his heart out. He might as well have been singing in a bar with everyone around him straining their vocal chords to be louder than the music. He was finishing up, telling someone named Wendy that they would walk in the sun some day, but the Boss' words of undying love were obliterated by the ringing of a call coming through the Bluetooth connection.

Nathan answered and a heavily-accented voice reverberated through the speakers. "This is computer security calling."

Nathan turned his head towards Marcie with a look of *does he really want to do this now?* The man continued. "We have discovered a serious security flaw in your computer. It needs to be addressed right away, sir." He pronounced "away" with a "v."

The breathless man on the other end paused as he waited to see if he actually had a fish on the line. Then Nathan intoned, "I'm so glad you called. I've noticed my computer has been acting up lately. How can you help?"

The man said excitedly, "We can get rid of the virus for you, sir. If you are sitting in front of your computer right now, I can help you, sir. I just need . . ."

Nathan calmly cut him off. "Okay, that's great. Thank you so much. I just need one thing from you first. Could you please give me your credit card number? I need it for two reasons." He looked at Marcie who stared straight ahead with a huge grin, knowing that the man on the phone was about to get schooled. Nathan continued, "I need to be able to send you a bill for my time that you are so glibly wasting. Secondly, you have reached an agent of the FBI, so I would like your credit card number so I can track you down, throw you and your buddies in jail for a while, and tell your mother what you are doing."

The man on the other end didn't hear the last sentence. He was busy screaming obscenities into the phone and abruptly ending the call.

Nathan reached for Marcie's hand. "That went well, don't you think?"

"It would be great if he learned something from it," agreed Marcie. "I guess he's one of the Yahoo boys from Nigeria?"

Nathan concurred that he was likely one of the young men who frequently use Yahoo's free email service to swindle unsuspecting Internet users. "He certainly sounded like it. The trouble is, their scheme works often enough to make it profitable."

They arrived at their destination and entered the restaurant. The second they walked in, it was like they had been transported to Saigon. A young woman in a long flowing yellow dress sat in an ornate chair plucking a 16-string instrument that looked like a long tube that had been sliced down the middle. The air filled with captivating and soothing tones from the instrument. She smiled brightly as they passed by. The room itself was richly decorated in reds and oranges, featuring silk lanterns hanging from the ceiling. Themed figurines and statuettes dotted the room. They were led to their favorite spot, a quiet corner separated from the other patrons by a curtain.

The restaurant name literally translated into "good soup" and Nathan and Marcie ordered two of the many choices on the menu. The specialties consisted of large bowls of broth, rice noodles, some herbs and either beef or chicken. They had instantly fallen in love with the restaurant and the personalities of its servers on their first visit, and considered their soup to be comfort food.

The curtain separating the room from the other customers didn't drown out the drone of the conversation in the restaurant, but it did offer some privacy. A small candle illuminated their menus and faces. Upon entering the restaurant, they had bantered about whether to shut off their cell phones. Surprisingly, it was Nathan who wanted to shut them off completely. They had agreed they would leave them on vibrate in case something happened with Annie's computer. Her fragility after everything that had happened to her made it imperative that they remain reachable. They were comforted by the knowledge that a police officer guarded her residence.

Their server was a woman who appeared to be in her early thirties with an effervescent personality. She also wore a traditional long floral print silk tunic over pants. All that reminded them that they weren't in traditional Vietnam was the bright blue dye in her hair. She poured each a glass of wine from the carafe they had ordered while they waited for their soup to arrive. Marcie asked, "So how did your day go? Any luck with the security cameras?"

He replied. "Yes, I talked to Welch and a couple of other people at the office about the possibility of checking the security cameras in Shanghai. They said they would contact Special Agent Chin in Beijing to set it up. It might take a couple of days. This whole thing's frustrating for everyone. Welch is going to see if he can reverse-engineer the spyware by accessing Annie's computer, but he says that process can take months. By then, this could be all over one way or the other.

"I did give him the list of financial institutions you put together, and we decided to split it up. Thanks for that, by the way. We're going to contact them first thing in the morning and Welch is going to work on mirror sites with the cooperation of all the financial institutions that the Logans use. Welchie talked a bit more about that Canadian high tech company that was hacked. He said the Chinese were in the company's systems for years before they were discovered. They downloaded business plans, emails and a host of other documents that they could use for competitive advantage. Even when it was discovered, senior management didn't believe it to be a serious issue until the company finally went bankrupt. Of course, now that hacking is more prevalent, managers are much more tuned into the fact that any sign of intrusion could be real."

Marcie sighed. "It's so invasive *and* pervasive. It's good we have people like Welch to watch out for these things." Marcie then added with an amused smile, "Did he give you any special golf tips?"

"I think he'd have to give me more than a few tips to help my game," Nathan chuckled. "But he did invite me out for a game when all this is over." He leaned back as the blue-haired server set his bowl in front of him. "I told him if he didn't mind me slowing him down, I'd go. Did you find anything about Hartman when you checked the online news?"

"There was a small article about Hartman dying at the hotel. It said he was an American but that's about it. I copied and pasted it into a Word file and sent it to you by email."

"Okay, thanks for checking. I haven't seen it yet. I didn't really expect anything to come out of that, but we have to follow everything through."

They ate their soup in silence, both focused on the delicacy in front of them and on their own thoughts. When they finished, they sat back sipping the remainder of the wine. The conversation turned to their honeymoon. Marcie said, "I've been looking at hotels in Tanzania, Dar es Salaam specifically, for our honeymoon. Interested in seeing some options?"

"Of course! What did you find?"

She took out her phone and opened the travel site. As she did so, she smiled sweetly. "By the way, I was wondering if the design we chose for our invitations with the oval pattern in the middle surrounded by red roses is giving you nightmares."

Nathan's brow deepened. "No, why would you say that?"

Marcie laughed. "Oh, I don't know. Oval office. Rose garden. Things like that."

Nathan chuckled at the reference to the White House. Marcie had just turned her phone around to show him the hotel options she had found when it vibrated in her hand. At precisely the same time, Nathan's phone vibrated in his pocket. Marcie swung the phone back towards herself as Nathan fished his out of his pocket and entered the password to open the screen. It was an email with a blind copy to both of them. As they read it simultaneously, their eyes widened as if synchronized and Marcie's mouth formed a silent "O."

Nathan rose from his seat as he returned his phone to his pocket. "I think the other shoe just dropped. I'll get the waitress. I think we'd better go."

CHAPTER 27

Craig Logan glanced at the clock as he put the finishing touches on President Hughes's agenda for the next day. It was 7:45 at night and the daylight that had been illuminating the room was rapidly evaporating. He reached across some papers scattered on his desk to click on the lamp. He still seethed over Hughes's lack of empathy for the situation he and Annie were in. It was clear the president was pissed off at the Chinese and wanted to punish them for their perceived lack of respect. That kind of thinking could be dangerous.

Nice to know your boss doesn't have your back, Logan thought, as the keyboard absorbed the brunt of his frustration. He hadn't expected the president to drop what he was doing—but he could have perhaps been sympathetic to his plight. Clearly, that's not who the president was despite their personal friendship. Hughes had his own agenda and he was going to make sure it went through, no matter the collateral damage.

Logan scanned the agenda. Except for a 10 o'clock meeting with the president of Nigeria and his entourage, it was full of meetings with personal advisers. Not a single chairman of any committee or House representative or anyone from the Senate or anyone else with any government experience on the agenda. It wasn't for a lack of trying on their behalf. The president had specifically told Logan that he wanted to meet with the closest members of his inner circle tomorrow, so that's what the agenda reflected. Based on the time allotted, even the meeting with the President of Nigeria seemed to be an imposition.

Logan printed the agenda and placed it in the president's folder. He thought about checking his emails, but he was exhausted. Whatever was there could wait until morning. Besides, he and Annie had agreed to talk at 8 o'clock. She had arranged to use Sami's phone to make the call. He was so happy when Nathan Harris told him the 5 p.m. deadline had been missed by the hackers. At least that was something.

The phone rang at precisely 8:00 p.m.

Logan answered, happy to hear his wife on the other end and relieved that she sounded sober. They expressed how much they missed each other and Logan felt a deep abiding emptiness, knowing she was so far away. He was going to surprise her with his desire to bring her to Washington, but he wanted to hear her voice and about everything that had been happening to her first. He just wanted everything to be normal for a few minutes. Annie told him about her rose garden and Craig shared some tidbits about his day.

Craig said, "Nathan told me nothing happened at 5 o'clock. That's a relief. Hopefully, that's the end of it. I hope Sami doesn't mind you using her phone to make these calls."

Annie replied, "It seemed like the world was lifted off my shoulders. It's so stressful, but Sami's great. She knows something's going on, obviously, but Nathan told her the other day when the police arrived that it needs to be kept confidential and she hasn't asked anything more. Sami's staying with me and a policeman is outside guarding the house. I feel like a prisoner, Craig. I'm glad the media handled it the way they did. It could've been embarrassing for you that the president's chief of staff's wife was arrested. They could've really done a number on it. The articles I read online just described it as a suspected break-in."

Craig sensed that Annie was holding her breath. Part of his job was to find out through the White House Communications Branch everything in the press that might impact the president. He had seen newspapers that leaned politically towards the other side of the Congress making a big issue of Annie's arrest in headline typeface usually used during times of war, but he wasn't about to tell his wife.

Finally he asked, "Annie, have you contacted the counselor like I asked?"

A sigh escaped Annie's lips. "I haven't yet. I will, I promise. It's been so crazy with everything that's going on, I just can't do it now. When everything settles down, I promise I will."

Craig had his doubts, but he simply said, "Please do, Annie. It's important to me and it's necessary for your health." He decided to change the subject. "Anything else from Nathan?"

"I gave Nathan and Marcie a list of all the banks we deal with and all our accounts. The FBI thinks they can protect us from the hackers being able to destroy our financial credibility, but they don't know about what else they may have in store. The hackers could do something to make us look bad." Craig was happy to hear Annie chuckle nervously when she added, "Although, I don't know how much worse it can get when I've been arrested at gunpoint by the police and you work for someone everyone seems to despise."

Craig couldn't help but laugh along with her. Warmth flowed through his body. They had always been able to laugh when things got bad until recently. In spite of everything that had transpired, this was the best conversation he and his wife had had in the last few days. He sat with the phone wedged between his shoulder and his ear. He leaned forward to power down his computer. He said, "Listen Annie, I've been thinking. I think you should . . ." A sharp knock at the door interrupted him before he had a chance to tell her about moving her to Washington. He glanced up to see a grim-faced head of White House security, Mike Tobin.

Craig's shoulders sagged. He didn't want to be interrupted now. The conversation was going so well, but he could tell that Tobin clearly had something on his mind. "I'm sorry, honey. I have to go. It's been great talking to you. Let's do this again tomorrow. I love you."

Annie said she was sorry he had to cut their conversation short. She had so much more to tell him and she expressed her reluctance at ending the conversation, but told Craig she loved him and hung up.

Tobin was the prototypical security person. He was tall and angular with broad shoulders, a square jaw and a crew cut. The former military man could have been assigned his role by central casting in Hollywood or featured in a billboard advertisement for joining the Marines. Craig thought to himself that he wouldn't want to cross the man standing at the door whose shirt buttons strained across his massive chest. But he was encouraged that the president had decided to talk to the Secret Service about his situation after all. He didn't know that this assumption was about to be shattered.

He addressed the giant as he got up to invite him into the room. "Mike, what can I do for you? Did the president ask you to come and talk to me?"

"No, sir, and I'd prefer you stay sitting if you don't mind."

Only then did Logan notice two other agents standing on either side of his doorway with their suit jackets pulled back to reveal side arms.

The warmth that he felt only moments ago was replaced by a chill that ran from head to toe. The lines in Logan's brow deepened as he sat back down as instructed. "Uh . . . okay . . . What's up, Mike?"

Tobin strode across the room with the agility of a cat, surprisingly quick for a man of his size. Logan made no effort to stop him as the big man grabbed the laptop from his desk. Logan was shocked to notice that the security agent wore latex gloves.

Tobin opened the laptop and turned it on. He turned the screen towards Logan and once the computer booted up, he asked him to enter his password. Logan silently complied, completely mystified by Tobin's actions.

The screen came to life and Tobin asked Craig to open his email. Silently, he did as he was told. He wanted to find out what this was about, but a creeping anxiety told him he already knew. Not the specific details, but this had to have something to do with the hack of his wife's computer.

Tobin watched over his shoulder and when the email account opened, the security agent took the machine back. His eyes were focused on the screen and he held the computer, guarding it. His hand clicked the mouse a couple of times before he finally held the computer out for Logan to see, but at arm's length so he couldn't touch it. He said grimly, "Are you aware of an email your wife sent this evening?"

"No, I haven't looked at my emails this evening. I've been busy working on the president's agenda for tomorrow and I decided they could wait until morning. You're acting strange, Mike. What's up?"

Tobin lifted the computer closer to Craig's eye level. Logan read the email and red blotches crept from the top of his shirt collar to his hairline. His stomach churned. He had to read the email twice to satisfy himself that the lateness of the evening wasn't playing tricks on him.

Sadly, it wasn't.

It was there in black and white and it seemed to be much worse because it was all in caps.

> MY HUSBAND, CRAIG LOGAN, IS THE CHIEF OF STAFF
> AT THE WHITE HOUSE. HE IS AWARE THAT PRESIDENT
> HUGHES IS ABOUT TO SIGN AN EXECUTIVE ORDER THAT
> WILL IMPOSE SEVERE TARIFFS OR BORDER TAXES ON
> ALL ELECTRONIC GOODS IMPORTED FROM CHINA.
> THE PRESIDENT HAS CHOSEN NOT TO CONSULT WITH
> ANYONE IN CONGRESS. HE IS ONLY WORKING WITH HIS
> SENIOR ADVISORS, NONE OF WHOM HAVE GOVERNMENT
> OR DIPLOMATIC EXPERIENCE AND THE CONSEQUENCES
> WILL BE SEVERE HERE AND ON THE CHINESE ECONOMY.
> EVERYONE WHO USES OR BUYS ELECTRONIC PRODUCTS
> MANUFACTURED IN CHINA WILL BE IMPACTED AND
> IT WILL PERMANENTLY DAMAGE THIS COUNTRY'S
> RELATIONS WITH CHINA. I AM PLEADING WITH EVERYONE
> TO CALL THEIR CONGRESSMAN IMMEDIATELY SO THE
> PRESIDENT DOES NOT SIGN THIS EXECUTIVE ORDER.
> PRESS RELEASE ATTACHED.

Logan gasped for breath. He looked at the time on the email and noted that it had been sent less than an hour earlier. The "To" section in the email was blank, meaning it had been sent blindly to a distribution list. *Could this be what Annie meant when she said she had more to tell me?* He found his voice even though it sounded panicked and unrecognizable to him. "Mike, my wife wouldn't do anything like this. I was on the phone with her when you walked in. She couldn't have sent this while I was talking to her. There's more going on here than you realize. My wife's computer has been hacked and we suspect it may be a Chinese spy or informant. The FBI is already on this. Nobody else in the White House has been told because we think there's a leak close to the president. There's a suspicion that someone internally told the Chinese about the executive order. You have to contact the FBI agent. He'll straighten it out. Have you opened the attachment? She wouldn't even know how to write a Press Release. She's never written one."

"We're not opening it. It's probably a virus and we're not taking any chances. We'll open it in the lab."

Logan's heart pounded in his chest. A bead of sweat formed on his forehead. He grimaced as he reread the email. His mind raced, trying to fully comprehend the implications when his cell phone vibrated on his desk. He glanced at it. The caller ID shouted *Washington Post*. He ignored it. The vibration stopped for a few seconds and then started again. *New York Times*. The media! *Could that be the distribution list? Oh my God, not the media.* He slumped back in his chair as the impact began to sink in. Somehow this email had been circulated to major newspapers around the country, and they were all looking for comment. They would be out for blood, demanding answers, screaming for an explanation.

Logan knew this was going to be a very long night.

CHAPTER 28

In the ensuing hours, Washington exploded with the fury and intensity of an oil well fire. The Secret Service confiscated Logan's computer at Mike Tobin's request for total analysis. He reasoned that he had to ensure the virus, if there was one, didn't spread. Logan knew his computer would be scrutinized more closely than a new strain of bacteria under a laboratory microscope. Logan had the impression he was on the verge of being frog-marched in handcuffs out of the office if he resisted, so he said nothing. Instead, he gave Tobin Nathan Harris' phone number and insisted he contact him to confirm the hacking and the FBI's investigation.

Normally, it would have been Logan's responsibility to wake the president if a situation was deemed necessary. Instead, Logan decided to contact Zyva Khan, the president's chief legal counsel. He needed to discuss how to handle the president, as well as to start preparing himself should he need his own legal advice. Khan was shocked to hear the details, but said she would wake up the president immediately, who instantly demanded a midnight meeting with his senior advisers, as well as Tobin and Logan.

Craig wanted to contact his wife. He knew deep down that she wouldn't do this. She wouldn't jeopardize him, his job, and the national security of this country. For that matter, he didn't believe for a second that she could have done it—she didn't have enough facts to even be credible. Sure, she'd heard enough from the hacker to piece together some elements of the story, but she didn't have access to everything. She couldn't have written a press release that would seem the least bit believable. Yes, Annie had a drinking problem, and she missed him a lot. But they had both agreed that he should take this position in Washington for his own career and their future. She wouldn't backstab him now. Bad as it looked, Craig Logan still trusted his wife. Somebody else did this to cause political pressure to be put on the president from within the U.S. so he wouldn't sign the executive order. Craig Logan was sure he and his wife were simply the pawns.

He wanted to give the FBI a heads-up before he called his wife. He called Nathan Harris. When Harris answered, Logan immediately asked if Nathan had seen the email. In a low flat voice, Nathan confirmed that he and Marcie were having dinner when the email came in and had left the restaurant immediately. He added, "I think it's probably gone out to everyone on Annie's contact list."

"It's far worse than that, Nathan. Calls are coming in from the major newspapers around the country. Annie wouldn't have journalists and reporters in her contacts. They must've been added somehow. This has all been fabricated. You didn't open the attachment, did you?"

"Before all this started, I might have. It looked innocent enough. Why? Is it a virus?"

"The Secret Service has my computer now. You should be hearing from their guy Mike Tobin. If he doesn't call you in the next hour or so, let me know and I'll get you his number." Craig Logan paused to take a deep breath. "I have a midnight meeting with the president. He's got to understand that Annie and I were *not* involved in this. Annie did not write that email or any press release!"

"Okay, no problem," Harris replied. "By the way, how did it go when you talked to the president about your situation? Was he interested in holding off signing the trade tariff order until we can learn more?"

"No," said Logan. "Unfortunately he's determined to go through with it."

The conversation ended with silence and they hung up, both wondering how they could possibly quell the burgeoning firestorm heading their way.

〈 〈 〉 〉

At midnight, President Jeffrey Hughes strode into the room occupied by a flank of very tired and disheveled senior advisers. Most had been awakened without warning and had dressed quickly to make the drive to the White House. There was an assortment of plain shirts without ties and some hadn't bothered to comb their hair before arriving. After being summoned, no one had taken the time to dress the part. Some who hadn't checked their emails wondered if war had broken out somewhere. The meeting took place in the Cabinet Room in the West Wing adjoined to the Oval Office. The attendees sat around a large elliptical mahogany table, a gift from Richard Nixon in 1970. President Hughes took his seat in a chair at the head of the table that was three inches taller than the others.

His face was as gloomy as a starless night sky. His chin jutted and a vein visibly throbbed in his neck. His head swiveled slowly from right to left, his eyes burning holes in every attendee around the table. He wasted no time going after Logan like a hawk on a mouse, demanding answers to explain the email. But very quickly, presidential legal counsel Zyva Khan, who sat directly to Logan's left, intervened. She was in her late thirties with jet black eyes that matched her hair. Usually impeccably dressed, she wore jeans and a t-shirt with sequins on the front.

"Mr. President, the FBI is apparently already looking into the matter. It appears Craig Logan's wife's computer has been hacked and whoever did it has been sending threats to her about this very issue. Somehow the hackers know about the Chinese tariff and are prepared to do anything possible to stop it. It looks like the email message was sent through Ms. Logan's computer to her contact list and many others, including the press." She motioned her chin towards Tobin. "Mike's people are looking at Craig's computer now and the FBI in Tampa is checking out Ms. Logan's computer. My understanding is that there's strong reason to believe the Chinese are behind this. They have the most to lose should the Tariff Executive Order go through. The FBI is also trying to trace the source of the original leak. It may be best, sir, at this stage that we try to control the situation and let the FBI do its job."

Tobin spoke up. "The FBI in Florida seems to be working on this so-called hacking on their own. We have not been informed of any hacking. This is all news to us in the Secret Service."

Logan was about to respond but Khan interrupted. "I've spoken with a Nathan Harris who is a consultant working closely with the FBI. Somehow it appears the Chinese have gotten details about the executive order and your intention to sign it in the next few days,

Mr. President. The FBI states they will advise the Secret Service here at the White House and Homeland Security in due time."

The meeting dragged on for over an hour. Khan managed to soften the president's tone, but Logan left with the impression that the country's leader had chosen to not mention the conversation that had taken place earlier in the day about the hacking. He decided it was best not to bring it up in that forum, but he would be telling anyone who would listen privately.

The meeting became an exercise in spinning the news about the impending tariffs. The official story would focus on the president's commitment to his supporters to create more jobs in America and he was proactively addressing that need. He had relied on his experts in the White House to advise him because they were all successful business men. He planned to brief the House after signing the Executive Order. And so on.

The President's penultimate instruction was to his communications staff to cancel the 2 o'clock briefing to the press. He didn't want his press secretary answering any questions until the order was official. The communications team wasn't surprised. There hadn't been a press conference with the president himself for ages and he closely controlled any White House interaction with the media.

Then the president dropped his parting instruction like a bombshell. He wanted a release issued immediately announcing a 5 p.m. press conference. At that time, he would sign a new China-U.S. Tariff bill that would effectively bring more jobs back to America because no one would be able to afford to buy any electronic goods imported from China. He wanted the executive order to implement tariffs on imported Chinese electronics on his desk and ready for signature before then. He stood up and stalked back to the Oval office with every pair of eyes in the room glued to his back.

‹ ‹ ‹ › › ›

The next day, the press release unleashed a firestorm. A flurry of phone calls took place among the president's elected party leadership. The calls were dominated by griping about the president's autocratic leadership style, but everyone agreed he wasn't doing anything illegal. After much debate, the party faithful agreed that they would support the president by offering their own spin on the reasons they hadn't been consulted. The unspoken message was that they would support him as long as it was politically expedient. It was tacitly understood by everyone that if their own approval ratings started to drop in the polls before the next round of primary elections and their jobs were at stake, that their support for the president and his style would evaporate like puddles of water on a hot day. That was just the nature of politics.

〈〈〈〉〉〉

The leadership of the other side of the House held their own meetings. They decided to lay low. While there was an opportunity to make political hay of the situation, which they would do as individuals in interviews, their strategic and united party approach would be to let the president hang himself by his own impulsiveness. By the time the primary elections came around, the effect of the tariff bill would be costing the public exorbitantly and voters would take it out on the president and his party. The consensus was that he was doing plenty of damage to himself, and a spotlight had been fortuitously shone on it by whoever sent the email. The opposition party knew the media would gnaw on it, devour it and spit it out at the public.

〈〈〈〉〉〉

The disparity between the views of the two sides of the House proved yet again the truth of an old political adage that read: where you stand depends on where you sit.

〈〈〈〉〉〉

Lower-level policymakers and procedure-writing bureaucrats cringed at the latest developments. For them, the president and his cronies had it easy. All the president had to do was sign a piece of paper. It then became their job to write the policy in a way that adhered to the law and contained detailed procedures on how to implement it. Documents and forms would have to be designed. It would all have to be done yesterday. At least the leaked information gave them a heads-up that something was coming. That was more than they normally had with this president. It would still take weeks to draft the policy and procedures and have them approved and distributed to the front-line workers.

⟨ ⟨ ⟨ ⟩ ⟩

The people on the front lines whose job it was to implement the policy sat across from their loved ones or in coffee shops at work shaking their heads, bemoaning the fact that they would once again be acting blind, unsure of what they were supposed to do. The frustration level would be through the roof. They all wanted to do a good job, but how could they when they didn't have the proper instructions and documentation to do it? It would take time for the policy and procedure writers to do their jobs. They had seen this before. They would be expected to implement the new tariffs without access to the proper forms to fill out or detailed procedures on how to do it. They laid the blame directly on the lazy know-nothing civil servants in Washington.

⟨ ⟨ ⟨ ⟩ ⟩

The newspapers and TV news networks dug in with their respective positions, mostly roaring with righteous indignation. Those who disagreed with the president's political views focused on Hughes's dictatorial style, bemoaned the cancellation of the daily press briefing as flying in the face of the First Amendment and called for him to lead like a head of state should. Those sympathetic to the president focused on the jobs the new legislation would create and railed against the leaks coming from the White House, even though leaks were their lifeblood. Expert economists and opinionated pundits filled the airwaves, all speculating on what the effects of the tariff on Chinese exports would be. It was the same movie, but everyone saw it differently.

⟨ ⟨ ⟨ ⟩ ⟩

Members of the public who were interested in politics would choose to read and listen to the detailed description of events that suited their particular agendas and become even more entrenched in their views. Those who were mildly interested would read the headlines, shake their heads and wonder to their friends if there would ever be a politician who would put country ahead of getting re-elected. Some would ignore it all, assuming it would somehow get sorted out before the next election when they would vote for the same party their family had been supporting for decades. A growing number would decide that it didn't matter who was elected—nothing was ever going to change—and continue with their lives, not bothering to cast a ballot or attempt to make a difference when the next election rolled around.

‹ ‹ ‹ › ›

Social media lit up. Facebook friends were unfriended because of their political views, and opinions flew back and forth by people who had no clue what was really going on. They viewed provable facts and accurate information as intrusions on their own beliefs. It was their right to comment. Period. And no one changed anyone else's mind.

‹ ‹ ‹ › ›

Writers for late night comedians and talk show hosts were the happiest of all. They didn't have to search for material. They just had to read each day's newsfeed and create what they considered to be their best monologues ever.

CHAPTER 29

W hat the hell happened this time?" It was the following morning and Nathan Harris expressed his frustration as he sat across the desk from James Welch. The leg he had crossed over the other swung back and forth as if suspended from a pivot with nothing to hold it in place. The habit manifested itself when he experienced anxiety or frustration. The latter had set it in motion.

He and Marcie had gone to see Annie immediately after leaving the restaurant the previous evening. She was shocked and despondent. She seemed to be operating on autopilot, clearly in a daze and not really caring what happened next. She had not even known about the email until her husband had called her on Sami's phone. And when she was told there was a so-called Press Release attached to the email, she just shook her head in disbelief.

Nathan didn't even think the full gravity of the situation had sunk in. The Logans would be the subject of scrutiny by the press and fingers would be pointed directly at them. Some people would thank them, others would think they were treasonous. Craig could lose his job. There would be new criticism of the president and pressure for him to be more transparent and co-operative with trading partners. The problems had only begun, and the extent of the fallout was yet to be determined.

Craig had told her not to talk to reporters. The phone rang incessantly while Nathan and Marcie were there but no one from the media had arrived. Annie had convinced Sami to go home earlier in the day. While Nathan talked to Annie, Marcie checked the kitchen for wine under the pretense of making a cup of tea. Relieved she hadn't found any, they sat with Annie until they finished their tea and went home. There was nothing more they could do. They were convinced from the smell of alcohol on her breath that she had bottles stashed away somewhere. Her promise to stop drinking had been sidetracked by the latest events. Neither of them got any sleep when they got home, and they were quite sure Annie wouldn't either.

Now Nathan sat across the desk from Welch. Nathan's swinging leg wasn't prompted by frustration with the man sitting across from him. It was the overwhelming magnitude of what had happened that drove him crazy. It was like they were chasing a ghost and the wraith firmly remained in first place. In fact, the ghost was so far ahead, Nathan was beginning to wonder if they could ever regain the lead. This was getting out of hand. Sending out that email from Annie's computer and getting it to the media could be considered a stroke of genius by the president's adversaries. It had unleashed a firestorm of events that could only get worse unless they could find a way to stop the hackers.

Welch frowned. "I'm afraid our clever Chinese friends, if they are indeed Chinese, incorporated a logic bomb, a piece of coding, in the virus they planted in Annie's computer. It must've been scheduled to go off if a certain event happened. It could be that the hackers thought their work was time sensitive and if they weren't successful by a certain time, the bomb would go off and the email would be sent. It's evident something triggered the bomb."

Nathan snorted derisively. "You mean they *haven't* been success-ful? My God. It seems to me we've been playing catch up this whole time. How much success do they need?"

"Nathan, as they said in the messages to Annie, the end goal is to stop the tariff from going through. That means stopping the president from signing the executive order. It seems from what you said that the president is not inclined to stop so they still haven't been successful. They're hoping to put enough pressure on President Hughes to stop him from signing it. The media. The public. The president's supporters. The hacker or hackers don't seem to under-stand that this president isn't influenced by members of Congress or his chief of staff, obviously. It seems common sense may not be too common in the Oval Office. "

They sat silently for a few minutes. Finally, James Welch asked, "How's Annie holding up?"

"I don't know. Marcie went over to check on her again this morn-ing. We saw her last night and she seemed to be okay, but she's pretty fragile. I'm worried that the attention from this could put her over the edge. The best thing we can do is stop this—for her sake, of course, but for our entire country's sake as well. Any suggestions on next steps for tracking the hackers?"

"I discussed the matter with Special Agent Walker and he's assigned other resources to contact the financial institutions used by the Logans. I'll have my staff set up mirror accounts to intercept any attempt by the hackers to hijack the Logans' data.

"As I think I've mentioned a few times, hackers bounce their signals all over the world and use various relays, so finding the source by tracing the signals backwards is really time consuming, but we've already started the process. We got some good news from Agent Chin in Beijing. The Chinese are cooperating and letting him view the security camera video from the hotel Eric Hartman stayed in. They'll censor the video first, of course, but hopefully, they'll let him see what he needs. I'm expecting a call at any moment."

Nathan's leg stopped bouncing. At least Chin's success was something positive. He threw out his own thoughts, "I think the hackers must've pretty well run out of patience with the Logans. Anything they do with them now is strictly for revenge. I think the fact they didn't contact Annie at 5 p.m. as they said they would and this email blast means whoever it is has elevated his targets. They're trying to undermine the president in this country as well as on the world stage. They might try hacking other top government officials now to increase pressure and stop the tariff from being implemented."

"That sounds right to me, Nathan. That's why you're the field operative and I'm just some nerd stuck behind a desk. I never get to shoot anybody like you do. I've asked for a permit to shoot a few computers, but my request has been denied. Can you imagine? Something about them not trusting me with a firearm."

Welch was about to add something when his phone rang.

As Welch turned aside to answer, Nathan chuckled at the computer expert's last comment and glanced around the room. The desk was barren as usual, except for the ever-present laptop. The equally ubiquitous putting trainer sat on the floor in front of the closed door. A putter leaned against one corner of the office. The shelves of the bookcase were adorned with a variety of painstakingly polished golfing trophies. The walls of the office were as barren as the desk, but for a framed picture of Welch with a star player from the Tampa Bay Lightning and another of him with a wide goofy grin on his face as he waved to the crowd from a seat beside the driver on a Zamboni. Harris wondered to himself how Welch had managed to pull that one off when his thoughts were interrupted as the computer expert set the phone on the desk.

Welch turned back to face Nathan, "We may have a breakthrough. The Chinese just sent some security camera files to Chin in Beijing. I don't even want to think about the promises he had to make to get them. He's already reviewing the footage, and he's picked up Hartman leaving the hotel in a taxi on the night he died. He's going to call the company to find out the route the taxi took. It shouldn't be hard to find his destination through GPS and hopefully pick him up on camera again that evening. Chin says Shanghai has more cameras on the streets than Vietnam has motor scooters. I believe his exact words were that the cameras are lined up on street lights like pigeons. And to think *our* citizens complain about privacy! Of course, none of this means anything unless Hartman had some interaction with the hacker. He could have had an innocent dinner or a business meeting with someone completely unrelated to all this. Or for that matter, it could just be that he went to their version of a red-light district for all we know. Maybe all the activity was too much for his heart."

Nathan demurred. "I don't believe in coincidences, James. There's just too much going on here at the same time. Hartman dies in Shanghai around the time the Chinese somehow get hold of information about the tariff. Then the hacks start with the Logans. I think we just might find something."

"I hope you're right," said James Welch. "Meanwhile, it'll take a bit of time for our man in Beijing to examine more footage. Got time for lunch? I'm famished."

〈 〈 〈 〉 〉 〉

Marcie's eyes widened as she turned the corner onto Annie's tree-lined street. Cars and news media trucks sat haphazardly on the street all the way past Sami and Mason Seaforth's house. A crowd mingled on the lawn. Some were sitting on the grass. She recognized the police officer standing on the doorstep, eying the group as they watched the house for any sign of movement. He was one of the officers assigned to watching Annie's house. Marcie left her car as close as she could and strode towards the group. As she did so, a man slipped away from the crowd and walked around to the side of the house. He trampled Annie's roses as he leaned towards the window, pointing his cell phone towards something or someone in the house.

Marcie waited until she was close enough that he could hear her. "HEY, YOU!" she screamed at the top of her lungs. "Get out of that garden, you're trampling all the flowers!" The man barely glanced around to see who was yelling. But the sound of Marcie's voice had the effect of drawing a pride of lions to a wounded zebra. Heads snapped in Marcie's direction and the crowd of reporters swarmed around her as one. The sensation was like being swallowed by a gelatinous mass as the crowd pushed her towards the center. Questions rained down on her. "Who are you?" "What are you doing here?" "How do you know Annie Logan?" "Is Annie Logan a traitor?" "Why would she send an email like that?"

The questions descended into white noise, a mixture of shouting male and female voices. Marcie couldn't breathe as she was jostled by men much larger than her. An overly-exuberant woman shoved a cell phone at Marcie, nicking her in the face as she attempted to get a quote for her deadline. Marcie reacted instinctively. She raised her left hand defensively to fend off the woman, nearly knocking the cell phone into the crowd. Her other hand was balled into a fist and ready to pummel the next person who touched her. Then someone grabbed her arm and pulled her away. It was the policeman she had seen on the doorstep.

The officer led her through the chaos toward the house. He leaned down and yelled loud enough that his voice rose above the noise, "Marcie Kane, right?" Marcie confirmed she was and he continued, "Ms. Logan told me you would be here and asked me to watch for you. I remember you from the other day." He leaned closer to her ear so she could hear him. "She gave me the key to let you in the house. I've called for a couple more officers to get things quieted down here. These jackals are getting out of hand. I don't know what's happened to the press. It's like they're all crazy and getting crazier. Anyway, here you go." He opened the door and gently shoved Marcie inside before slamming it again.

The room was silent when she entered, but she sensed someone was there. Her suspicions were confirmed by soft footsteps padding down the hall. Marcie was surprised to see it was Sami Seaforth who came around the corner since Annie had told her to go home earlier. A jolt of fear ran though her.

"Is Annie okay?" she asked, setting her purse down on the coffee table.

Sami replied, "She's fine. She's just resting. When I got home last night, I saw the email like apparently half the rest of the world. I decided I should come over again this morning. Annie said the media showed up around 3 a.m. They're scaring Annie half to death. And me too, for that matter. I'm glad the policeman was sitting outside when they arrived. He's been controlling them as best he can."

"It must've been scary for Annie." Marcie agreed as she touched the spot on her cheek where the cell phone had hit her. "The policeman rescued some aggressive female reporter before I had a chance to lay her out." A spot of blood appeared on the tip of her finger when she pulled it away from her face. She dug a tissue out of her purse and dabbed at the scrape.

"So, is Annie really okay? She hasn't been drinking, has she?"

"I think she may've been. She tries to hide it. She's emotionally distraught and she's not getting much sleep. She just said she wished Craig had never taken the job in Washington and I can't say I blame her. This is horrible, Marcie. Has there been any progress on finding who's doing this stuff?"

"Nothing solid. The FBI is working on it. That's all I know."

"Let's hope they solve this quickly, Marcie. I'm not sure how much more Annie can take."

CHAPTER 30

Nathan and Marcie reconvened at home later that afternoon. They hadn't seen as much of each other as they would have liked since all this had started. Marcie's vacation was slipping away without them accomplishing any of the things they hoped to do. She had decided to leave the sleeping Annie with the very capable Sami and get some rest herself.

Nathan and Welch had eaten a quick lunch at the cafeteria in the FBI building. The food wasn't bad. It filled a hollow spot and that's all they really needed for now. Welch suggested Nathan might as well go home as they wouldn't likely hear anything more from agent Chin until he had talked to the Chinese taxi company and reviewed more of the video.

Nathan and Marcie sat on the sofa with the laptop on the table in front of them. They had the screen open to the travel site Marcie had been looking at earlier.

They enjoyed sharing this moment as they talked about their wedding, the band they had hired, the layout and decorations for their special day and some of their potential honeymoon destinations in Tanzania. Marcie had put a beef stew in the slow cooker and as the afternoon wore on, the combination of meat, vegetables and various spices filled the condominium with a delicious aroma, prompting their stomachs to growl in anticipation.

Then suddenly, across the bottom of the computer screen rolled a "Breaking News" banner. Nathan sat back with a start. "I wonder what it is this time. Something completely unrelated to our nightmare would be good for a change. I just want some time away from all the crises. It seems like everything is breaking news these days. The media wants our attention 24 hours a day, but more and more, it's like crying wolf. Eventually, we'll all just stop watching."

Marcie leaned over and nibbled his ear. "Mmmm, well . . . how about now?"

Nathan sat up to take a closer look at the computer screen. "As much as I would like to ignore everything right now, Marcie, I don't think we can. There's too much going on." He grabbed the remote and turned on the television set. "Let's just see what it's about and then maybe we can forget it."

The news anchor chattered excitedly about a new executive order the president was about to sign, a ceremony that would be followed by a press conference in the Rose Garden. Nathan and Marcie exchanged worried glances. The anchor had silvery white hair swept back from his forehead, which contrasted effectively with his dark suit, white shirt and matching tie. He had the distinguished appearance of someone you should believe, or at least that was the intention. The man was surrounded at the anchor desk by eight opinion-givers, four on each side, ready to seize any opportunity to speak their minds and show off their knowledge. These were paid experts the network brought in from time to time to comment and debate on the issues of the day. Nathan didn't recognize them all, but there were four who were reporters, one former professional campaign manager who was decidedly pro-President Hughes, and a former Congressman who supported whichever side of the discussion was most popular that day. No wonder he had been a successful politician, thought Nathan.

Sitting formally at the desk and reading from his teleprompter, the news anchor reported in a resonant broadcast voice, "President Hughes is signing an executive order today that will impose steep tariffs on the importation of Chinese electronic components and systems. If you've just joined us, the signing will take place around 5 o'clock this afternoon, followed by a presidential press conference. I would like to point out this is the first press conference the president has personally done in weeks, so he must be feeling pretty good about it. The signing was pre-empted by an email issued last night from a computer belonging to Chief of Staff Craig Logan's wife. We have a lot to talk about and you can see the cameras are ready at the Rose Garden. Jim Ansel is on location. Jim, what can you tell us?"

Ansel reiterated everything the anchor had just said and asked his cameraman to pan around the garden, which was packed with journalists. He finished by saying, "We're trying to get a statement from Annie Logan, the wife of Chief of Staff Logan. Over to you, Sarah."

Marcie recognized the pushy female reporter from the crowd who had shoved her cell phone into her face for a quote. She wondered if the woman realized she would have lost a couple of teeth if not for the policeman's intervention. The woman was voicing over footage that clearly showed Marcie walking towards Annie's house, telling viewers she was a family friend who had come to visit Ms. Logan. The portion of the footage where the cell phone slammed into Marcie's face had been conveniently omitted. Marcie touched her cheek where a scab had already started to form and mumbled, "Still think I should've clocked her. Maybe I should sue her."

Nathan turned to her and laughingly said, "From what you told me, the policeman intervened. I think you might've been in trouble if you had started a fight with her, though. She would just say she was pushed by you. If there was any video, I think it's disappeared by now, and no other journalist is going to confirm it happened. If you had managed to punch her, you would be the one being sued but you could've been an Internet sensation, maybe even have gone viral."

Marcie grumpily shrugged as the anchor turned to one of his guests and figuratively tossed him some red meat. "What impact do you think this will have on the sale of electronics in the U.S.?"

The economist talked about how tariffs never work, how the cost of electronics would skyrocket, and China would have to find other importers. The Chinese economy would suffer greatly, but so would the American economy. It was a lose-lose situation. Six other heads, including the former Congressman's, nodded gravely. The former campaign-manager-turned-opinion-commentator, chimed in, trying to stake his time on camera, "Now, wait a minute, let's bring some sense to this discussion. President Hughes is taking a stand against China and their cheap labor force and inferior products." His voice ascended like a thespian who knew he owned the stage, however briefly. His righteous indignation was mounting. He thundered, "This president's going to bring jobs back. He's . . ."

Nathan marveled at the man's temerity to take on seven adversaries on national television and stick by his principals no matter what. He had to give the man credit, whether he agreed or not. But the rest of his words were lost as the anchor interrupted, drawing the audience's attention to the Rose Garden where President Hughes stood at a microphone surrounded by his executive committee. Nathan examined their faces with the scrutiny of the experienced field agent. He saw tension in most of them. Although they all smiled for the cameras, Nathan observed underlying expressions betraying that some didn't want to be there. The chief of staff's absence was obvious to Nathan.

President Hughes beamed and announced it was a great day for the United States. "This is the first step toward taking back our country, my fellow Americans. We're taking back manufacturing. We're taking back jobs." As he droned on, Marcie was quite sure many of the president's base were nearly tripping over themselves in their homes in their efforts to stand at attention and salute their television sets. It was a masterful performance by a man who could play to a crowd. Marcie thought it was mostly nonsense, but when this man said it, many Americans would think it was wonderful nonsense that must be believed.

The president finished his statement, took a few softball questions lobbed by friendly plants in the audience, and accepted enthusiastic congratulations from the loyals around him. It made for great TV. Even the sun broke free from the clouds holding it hostage as he made the rounds to accept handshakes and pats on the back. He was in his glory. This was all about him and he bathed in it. The coverage went back to the anchor desk where the host threw out a question about it being a good, solid day for the president, and then everyone started talking at once.

Nathan pressed a button on the remote and the TV screen went black. Marcie and Nathan looked at each other. Marcie chewed her lower lip. Nathan frowned. They both had the same silent question.

What will this mean for Craig and Annie Logan?

CHAPTER 31

Yang Lee sat once more in the conference room in the Chinese government office building, summoned by Ji Cheung, the 4th Vice Premier of the People's Republic of China, the man representing a government that expected results. This time, another man sat in the corner of the room. Lee hadn't been introduced, but the man sat quietly, filling the chair with his muscular bulk. He wore the uniform of the People's Liberation Army and his large closely shaved head sat on his shoulders like a pumpkin. There was no hint of a neck.

Lee knew why the man was there. He had seen it before. He was there for intimidation—a warning to Lee. He served as Cheung's personal bodyguard. That meant Cheung feared Lee and that brought a brittle smile to his face. Lee was certain the Chinese government wouldn't sanction violence in this situation. There were too many moderates in the Politburo now. However, Cheung was a throwback who might take matters into his own hands. Lee had to be alert. Frankly, Lee wasn't intimidated. He smirked inwardly that Cheung would actually think intimidation would work on him.

Nevertheless, the presence of the man meant that this conversation would not go well. He thought he was summoned to discuss progress and he had prepared himself for Cheung's displeasure, but the large man in the corner suggested something more. Cheung's countenance was dark, his lips pressed together. Lee wondered if the government man had information that he hadn't heard yet. Cheung didn't say a word, his hands pressed together in the shape of a teepee in front of his face.

Finally, Cheung murmured, "We have been informed that the enemy of our country, President Hughes, has signed the vile executive order implementing tariffs on our electronic exports. Now it is subject to their judicial review process, but unless it violates their

Constitution, it will become law. We hired you to fix this Mr. Lee, but apparently, you have failed miserably."

Lee was stunned. The signing had happened even quicker than he expected. He should have checked the news before coming. He struggled to regain his composure, but he stammered. "This is the first I've heard of it, Mr. Vice President. I . . ."

Cheung cut him off. "We don't abide failure of this magnitude, Lee. You understand that."

There was more, but Lee stopped listening. *Who does this pretentious bureaucrat think he is?* Lee was tempted to get up and walk out. He glanced at the man sitting in the corner who cast a menacing look his way. The man was there to protect Cheung and intimidate Lee. He had no interest in tariffs and bureaucratic mumbo jumbo. At least he had military status and training, Lee thought. He had *earned* his rank. Lee respected that. Who was Cheung? A sniveling friend of someone in power? He was *appointed* by the president and prime minister. Lee nearly spat as he mentally worked himself into a frenzy over this man criticizing him for not completing what was turning out to be an impossible task.

He tuned back in and realized that Cheung expected a response from him. His confidence returning, he countered, "No one, including his closest advisers, thought the president would implement this so quickly. He doesn't listen to his advisers, and he also doesn't listen to people with more experience. However, all is not lost. There are still ways that I can fix this."

"You don't think we prepared ourselves for this, Lee? We have devised many weapons to punish the Americans. They want help controlling tiny rogue nations like our North Korea friends next door? The United States can't seem to deal with the problem, but we have the power to refuse to help. We will now continue to assert our rights in the South China Sea without negotiation. We will find other new and plentiful trading partners that will make our trade with the United States pale in comparison. You see, Mr. Lee, we had many options waiting for us in the event you failed. And it seems you have indeed failed despite your assurance to the contrary.

"But what bothers me even more, Mr. Lee is that your actions may have *encouraged* the president to sign this abominable law even sooner. Your email may have backfired and made things worse.

You have involved the media and the public, but it did not stop the American president from signing the tariff legislation. And if it goes through as expected, despite our plans to punish the Americans, the repercussions will be disastrous for our country." The room fell quiet. Then Cheung spoke again, this time with a softer, more insidious tone. "We cannot tolerate such failure, Mr. Lee. My moderate friends in the Politburo wanted to take a more diplomatic approach, but your failure has forced me to take action in another way. You do understand what I'm saying, Mr. Lee?"

Lee sucked in a deep breath through his clenched teeth. He could feel his anger rising exponentially at this affront. Adrenaline raced through his body as the man across the desk continued to criticize him. There was no need for this ridicule. "I can still disrupt their plans if you give me more time." His jaw muscle flexed visibly. "I think a major threat or disruption can get them to put this on hold. It would give you time to force negotiations with the president and convince him of the error of his ways on trade tariffs."

"You think? You *think*?" Cheung rose slightly from his chair, his face red. He pounded the desk for emphasis, and his voice rose dramatically. He sat back and pulled a handkerchief from his pocket to mop his brow. "How do we know you will not fail again? You have become a liability to us."

Lee tensed. All this talk about backup plans from Cheung was bluster. *If* there really were plans in place, they would be difficult to implement and they would take time. Cheung was in trouble with the Politburo, the 25-members who oversee the Communist Party of China. He must have guaranteed them that Lee, and therefore he, would succeed. When that didn't happen, Cheung knew now he must be seen by his colleagues to be taking bold action. This prominent member of the Chinese government and appointee of the Premier and Prime Minister had commissioned Lee to interfere with the actions of the American government, and now Cheung blamed him directly for the failure. Cheung had lost face with the Politburo and now he had to clean up the mess.

Although Lee knew the moderate thinking Politburo members wouldn't sanction violence against him, Cheung came from a different political climate and wouldn't hesitate. He now understood why the large military man sat in on the meeting. Lee's focus had been on the man in front of him and he almost missed the stealthy movement from the other side of the room. He sensed without looking a sudden change in the air and tensed. He continued to stare at Cheung across the desk, but his peripheral vision told him that the burly bodyguard was moving quickly towards him, circling in from the back.

The man closed fast as Lee shot from his chair, deliberately knocking it backward toward his onrushing attacker. Lee's flailing arm as he whirled around swept a lamp on Cheung's desk crashing to the floor. The sudden movement surprised the soldier, and the falling chair momentarily blocked his path. Lee hadn't been in a physical confrontation since his bullying-victim time in school, but street fighting wasn't something he'd forgotten from those days. This was a matter of self-preservation. He'd acted on pure adrenalin as a school kid, and he was doing so now. Images of his abusive classmates flashed through his mind. He didn't flee then. He certainly wouldn't now.

Lee's reflexes were fast. He was now facing the man and caught a glimpse of a garrote stretched between his outstretched hands. The onrushing man had sidestepped the chair and was trying to get the thin wire over Lee's head, but Lee's hands shot up to insert his arms between the garrote and his vulnerable flesh. He thrust his arms forward against the garrote with every ounce of his strength, and at the same instant shoved the surprised man, pushing him backwards towards the overturned chair.

The unexpected move worked in Lee's favor. The military man tumbled backward over the chair and as Lee fell with him, he removed his right arm from its position holding the garrote. The sudden release of the hands holding the garrote caused them to drop. As they did so, Lee reached for the lamp he had knocked off the desk. The attacker struggled to regain his balance while trying to force the garrote up under the bare flesh of Lee's chin. The shade had fallen free of the lamp and Lee struggled to grab the urn-shaped metal base. It rolled agonizingly away at his touch, almost out of reach. Finally, as he stretched, his fingers closed comfortably around the thin bottom section of the base. The electrical cord yanked free from the wall socket as Lee swung with all his might, bringing the base crashing down on the man's skull, opening a large gash. To Lee's surprise, the big man grunted and completed his fall heavily to the floor over the chair with the garrote spilling aimlessly to the side. Lee hit him again and again before tossing the lamp aside.

Lee picked himself up, pulled the chair out from under the unconscious man, righted it and sat down as if nothing had happened. His heart raced, but he tried not to let it show. He didn't want this pompous bureaucrat sitting in front of him to know that what he had done was pure luck. He wanted Cheung to believe he was in complete control, though the truth was, it had only been outrage and good fortune that had saved him. The Vice Premier hadn't moved a muscle in the seconds that everything had transpired in front of him. His face was pale but inscrutable as he regarded Lee.

Lee tried to steady his voice. "Now, as I was saying, I trust you will allow me to take action to regain your trust and that of the Politburo again. You can do what you want about the trade issue or negotiate for a better arrangement. You can keep your money. That's of no concern to me. My immediate goal is to rebuild my reputation."

The Vice Chairman remained frozen in his seat.

Lee added, "You will hear from me again when I have results to give you."

He got up and stepped over the military man on his way out the door, who moaned as Lee went by. Lee glanced to a side door that he knew would lead to a private alley in the back of the building where they would have disposed of his body. He had thought those days were over for the Chinese Communist Party, but apparently not for all. Neanderthals still existed in the party. When he closed the door behind him, Lee leaned against the wall and bent over, trying to regain his breath and calm his racing heart. He had to leave this place and fast. He fought against the nausea rising in his throat. Finally, as he exited the building, he knew what he had to do next. It didn't please him, but he now knew it was necessary. He made a phone call to arrange a meeting and tossed the phone into the Huangpu River.

CHAPTER 32

The weight of Bai Hu's gaze traveled across the desk, settling heavily on Yang Lee's shoulders. Lee was now sitting in the office of the Chairman of Hu Electronics. He had gone to his workplace to pick something up and calm himself after visiting Ji Cheung, and now he had just admitted to the old man, his other employer, that his attempts had not been successful so far.

When Lee arrived, Hu was sitting upright in his chair as he always did, but the old man seemed to visibly age at the news in front of the hacker's eyes. His shoulders slumped noticeably, giving his normally straight body a rounded appearance. It looked like the muscular structure of his body had suddenly disintegrated. The eyes are often tools for the Chinese to discern emotion. Rather than the expressive smiles and frowns usually seen in western culture, the main clue to the mood of the inscrutable Chinese is the eyes. But the old man's eyes, normally so bright and full of intelligence, were now rheumy. He looked at Lee through a fog of defeat.

Lee had expected a reaction, although this was more than he thought it would be. Hu came from a generation where gaining and losing face was of utmost importance. While always foremost in Chinese culture, someone of Hu's age would live and die by it, possibly literally. Lee had seen great pride in Hu's face in their previous meetings but now he saw a very different reaction.

Face was determined within various spheres, such as the workplace, family, friends and society at large. Measuring sticks were used, such as age and status in a company and the level of success was often determined by where a person lived or the car they drove. Hu's strong reaction suggested that he perceived he had lost face and Lee was the cause of it. Lee sensed that he had failed on two counts in Hu's eyes. In business, part of having face meant demanding the utmost respect from subordinates. Hu considered Lee to be a sub-ordinate—a hired hand like a worker in one of his factories—and a failure who therefore had not respected him. Secondly, since the bulk of the company's exports went to the U.S., Hu's vision of his company losing significant revenue could spell the ultimate demise of Hu Electronics. That was unacceptable. Bringing embarrassment upon a company and its owner was the second failure. It was strike two, but in this game, Lee sensed there was no third strike option.

Hu finally spoke with a steely edge to his words. "Do you have another plan for dealing with the arrogant Americans?"

After what he had just been through, Lee was in full defensive mode. Whereas Lee had respected Bai Hu for a long time, he now saw a pathetic wizened shell of a man. He knew the man in front of him had dangerous associates and could put them into play, espe-cially when saving face was at stake. His teeth clenched so hard pain shot through his jaw. Taking a cue from something Cheung had said, he uttered through barely open lips. "I'll take care of it, but are there not other countries that you can trade with? Losing trade with the Americans would be a significant blow, but perhaps it will be short-lived. And in the meantime, you may pick up new global customers in other markets. It may not be the worst thing that could happen to your company."

Hu stared across the desk. His voice was hoarse now and he was shaking. "Look at me. I'm in my eighties. My time is running short. I want to pass on my company to my granddaughter. She's ready to assume control. But your failure has jeopardized my status in society for my remaining years and will force my granddaughter to seek new revenue streams. She is a smart woman, but it will take time. This is a setback from which it will take years to recover."

Lee frowned, but came to a decision. He was already in danger from Cheung and knew he would never be safe if Hu blamed him for the failure to stop the trade tariff order from being signed. He would be looking over his shoulder constantly. He said, "Sir, I understand." He wondered if the beautiful young woman who had shown him to the office was Hu's granddaughter. "I assure you the Americans will pay for this transgression. In the meantime, I want to make a peace offer-ing as a way of begging your forgiveness." He pulled two cigars from his suit jacket pocket, offering one across the desk to the old man.

Hu took the torpedo-shaped object with a shaky hand covered in nearly transparent skin that only partially obscured blue veins. He examined it closely and sniffed its length, nearly sighing in satisfaction. Lee had no clue about the etiquette of enjoying a fine cigar, so he planned to mimic Hu's actions. He too slid the length of the cigar under his nose and took a deep breath. He had to admit, it smelled pretty good.

Hu pronounced, "A Montecristo #2 from Cuba. You have very good taste, Mr. Lee."

Lee had done his research and imported the cigars for just such an occasion. He was always prepared.

Hu opened a side drawer in his desk and removed a box. He slid the lid open to remove a wooden match and offered the box to Lee who did the same before handing it back. Lee waited to see what he was supposed to do next. Hu brushed his match along the side of the box to light the cigar, and held it at a 45-degree angle to the flame. He rotated the cigar until embers appeared. "As you already know, this is called toasting the cigar, Mr. Lee." Yang Lee nodded in accord, as if he would know such a ritual as well. Too late, he realized he was supposed to strike the match on the box. The old man handed the box of matches back to Lee who replicated the actions.

Hu took the cigar into his mouth and took short puffs while holding the flame on the end of the cigar to fully light it. He didn't inhale the smoke, but continued to puff briefly, enjoying the initial taste of the cigar. Finally, he took some long, deep puffs into his lungs. "Ah, it is smooth and spicy. A perfect balance." Hu lost himself in the experience of smoking one of Cuba's finest cigars.

Lee puffed on his cigar as he watched Hu, fascinated at how someone could be so absorbed in this simple act. It was like the man was floating on air. He set his cigar on an ashtray on the desk as Hu suddenly coughed. The coughs became more intense, and Hu's eyes widened as he gasped for breath. He shot a look of terror at Yang Lee before his eyes filled with hatred as the realization of what was happening dawned. But there was no way to stop it. Hu's body convulsed hideously, throwing him backwards against his chair, nearly toppling over. He clawed at his chest and his face turned a sickening shade of blue. Finally, he pitched forward onto the floor, motionless.

Lee watched without expression. He glanced over his shoulder to determine if the noise had attracted any attention. He retrieved his cigar from the ashtray and crushed the end. He rose from his chair, maneuvered around the desk and bent down to check the old man's pulse. Nothing. Bai Hu was gone, courtesy of the man he had hired to help save his company. Lee reached under Hu's body to recover the aconite-laced cigar. It was the same chemical he had used on Hartman, but Hu's age and possibly weakened heart, brought death even quicker than it would have to the American.

The cigar had burned a small hole in the carpet, but that could have happened any time. He smothered the lit end of the cigar between his fingertips and placed it in his pocket. He replaced it with the one he had been smoking only seconds ago and set it down beside Hu's body. He drew himself up to full height and calmly walked to the door of the office as he prepared for his next move.

Jerking the door open, he yelled, "Please, someone help! Mr. Hu is having a heart attack! Please come quickly."

The same beautiful young woman came running as fast as her tight cheongsam would allow. Lee drew in a deep breath as she bent down, the slit of her dress exposing her legs to her thigh. His eyes quickly shifted to hers as she looked up with her mouth open. He repeated, "I think he had a heart attack. He was smoking a cigar when he clutched his chest. I put the cigar out, so it wouldn't start a fire. You must call the emergency number immediately. I have another meeting I must attend, but please call me as soon as you know of Mr. Hu's condition. I am so concerned for him. You have my number."

He turned and left the flustered young woman before she could find her voice and strode through the office door past her desk to the elevator. The only record of this visit or any other he had made to the office of Bai Hu would indicate that a Tony Chong was the visitor. Hu had kept Lee's true identity quiet due to the nature of his work. The only number on record in the office was from a burner phone that no longer existed. No fingerprints would surface because Lee didn't have any. If the police became suspicious and checked the cigar, they might find Lee's DNA on it but why would they even think of that? All evidence would indicate that the old man had died of a heart attack while enjoying his favorite pastime, smoking a cigar. Lee doubted there would be any reason for the authorities to believe differently, other than that the only witness to his death had disappeared as if he were a ghost.

〈〈〈〉〉〉

Lee exited the building into the usual thick atmosphere, heavy from the exhaust of the two and a half million cars registered in the city and the sultry humidity that enveloped the area like a horse blanket. The heavy air suited his mood. His face was shaded by one of his lightweight fedoras. He wasn't really a hat person, but they served his purpose when necessary.

He hadn't wanted to kill Bai Hu, but he knew what losing face or losing his company would mean to the old man. The chairman would have held Lee responsible for everything and he would try to exact revenge. Yang Lee couldn't have that. He had enough enemies already. He didn't know if Cheung would send the military man after him again and he didn't need the electronics company owner sending trained assassins trailing him. It was a risk he couldn't afford to take.

Lee strode down the street—a man on a mission. Overnight he had gone from a man who was valued among the people who knew him to someone who could not be trusted to do a job. They had given him an impossible task, but he had accepted it willingly, thinking that he would always find a way. So far, things hadn't gone well at all, but it was time to turn the situation around. This was critical. The presumptuous president of the United States had gone ahead and signed the damn executive order without regard for how it would affect the Chinese, and now he, Yang Lee, was a pariah in his own country. He was in grave danger unless he came up with a plan of action that would reverse the U.S. position. He had to take bold action to regain his reputation. There was only one way forward and he wouldn't be able to do it from here. This called for more drastic measures.

CHAPTER 33

The phone vibrated itself to the edge of the night table beside Nathan. He pried his eyes open and sat up, the covers falling off his bare chest to his waist. His heart pounded from the sudden movement and a twinge of nausea shot into his throat. He hated middle-of-the night phone calls.

He answered sleepily as he glanced at Marcie whose heavy breathing indicated that the sound of the phone had not wakened her. The covers were pulled to her chin and Nathan smiled at her peaceful features, so relaxed in repose.

He checked the screen, which displayed the words 'private name.' He had no clue who was calling him this late. When he answered, James Welch's voice came through the speaker. "Sorry to bother you at this hour, Nathan, but you might want to get over here. We've had what could be a breakthrough. Special Agent Chin in China has been able to trace Eric Hartman's movements—and guess what, he met a male a few times for drinks and he handed a package over to the same person on the waterfront in Shanghai on the night of his death."

Nathan was fully awake now. "Okay, I'll be right there." He hit the key to disconnect. He closed one eye as he looked at the clock. It was 2:10 a.m. Even in his foggy state, he was able to calculate that with the time difference, it was mid afternoon in Shanghai. He had been sleeping in his boxers, so he pulled on some jeans and an old James Taylor concert t-shirt and padded quietly to the bathroom in his bare feet. After splashing some cold water on his face, he went to the kitchen to leave a note for Marcie.

He didn't hear her follow him and he was startled when she put her arms around him. "What's up?" she slurred sleepily in his ear.

"Welchie seems to think we have a possible breakthrough. It must be important because he wants me over there."

"Okay, want me to make you coffee or come with you?"

Nathan's pulse sped up with the familiar feeling of love for this woman. "No, just go back to bed. I'll call you when I know what's going on. I'll pick up some swill at the all night place on the way." They embraced, and Nathan left the condo to go to the FBI building.

It didn't take him long to reach Welch's office. Traffic at that time of night was negligible and he hit every green light. He wished it could always be like this. He walked into the office and found Welch intently peering at his computer monitor. The FBI agent had headphones on. He signaled to his friend as he walked through the door.

"Good morning to you too." Welch pulled one of the headphones aside and smiled lazily at Nathan. "I have lots for you to see. Just a minute until I end this call."

Welch listened intently for a few more minutes while moving files on the computer into a folder and then ended the call.

"That was Chin in Beijing. He was able to determine the route Hartman took in the taxi and he ended up on the waterfront, which is called the Bund. Hartman walked for a few minutes and then sat beside a man on a bench. It's the same guy he met for drinks. Watch this."

Welch clicked on a folder, opened a file and a video from a security camera somewhere overhead showed a stout man crossing the street and plowing through the crowd. As Welch had said, he sat beside a man he seemed to know. Welch identified the stout man as Hartman.

Nathan leaned closer to the screen to observe everything that was happening. The man Hartman sat beside was impeccably dressed, including a fedora-type hat that obscured his face. Every time it looked like his face would come into view, the man tilted his head away from the camera.

"Huh," Nathan said. "This guy seems to know where the cameras are. Is there a better angle or do we ever see his face?"

Welch put the video on pause. "This is as good as it gets as far as facial recognition is concerned. They might be able to do something with the angle of his chin or shape of his ear. It's a long shot, but keep watching."

He restarted the video. Nathan watched, fascinated, as Hartman handed an envelope to the unidentified man. The man handed a tablet to Hartman. Hartman tapped on the tablet, nodded smugly and handed it back. He pulled something out of a paper bag the man had given him and devoured it. He got up from the bench and wolfed down more of the treats as he sauntered along the sidewalk. He drifted out of range of one camera, but was soon picked up by another that showed him emptying the contents of the bag, tossing it towards a garbage can and missing. The camera followed Hartman to a street corner where he waved down a taxi. He seemed to grimace just before the taxi arrived. The video cut to the taxi arriving at the hotel where Hartman had been staying. Hartman got out of the taxi, obviously in distress. He clutched his stomach and rushed into the hotel. A camera mounted somewhere in the hotel lobby captured him as he hustled to the elevator and frantically pressed the button to summon it. The video ended with Hartman lurching down the hall, trying desperately to activate the door lock with his key card until he got it open and disappeared into his room.

Nathan asked, half in jest, "No video inside his room?"

Without a hint of sarcasm, Welch replied, "Not at this hotel."

Nathan shivered at the thought. "Okay, so we have Hartman passing off an envelope to somebody we can't identify in Shanghai. Then he appears to get a stomach ache from whatever he ate. Circumstantial, but not really compelling. Could be he was poisoned. Could be whatever he ate didn't agree with him. Could've been a copy of the executive order he gave the guy. Could've been pictures of his wife. I could go on. We don't have much."

Welch held up his hand. "Well, as they say, wait, there's more."

Welch hovered the cursor over another folder and clicked.

Now the camera focused on the well-dressed man.

Nathan's apprehension rose. There were gaps in the timeline. The guy clearly knew where the cameras were and how to avoid them. But the people who had dissected the video were equally professional. They had pieced together his route and even though his face was always obscured, they were able to track him to a high-rise in downtown Shanghai. That's where the video recording stopped.

Nathan pulled back from the screen feeling disappointed. He initially wondered why he had pulled himself out of bed. Then his FBI mind kicked into gear.

"Okay, there's enough here to look into. We need to have a toxicology test done on Eric Hartman's body. I don't know whether the body is on U.S. soil yet, but we need to find out. I'll contact Charles Walker to bring him up to speed and get that moving. Since he signs my contracts, I better make sure he's informed. I think there's a possibility that Hartman was poisoned by the well-dressed dude in these videos. We also need Chin to talk to people in the high-rise building who may've seen the guy. We need a composite sketch to identify him."

Welch watched Nathan as he spoke. Nathan's mind was now operating at warp speed, as it often did when he sensed a case was progressing. He added. "Can you send an email to Danny Chin? Ask him to check the energy bills for that building. See if there's an unusual amount of electricity being used in one of the apartments. It's a long shot, but I'm wondering if this man could be the hacker. If he is and that's where he's operating from, he might be using unusually high-powered computer equipment so there could be an unusual heat signature coming from somewhere in the building. Tell Danny we need to know now. Also, if we find a spike in the power, I want a team on standby in Shanghai to go in and talk to this guy. We can't wait. I don't know if he's dangerous, but they need to be prepared with some firepower. Do you think Chin can pull a few more strings? Tell the Chinese police that if they don't cooperate, we'll turn this into a bigger international incident than it has already become since the executive order was signed."

Welch sat wide-eyed watching Nathan. "Whoa, slow down my friend. We'll talk to Danny on Skype, so you can give him your wish list yourself. Did you drop some acid when I wasn't looking? Jeez!"

"Sorry, I just think we might have a major lead here. My mind took a little longer than my body to wake up. Get Chin online. Let's get this moving."

Nathan spent the next few minutes outlining his plan to Special Agent Chin in Beijing. He wished the man operated out of Shanghai, but that couldn't be helped. When they disconnected, Welch said, "Let's go get more coffee."

After half an hour, they arrived back in the office. It was another 45 minutes before the bouncy Skype tune played on the computer announcing a call. It was Danny Chin.

"I pulled some strings and got the information you requested. Things can happen quickly around here when you know the right people. It's a closed society until it suits them. Then they can be quite open. You can expect a request for a favor from the Chinese police force soon to do something on their behalf. They'll expect a positive response."

Nathan shrugged his large shoulders. "Okay, Walker can deal with that when the time comes. What did you find out?"

"There are two apartments in the building that have higher than average power bills. One bill is nearly through the roof. I'm thinking drug op, but who knows? Either one could potentially be our man."

"Can we get someone in there to ask some questions?"

"I mentioned to the head of the police department that we wanted to talk to someone of interest in two apartments in the building. I said the person or persons could be dangerous, but we don't know. They're going to set up a video feed, so we can watch."

Nathan: "Are they sending a couple of guys just in case?"

"They seemed to be having a slow day. They're sending the Shanghai Special Police Force. He said they have some new recruits who need to get some on-the-job training in the field."

"What exactly is the Special Police Force?"

The agent chuckled. "We have the same thing in North America except we call it Special Weapons and Tactics. You know . . . SWAT."

CHAPTER 34

Yang Lee arrived at the stark gray building where he worked and rode the elevator to the floor of his apartment. His heart thumped. For a man with a normal resting heart rate in the top percentile of his age group, this was highly unusual. His palms were sweaty, and a sheen of perspiration appeared across his forehead. The coolness of the air conditioner drifted through the elevator, yet it didn't seem to help. Tightness pulled his shoulders together.

This was unfamiliar territory for him. He hadn't experienced stress since a teacher reprimanded him for punching another kid in grade school. Even then it was more exhilaration. Nothing like this.

The elevator ride gave him time to examine his stress. So much had gone wrong with this assignment. He'd been given an impossible deadline. Maybe he had taken the wrong approach by going after the woman. Maybe he had underestimated the resolve, or stupidity, of the U.S. president. He had to grudgingly admit to himself that he might have overestimated his own abilities this time. All his successes had come easily and now this one had blown up in his face. One mistake in a brilliant career and he was in trouble. A lot of trouble.

What he was about to do was necessary to regain his reputation. He had to do something spectacular so that he would be brought back into the game. It wasn't about money now. It was about reputation and prestige. It was about status. It was about—wait a minute, thought Lee. That sounds like the definition of saving face. He shook his head and smiled inwardly. Maybe there were some of the old ways left in him after all. It must have been passed down from his parents, although he never thought of himself as adopting the Chinese spirit.

In carrying out his new plan, he would get the Politburo off his back. He wasn't worried about Hu Electronics now. He had already taken care of that problem. The granddaughter would inherit the company. Lee was quite sure she could rebuild the company by finding other trading partners. The old man could have done it, too, but Lee knew that he was the type of man who would want revenge first and he hadn't been about to wait for that to happen.

Lee stepped out of the elevator and opened the door to his apartment where he was met with the heat emanating from his beloved computers. He sighed as he stepped through the door. He shrugged his shoulders and rotated his neck with a loud crack, trying to relieve some of the tension. He interlaced his fingers and turned them outward with his arms extended and stretched. His knuckles popped.

Still tense, he decided he soon needed to call the House of Pearls, his favorite escort service, for a massage.

He checked his latest downloads from various computers in government offices, corporations and public figures around the world. A couple of things caught his eye that could prove useful at some point. He looked over some hacked messages that a movie star had sent to another well-known celebrity. They were intimate messages, complete with photos. And they weren't to his wife. And the recipient was male. He might follow that up sometime just for fun.

He opened the drawer of his desk and removed a tiny USB flash drive. There were two and he selected a gray one with red markings. It had a capacity of one terabyte or 1,024 gigabytes. It was the largest capacity and fastest flash drive yet developed and not yet available to the public—but it was available on the deep web, an area of the internet not accessible by the average person or through search engines. He inserted it into the computer and started the process of backing up the data collected by his computers.

While the data downloaded, he walked to a cabinet and removed bottles from the shelves. He boxed up all but two. He couldn't flush them down the toilet without poisoning half of Shanghai. That thought didn't really bother him, but it would draw unnecessary attention. He would drive to the country and bury them in a spot under a tree that he always used when he left town for a few days.

Next, he opened another cabinet to expose a 9mm Norinco CF-98, a popular handgun of the Chinese People's Liberation Army. He had never fired it. Too messy. It wouldn't bother him to bury it. Lee wouldn't have any trouble getting a gun if he needed to where he was going, but his chemicals would be weapons enough. Tonight after dark, he would get rid of everything he didn't need.

The computer beeped to indicate everything had been downloaded. His hands flew over the keyboard as he checked various files on the flash drive to make sure everything had backed up properly. This would be his only backup until the next job was done, so he had to make sure everything was there. Satisfied, he threw the flash drive in the box and opened the drawer again to find a similar one in gray and blue.

He picked it up, but hesitated. The tension still occupied his body. He was a spring wound tightly inside a box about to be opened. As soon as he finished here, he would order that special massage he craved. He thought of the lithe beauties they sent from the escort service he used on many occasions. It was always a special treat, and he knew this time would be no different. They never said much, just got down to business.

His thumb caressed the flash drive as he thought about the pleasures. Finally, he inserted it into a slot on the computer and performed another routine with the keyboard. A program began working.

He carried the two chemical containers he had not boxed into the bedroom. He put on his lead lined gloves and a mask and poured minute quantities of the chemicals into separate ceramic vials and inserted each through a specially designed slit in the lining of his suitcase next to the frame. He had carried his chemicals through security many times before without incident. The material used in the vial and its proximity to the frame of the suitcase ensured it would never be detected. The remainder from the containers would be buried tonight. The gloves and mask would be buried separately.

Lee walked back to the living room where the computers stood and checked the screen. He felt a twinge of sadness, but it was necessary. The USB he had inserted had some crucial programs he needed to take with him. It also had a program that would wipe out everything on the computers. There would be no trace of any of the hacking he had ever done. Once everything had been removed, the hard drives would be destroyed. It was unlikely the authorities would ever catch up to him, but just in case . . . It might be possible for someone with exceptional computer skills to recover some of the data, but not all, and it would take sophisticated equipment and months, if not years, of work.

He would buy new hard drives and reinstall the backups when he returned, but he would need some of the software where he was going.

He would soon again be known as the most dangerous and reliable in his field in all of China.

Lee pulled open another drawer containing a variety of passports and identification documents. He acquired his illegal documents through a contact on the deep web who was adept at forging quality travel identification. The ID was backed up by paperwork that confirmed his identity. He had traveled the world on various assignments using the false documents and no questions had ever been raised. He had great confidence in his contact's artistry with forgery. He selected a passport, driver's license, health card showing he was on the Affordable Care Act, and other related documentation to prove that he resided in United States. He would be Ches Wong, born and raised in San Francisco. His identification proclaimed he was the president of an import/export business. The rest he put in the box to be buried.

It took time for the program to do its job.

The message on the screen read, "15% of files deleted. Please do not shut off the computer."

CHAPTER 35

Welch stared at the split screen at the front of the boardroom. "Okay, the Special Police Force might be a bit of overkill, if you'll pardon the expression."

"If this is our guy, I'm quite happy that they're coming down on him hard. He deserves everything he gets for what he's put the Logans through, not to mention trying to influence the activities of our government," Nathan replied.

Each screen displayed teams of heavily armed men sitting opposite each other in a van. A camera mounted on the helmet of each team leader showed their superiors in Shanghai and the observers at the FBI office 8,000 miles away in Tampa exactly what was happening in real time. Nervous energy mounted among all the participants, including those observing on their remote screens.

Nathan and Welch had been joined in the communications room by senior officials from the FBI field office, including the man in charge, Special Agent Charles Walker. Everything was happening quickly. Though Nathan had been keeping the senior officials fully apprised, he continued to bring them completely up to date on the rapidly developing events while they watched. When he finished, the room fell silent while they stared intently at the large screen on the wall.

The men in the van jostled back and forth as they made their way across the city. The older men's faces displayed nothing but a steely resolve. The younger faces exhibited apprehension. They sat on benches in what appeared to be a re-purposed delivery van or bus. It was dark inside, and the transmission was fuzzy, but Nathan could make out that their attire was like any SWAT team in North America. They carried their personal preferences in firearms, flash-bang grenades, tear gas, pepper spray, high powered flashlights and a variety of communications equipment. Nathan knew that when it came to body armor, it was always a balancing act between comfort and heat, protection and freedom of movement, and these men appeared to be wearing Kevlar to protect their torsos and heads. They were ready for anything.

The truck stopped in front of the building and the men poured out like ants from a hill that had been flooded. The hazy images bobbed up and down. Running feet on a sidewalk. Glimpses of the backs of the heavily armed running men. The front door of the building swinging open. Men streaming inside one after the other. Startled faces in the lobby of the building. Heavy breathing as the men ran. Shouted instructions. Gasps from scared people expecting to go about their daily lives today.

Although the language was foreign, Nathan knew what was being said. The team was ordering people to stay put in the lobby, so they could be questioned. The building was in lockdown. Anyone in the elevators on their way down would be allowed to come to the bottom and told to stay with the rest in the lobby. The apartment building lobby was now owned, at least temporarily, by the Chinese Special Police Force.

The men ran into the stairwell and up the stairs.

So far it was an impressively efficient operation carried out by highly trained men.

The teams on the split screen went in different directions. One team stopped on the fifth floor to carry out a raid on apartment 504, the site of one of the unusually high energy bills. All eyes in the communications room shifted to that half of the screen. The men worked their way efficiently along the wall with guns at the ready. They operated as one, quietly and confidently, towards their objective. They gathered on either side of 504 and one of the men knocked on the door. Nothing. He shouted a command. Still nothing. He knelt to pick the lock just as a bullet sheared through the door and splattered against the wall where his head had been just seconds earlier. The camera swung around briefly as the team leader swiveled sideways, yelling at people poking their heads through doors to get back inside. When the camera swung back, the team members were pulling their infrared goggles over their eyes. One planted an explosive device on the door.

The observers in Tampa were mesmerized by the action. This was completely unexpected. The hacker was trying to shoot his way out? Where did he expect to go with a SWAT team outside the door?

Nathan glanced at the other screen where the team had reached the eighth floor and were approaching the door to 812.

Three floors below, as the observers watched, the team blew open the door and the staccato sound of an automatic weapon echoed around the room through the speaker system in Tampa. A huge blast was quickly followed by a cloud of smoke erupting through the door as a flash-bang grenade tossed into the apartment by a member of the team exploded.

The observers could only make out dark images in the thick smoke clouding the air as the team made their way into the apartment with as much noise as they could muster. Shouts to intimidate and to warn. Four shots rang out, and two images slumped to the floor. The camera swung back and forth, catching members of the team clearing the bedrooms to make sure no one else was there. Images flashed on the screen of the two bodies. As the team leader examined them, the observers could see through the haze that both were men who appeared to be in their forties. The deadly aim of the Chinese Special Police's return fire had ensured that they would not be doing whatever it was they were involved with again.

What they were involved with soon became clear. The team leader's camera focused on a number of plants in the living room under heat lamps. There was the explanation for the high energy bill. Bags of cocaine with a huge street value were lined up on the kitchen counter. Used needles sat in the sink in the bathroom. One of the higher-ranking FBI officials commented, "They were probably high. That's why they thought they could shoot their way out."

One thing quickly became clear. There was not a computer in sight.

The observers focused their attention back to apartment 812 where the second team had gathered around the door. They knocked and announced who they were and again no one answered. Nathan wondered if the same thing was about to happen. After the reports of gunfire on floor five, this team was being extra cautious. They announced their presence three times before one of the team squatted to blow the door. It exploded off its hinges with shards of wood flying in all directions. Nathan thought of Annie and how frightened she must have been when the police knocked down her front door.

The team leader's camera beamed the image of the apartment back to their own headquarters in China and to the FBI agents in Tampa. The story was different this time.

It looked like someone had left in a hurry. Cabinet doors hung open and drawers were half pulled out. But the most interesting thing to the observers was the bank of computer towers occupying the shelving unit against the wall. Monitors sat on the desk. This was no operation of a pimply-faced kid. These were commercial-grade computers belonging to an expert who knew exactly what he was doing. A quick check of the apartment confirmed there was no one there.

The team leader placed his hand on one of the hard drives and said something in Chinese. Another voice crackled over the speaker system. "Nathan, are you there?" It was Danny Chin who was online from Beijing.

"Yes, I'm here, Danny. We can hear you. This could be what we're looking for."

"The Team Leader says the hard drives are warm. Someone was just here." Chin listened as the leader barked instructions. He added, "The team leader just sent more men down to search the building and question the people in the lobby. He might still be here."

"Can you ask the leader to turn on the computer? Let's see what's there."

In response to Nathan's question, Chin translated for the team leader who sat in front of the desk looking for a power switch. The observers in Tampa waited in anticipation. The only sound in the boardroom was that of a fly buzzing until it landed somewhere. Then all was quiet as they held their collective breath. The speakers came to life giving the observers hope. Chin translated the Chinese message on the screen. *I/O Error—Hard disk drive failure.* He added that there appeared to be nothing left.

Nathan was sure this was the location of the hacker. This was where he found the keyboard courage to launch his attacks. Nathan didn't believe in coincidences, and there were just too many things pointing to this location. He wanted desperately to nail this guy. He just hoped that someone in Shanghai could recover the missing data. Whoever the hacker was, he must have sensed they were closing in and shut down his operation. But if he wasn't still in the lobby, then where was he? And more importantly, where was he going next?

CHAPTER 36

Nathan and Marcie sat at the dinner table in their condo. They had finished their meal and were in no hurry to clean up the dishes. It was late in the evening since Marcie had stopped off to see Annie on the way home from running some errands. When she arrived home, Nathan had already prepared a dish with pasta, shrimp, zucchini and cherry tomatoes simmering in a roasted garlic aioli sauce, but she had shooed him away from the stove to finish up while he opened a bottle of red wine.

After the meal, Nathan leaned back in his chair and patted his stomach as he jokingly complimented himself for the fine dinner. Marcie wholeheartedly agreed by raising her half-empty glass, and Nathan shifted forward on his chair to reciprocate. They clinked glasses with a hearty "Cheers," toasting nothing more than that they were together once again and. Marcie was back at work, and Nathan continued to be updated by Welch when new developments came up about the hacking case. Nathan was far more preoccupied now with the online exploitation case since it was gaining more traction.

As always, Marcie was curious about Nathan's work. She understood her job in social work contributed to the well-being of her clients, but she sometimes envied the action Nathan found himself in. She had learned how to shoot from her ex-husband, He Who Shall Not Be Named, and had a concealed weapon license. She was also good at martial arts after taking courses in self-defense. Marcie could definitely hold her own if necessary.

Nathan hadn't talked much about his case load since the raid on the apartment. She loved to hear about his cases, but she knew that as a consultant for the FBI he was sworn to secrecy. Their time alone had been spent enjoying Marcie's vacation and talking about their upcoming honeymoon in Africa. She was dying to hear more, and she thought now would be a good time to bring it up.

She didn't beat around the bush. She started with the case he had been working on before Annie's computer was hacked. "How's the exploitation case going?"

Nathan chuckled. He knew his fiancée loved hearing about his cases. "I thought you'd never ask. It's going slowly, but there's good news on the trafficking case. We have one young girl who's willing to testify in the case I worked on. You know how rare that is. They often think their work here, no matter how bad it is, is still better than going back to their impoverished existence back home. If she follows through, we might be able to close down another ring." He shrugged. "It's a full-time job. It's frustrating as hell, but we'll keep chipping away at it."

Marcie asked, "Are you going to keep on taking contracts with the FBI? I thought you were interested in private sector work. White collar crime, money laundering, stuff like that."

"I *did* say that. I thought I would be working more for corporations when I got my private license, but this has been a good gig."

"Well, Special Agent Walker at the FBI seems to think you know what you're doing. You certainly have him bamboozled." Marcie peeked over the top of the wine glass held with both hands in front of her face, containing a grin. She saw the laugh lines deepening on Nathan's face. Then she added, "Anything new on our friendly ghost?"

"Marcie, you know I can't tell you much because of the secure nature of the case, but you already know about Eric Hartman, so I can fill you in on that part. Our friendly ghost has disappeared, hopefully for good, but not likely. My gut tells me there's more coming. The medical examiners actually did find poison in Hartman's body. In fact, it turned out his insides were a mess, which led them to investigate further. It's really amazing how a routine examination failed to uncover anything. I guess on the surface, it looked like he'd had a heart attack and given his weight issues, it made sense. So that's as far as they went. Hartman's death would've been recorded as cardiac arrest if we hadn't followed the trail of the security cameras." Nathan looked at Marcie with affection. "Kudos to you for suggesting that angle, Marce. Anyway, after running additional tests, they discovered something called aconite in Eric's stomach lining. Aconite's deadly and doesn't leave much of an external trace. They also discovered specks of the same poison in the apartment where they found the computers. It appears whoever stayed there is a very dangerous man, or men if there was more than one person staying there. That's probably more than I should tell you, but you've been involved up to this point so I'll take the chance." He laughingly added, "You know what they say about telling you more."

"I know, you'd have to kill me." She laughed. "Good luck with that. I know how to use a gun too you know." Marcie swatted at a wayward fruit fly floating in front of her face. "Where do these flies *come* from? It's like they suddenly appear out of nowhere." A quick snatch of her hand ended the insect's flight before it could land in her wine. At that precise moment, the office landline rang.

Nathan was relieved as he got up to answer the phone. He hated keeping anything from his fiancée, and he knew she would want to hear more. He walked quickly into the office. Very few people had his encrypted phone number, so he wasn't surprised when it was Walker wanting an update.

After the initial greetings, the agent in charge got right to the point. He told Nathan that Welch had gone home for some much-needed rest so he didn't want to bother him. He asked, "Anything new on the computers?"

Nathan replied, "You beat me to it, Charles. I was going to call you after dinner to fill you in. James called me just before we sat down. Not a trace on the computers, I'm afraid. They've been wiped clean. The technicians in China are working on them but it could take months. Apparently, whatever he did to destroy the hard drives was pretty successful. It even cracked them, which makes it doubly difficult to recover the data. If the police there ever do catch the ghost, they'll have to focus on the poison to make a case. If we're lucky, by disrupting his activities, the hacking may have stopped at the same time, but the Chinese authorities don't even know for sure if it was one or two people who worked at the apartment. There's no sign that anyone lived there, so he has accommodations somewhere else. They're working that angle, too. It could be that one person was responsible for the hacking and another poisoned poor Hartman. Of course, the Chinese government are disavowing any knowledge of any of this. Let's hope that's true or this could really blow up politically."

"Who was the apartment registered to?"

"Someone who doesn't exist. The police were able to put together a rough composite sketch of the person they think is the one who met Hartman by talking to the neighbors at the apartment, but they all said he pretty much kept to himself. You know better than anyone that we hear that all the time. The person who goes on a murderous rampage is always the quietest one on the street and always kept to himself, according to the neighbors. This guy was no different. He always wore a hat pulled down over his eyes, so the sketch is very rough. It doesn't help much. It's been given to Homeland in case he tries to come to America. They will pass it on to Interpol, so the borders are covered."

"Does your instinct tell you he would try to come to America?"

"I don't know of any reason why he would. He tried to stop the executive order from being signed and failed. But according to a profiler in the Chinese National Police Agency, that's the whole point. The profiler told our man Danny Chin in Beijing that one thing we shouldn't do is underestimate the lengths to which Asians will go to complete a task. They are very determined people so he or they might come here to try to make up for the failed attempt at preventing the order from being signed. Also, he will need to recover some of the face he lost by failing to accomplish his mission. Of course, that could mean another mission somewhere completely different, but the profiler seemed to think this case is not finished and I tend to agree."

Walker said, "Well, thanks for the update, Nathan. I know you and Welchie are on top of it. Have a good night."

Nathan hung up and left the office to find Marcie still in the kitchen. He told her it was Walker looking for a status report and asked, "By the way, how was your visit with Annie?"

"She's looking better, but she's so fragile. I think she's trying to control her drinking, but she could revert at any second. I don't think she's seeing anyone yet about it, and I'm not sure how committed she is to do it, frankly. She was in a good mood, though. Her face had a little more color. Thankfully, the media has backed off. I guess the news cycle on Annie's computer hacking has petered out since they're all focusing on the trade tariffs. There were a couple of cars on the street with people in them, but that's it. I assume they were reporters waiting for her to leave the house, so they could ask her questions.

"She's just lonely and a bit lost. She feels trapped in the house. She'll eventually recover from the drinking if she gets support soon, but Craig Logan doesn't seem to have time to give her much. He's coming home in a couple of weeks to take a short break from the insanity of the White House, so she's looking forward to that. Apparently, he told her he has a surprise for her. I don't know how many more surprises she needs, but she's feeling confident about using the computer again since the hackings seem to have stopped. I think she'll be careful about who she accepts online invitations from in the future, and I'm pretty sure her camera will be covered from now on."

Nathan was happy that Annie was enjoying at least a little peace. "I agree, it looks like the media is focusing now on the president's unexpected signing of that executive order and how China is going to react. I think they'll keep trying to get a quote from Annie, but that's about it."

They continued to talk about Annie for a few minutes. As Marcie got up with her plate and glass in hand, she asked, "Are you tired?"

"I'm never too tired," Nathan replied with a smile as he followed her into the kitchen with his plate.

"Cool your jets, big boy. I was thinking of watching a movie on Netflix."

"Oh, a movie, huh," he said, feigning disappointment. "Like what? *Fast and Furious?*"

"Nice try. You picked last time. I was thinking of something with some action, sensitivity, maybe even a little romance thrown in. You'll have to cover your eyes and ears during the naughty bits, though."

Nathan's eyebrows shot up and down. "Naughty bits? All right! I'm in."

After inserting a DVD into the player, Marcie leaned her head on Nathan's shoulder and snuggled under his arm on the sofa as *Bridget Jones's Baby* started to play. Nathan sighed loudly in a futile protest. She molded herself to his body, feeling completely serene. She had found her soul mate in this man. She leaned up to brush her lips against his cheek. She was so glad that things were getting back to normal.

CHAPTER 37

Craig Logan sat in the Oval Office waiting for the president. He had prepared the daily agenda and short briefing notes on the latest developments around the world. There were hot spots in a number of areas, and President Hughes was to meet with the Prime Minister of Canada later in the day. Logan knew the president would look forward to the meeting and the briefing after because that's when he was at his best. He loved the camera, and his charisma appealed to his base supporters. The purpose of the meeting was to continue discussions on protecting the Arctic without harming American companies that were in joint oil exploration with their Russian counterparts.

For some reason, Hughes seemed to have a fundamental need to be recognized as the most qualified leader of the free world ever to hold the presidency, although his poll numbers were headed in the opposite direction. Logan perceived that Hughes blamed most of his recent troubles directly on him.

He greeted Hughes formally. "Mr. President."

Hughes acknowledged Logan without a smile, "Craig. Sit down. What do we have today?"

Logan thought to himself that the president, who was in his early sixties, had aged about 10 years since taking office. Logan was convinced that there were ageing lines that hadn't been there before. Excess skin was apparent under Hughes' chin and jaw line, and there were dark circles under his eyes. The change was dramatic and disconcerting. He'd seen it happen to other presidents on TV, but it still jolted him to see it firsthand. Logan pushed the thought out of his mind and began going over the various meetings on Hughes' agenda. The president showed little or no reaction as he listened to his chief of staff drone on. Logan pointed to the meeting scheduled with the Canadian prime minister. "This meeting will be a short one. The prime minister is on his way to Australia, so it will consist of a short photo opportunity for the press, a brief behind-closed-doors meeting for you and the prime minister, and then a short question and answer period in the Rose Garden. The communications team is putting together some speaking notes for you, Mr. President, and it's probably best to stick to the notes the team gives you, sir." He hesitated, but decided to plow ahead. It was something he'd been asked to address with the commander in chief. "With all due respect, sometimes when you deviate off the script and add your personal asides, the media misinterprets you and we end up with bad press or misquotes." To soften the blow, he added, "In the interest of time, since this *is* a short meeting, we believe it would be best to stick to the prepared script."

The president leaned forward and looked levelly at Logan over his reading glasses. In a tone barely disguising his irritation, Hughes replied, "Frankly, I don't really care what the Comms team thinks. I got elected by the people of this country because of my straight talk. I don't follow scripts and never have. That's how I got here, and that's what my political base wants to hear. They like my style. They call me different and renegade and charismatic, and I intend to continue doing just what I've always done. I'm not going to start playing by everyone else's rules just because someone might get upset." He paused and leaned back in his chair. "What's this Arctic thing all about, anyway?"

The topic of Arctic drilling had been raised on numerous occasions, and there were accompanying notes provided for Hughes to look over. Logan sighed inwardly. The president wasn't going to read them. He wanted the short, simplified version, and he wanted a summary of valid points so he could approve or disapprove. Logan explained that taking a tough line with Russia over various indiscretions could result in American oil companies working on joint ventures with them becoming collateral damage. That could well be a political nightmare.

Hughes dismissed the discussion by saying, "It sounds like something the Canadians should be dealing with more forcefully. I'll put a little pressure on with my remarks. Maybe we need to embarrass the prime minister a little."

Logan cleared his throat to advise a different approach entirely, but then decided against pursuing it. Inwardly, he knew the communications team would be furious if Hughes followed through with that idea in front of the media. But of course, it wouldn't be the first time with this president.

He continued with the agenda. "Mr. President, your upcoming meeting with the chairman of the joint chiefs of staff is an important one. There's a detailed dossier for you to go through." The joint chiefs of staff was a body of senior uniformed officials in the Department of Defense that advises on critical military matters. Hughes needed to be prepared. "They're concerned about rising tensions in the Middle East. Iran is stirring things up, and the joint chiefs think you should make a statement strongly condemning their actions."

Hughes's mind was clearly somewhere else. He waved his hand in the air. "I'll go with whatever they want. They're the military experts. Tell them to put together a statement for me and I'll sign it."

Logan could feel the heat of frustration rising through his collar. "Sir, may I speak frankly?" Without waiting for a response, he continued. "Wouldn't it be advisable to hear what the chairman has to say, first? Perhaps it would help you make your decision if you understood in more depth what he thinks Iran is trying to do."

"Craig, you know I have complete faith in our military. I'll agree with whatever they want to do. Is there anything else with today's agenda? There's something I'd like to discuss."

"Well, there is the other thing about the executive order on tariffs. There are situations arising because there's still confusion related to its implementation, but more than that, there's some concern for our diplomatic community in China. The feeling among people who have their ear to the ground on this one think there will be retaliation of some sort. The Chair of the Foreign Relations Committee, Jason Thompson, would like to speak to you about that to get some guidance on how you would like to see it unfold. Perhaps direct discussion with the Chinese would help to ease tensions." Craig thought inwardly it was too late for that.

President Hughes stifled a yawn. "Tell Thompson to come up with some recommendations from his committee. That's what they're for. I'll meet with him when he has recommendations for me."

Logan had seen this before. If the committee proceeded without the president's input, there was a good chance they would waste time working in a direction the president would not support. Worse, he would blame them for not making any headway. Craig snapped the leather binder holding the agenda closed while doing his best to hide a resigned look. "Sir, that's all from me for today. You had something you wanted to discuss."

The president said, "I've been watching the news networks and they are announcing poll numbers that are obviously wrong. They say my approval rating is very low. I think we need to do a series of rallies with some of my supporters around the country to whip up a show of support. Could you set something up? Oh, and I think the Comms team should do a series of TV interviews reminding people that the election polls were completely off, and obviously these new polls on my approval rating are wrong too. Besides, I want to see how they handle their interviews. Some of the answers they are giving haven't been great lately. They'd better smarten up."

Logan groaned inwardly again. He knew he'd been doing that a lot lately. Hughes was more concerned about his personal political image than he was about running the country. His agenda was jam-packed with issues requiring serious decisions, there were more than three years left in his term, and yet the president was more interested in firing up his constituents for a show of public support. Oh well, Logan thought, it was his job to serve at the pleasure of the president and he'd accepted it, so he would start working on setting up the rallies.

"I can do that. Do you have any preference as to where you would like to start?"

"Yes, I do. I've been getting some pushback recently from the Governor of Florida. Let's start with a dinner with him and his key followers and some special guests. Then we can have a rally with a large crowd of supporters the next day."

‹ ‹ ‹ › ›

When they finished discussing the first political event in Florida and laying out a strategy for future rally-style events, Craig Logan went back to his office and tossed his copy of the agenda on his desk. He took off his jacket and laid it carefully on the back of his chair. He looked in the mirror just to make sure he wasn't aging at the same rate as his boss. There were new lines on his face for sure that hadn't been there before. He loosened his tie as he slumped into his chair, thinking about the meeting he had just suffered through. He thought about his role at the White House. He picked up a pen and jotted down names. He came up with eight. He sat back and considered the list.

There were eight people in the West Wing who had walk-in privileges to see the President of the United States. And *he* was supposed to somehow control the president's agenda and the consistency of the messages coming from the White House? Everyone had been personally given that prestigious status by the president himself. Then the president had impulsively signed the executive order.

Although the Chinese had remained quiet, he was sure there would be retaliation of some sort. Something was definitely going to happen. Craig shook his head. Then he thought of the first person blamed for the email that had been sent from his wife's computer. It had been him. Sure, it appeared to come from there, but who had *his* back? The answer was shouted at him from somewhere inside his head. No one! He contemplated his time in this office and how much he missed Annie. He should be with her, but he had been barely able to even talk to her recently. She needed his love and support, and he needed to be there to help her with her drinking problem.

Craig leaned back in his chair with his hands clasped behind his head and stared at the ceiling. He thought about the role of the chief of staff. He really had a constituency of one. His job was to serve the president and implement his agenda. But that's where things seemed to be falling apart. No one was sure what this president's agenda was. Someone once said if the chief of staff spends more time with the staff and less with the chief, they will do all right. Maybe that's where his focus should be.

He made up his mind. Working on the event planning could wait for a few minutes. He pulled himself forward in his chair and began typing.

CHAPTER 38

The man's breath reeked of tortilla chips and stale beer. He had been eating and drinking steadily since the airplane left the airport. Thankfully, the briefcase full of snacks he had brought onto the plane was nearly empty. A few hours into the flight, he was already fully inebriated. He leaned closer to Yang Lee, invading his space. Lee's success with the military man in Cheung's office had given him more courage. He thought of the many ways it might be possible to kill the man. One quick shot with his elbow to the man's temple would render him unconscious for a few hours, but then what would happen when he woke up later with a huge headache? Lee stopped fantasizing and settled into his seat. Still six hours to go on this horrible flight.

Lee's mood was already somber when he boarded the plane and this obnoxious man wasn't helping. He leaned his head back on the seat with his eyes closed, hoping the man beside him would shut up and do the same. He had chosen not to fly first class to avoid unnecessary attention. What a mistake. His mind wandered again as he tried to relax. This time he replayed recent events in his mind to satisfy himself that no omissions had been made. On the rare occasion when he had made mistakes, he planned and acted on ways to cover them. That was one of the keys to keeping him alive so far.

It had been a very close call. Too close. He had been warned by a contact at the Chinese Special Police Force, whom he paid very well, that the police were on their way to raid his apartment. He had seen them enter the apartment building just as he was leaving, carrying the box. He had to hurry his departure. A reel of everything he had done before the police had arrived spooled through his head.

The hard drives had been wiped clean and destroyed. The data might be recoverable, but it would take a very long time. He worried a little that there might be traces of the poison left behind, but that shouldn't be a big problem. He had taken great pains to ensure that if his apartment ever was raided, they would never figure out who he was. He liked to think of himself as invisible. If he had known, he would have liked the name assigned to him by the FBI. The Ghost.

He had taken the high-speed train to Deqin Station and then hiked to the Bamboo Forest of Moganshan. It was a long hike, and he was sweating profusely when he got to his destination. Tourists often came to the hiking trails in the area, but no one would ever stumble across his spot this deep into the forest. He needed a hand-held GPS to find it, and it led him directly to the location.

The box he had carried into the forest contained his supply of chemicals, except for the ones he had hidden in his suitcase. Lee had also included the identification he wouldn't need, the gun and the data backups in the box. He had scraped away a layer of dirt and the leaves that had fallen off the bamboo trees when the weather turned cooler, exposing a large container. It had taken him many trips to dig the hole and assemble the large waterproof box that would become the hiding place for the tools of his trade. He had lifted the lid and satisfied himself that it had been untouched since he was last there. The open lid had exposed more vials of chemicals and more IDs. He had pushed them aside enough that he could fit the new box into the container.

After leaving the forest, he had spent the night in a hotel room where he'd left an already-packed suitcase. Since the police had found his place of work, he didn't want to go back to the apartment where he lived. He would stay away from there for a while. He would just leave the handheld GPS in the hotel somewhere. The hotel manager would just think it belonged to a geocaching hobbyist. He loved the thought. He did geocaching of sorts too, but instead of the caches of troll dolls or small souvenirs that the hobbyists bury, his cache was far more sinister.

Now, as luck would have it, he was stuck with another boorish American businessman who couldn't stop talking about his managerial job at some automotive assembly plant in Bowling Green, Kentucky. Before he put his head back, Lee had learned far too much about the man—where he had gone to school, his wife and kids, the boss he hated, his favorite TV reality shows—the list went on and on.

Of course, Lee didn't remember any of it, other than that the man was responsible for some sector of a plant that manufactured Corvettes. Now *that* was interesting. It was one thing the Americans got right. Lee had admired the sleek automobile since he was a kid.

He didn't want to draw attention to himself by aggravating the man after sacrificing a seat in first class. He opened his eyes again and the man continued to talk, although he was slowing down. He humored the man for a while and then fished in his briefcase for his headphones. He found they drowned out the drone of the aircraft engines and by doing so, helped reduce jet lag. They were also great at drowning out unwanted commentary by seat partners. He had found a movie in Mandarin and pretended to watch intently. His mind was elsewhere again now. Plotting revenge.

The cabin filled with the aroma of food as the flight attendants shepherded the cart down the narrow aisle. At least he's quiet when he's eating, thought Lee, as the cart arrived at their row. He removed his headphones so he could hear what was being said and the grating voice of the man beside him choosing his meal assaulted his ears and wormed its way into his brain. His shoulders tensed as the voice landed on his last nerve. Lee picked at his food with gritted teeth, managing a few bites.

Mercifully, after finishing his meal, the man asked Lee to move so he could make a trip to the aft bathroom and then promptly fell into a sound sleep upon his return. Lee hoped he would stay that way until they landed. He took a *Washington Post* from the arm full of newspapers carried by a steward passing by. Maybe the newspaper from the home of the politicians would inspire him and give him a more specific purpose.

He scanned the headlines, but nothing immediately drew his attention. And then, suddenly, there it was. A small article buried in a corner of the paper. It was a nothing announcement—just a filler. The president was planning some rally-style meetings around the country to generate support. Several possible cities were mentioned in the article. This just might serve his purpose nicely. He would need more information, and detailed planning would be required, of course, but this could give him the revenge he so desperately desired and salvage his reputation as well. It was like the answer had been dropped in his lap.

This was more like it, thought Lee, smiling slightly in his seat. This was the good fortune he was accustomed to. He carefully ripped the article from the corner of the paper, pulled back the elastic top of the compartment at the back of the seat in front of him and stuffed the folded newspaper inside. He tilted his seat back as far as it would go. He listened with his acute hearing to the woman seated directly behind him complaining to her traveling companion about the inconsiderate passenger in front of her. He put the headphones back on and settled into a restful sleep.

After they disembarked, he joined a long line snaking its way towards the customs officer. When he finally reached the harried official, the man checked his ID and asked the usual questions. The officer glanced at the sketch from Homeland that had been scanned and circulated among customs offices around the country, looked at Lee and determined it to be so vague it could be a picture of half the male passengers deplaning from any flight from Asia. It was of little use to someone who has a few seconds to make decision about who gets into the country and who doesn't. He snapped Lee's passport shut and handed it back. "Welcome back to the U.S., Mr. Wong."

A banner hanging over the entrance to the baggage collection area greeted Yang Lee, aka Ches Wong. He picked up his suitcase from the carousel, looked up at the sign and smiled thinly.

WELCOME TO THE NATION'S CAPITAL, WASHINGTON, D.C.

CHAPTER 39

Yang Lee didn't waste time in Washington. He rented a car and headed straight for Tampa, Florida, one of the destinations for the president's rallies. He had decided it would be too risky to try anything spectacular in the nation's capital. He sat at the desk in a nondescript motel room in east central Tampa. He chose it because it was a typical two-story building in an average neighborhood with the shrieks of children rising from an outdoor pool. It was the least likely place to attract attention he could find.

On his way to the motel, he had paid cash for a laptop and tablet at a local electronics store. The laptop powered up as the Doppler effect of thundering little feet outside his door approached, passed and receded down the hall to their parents' rooms. The second they were no longer in hearing range, he forgot about them. Air escaped his pursed lips at the length of time it took the low-end computer to start, but it served his purpose. When it finally booted up, he logged on to the unsecured motel WiFi signal and installed a piece of software he had brought along on the USB flash drive. It created a twin electronic access point to the one used by the motel.

Yang Lee turned up the volume on the computer and busied himself rinsing the coffee pot in the bathroom sink. He didn't trust the cleanliness of any motel, and this one was no different. It had the usual double bed, one soft chair and a small TV sitting on cheap furniture. An uncomfortable office chair sat in front of a rickety desk lit by an old-fashioned lamp. A search of the drawers in the desk turned up a Bible, a note pad and a plastic pen. He washed a cup thoroughly and after the coffee maker stopped brewing, he poured the steaming dark liquid. He shook the packets of sweetener and powdered milk into the coffee to make sure he had every grain. He was certain he knew how the coffee would taste. A sip confirmed his suspicions. Disgusting but nevertheless, he decided it was better than nothing and swallowed a few mouthfuls. Just as he set the cup down, he was rewarded with a sharp ping coming from his laptop. Someone was trying to connect to the fake access point he had created so they could log onto a website.

It was of no consequence to Lee what site the person wanted to log on to. It could be banking information for all he cared. Lucky for the person logging in, Lee didn't need to steal his identity. He had what he needed. He jotted down the user name and password of the person trying to connect. Next, he deleted the fake access point. He smirked, knowing that in the next few seconds the person who had been trying to log into the site would be on the phone to the front desk complaining about the WiFi service, or lack thereof. He would be annoyed when he would be told the WiFi was working just fine and surprised when he could log on successfully the next time.

Lee connected to the motel WiFi, accessed a virtual private network service and created an account using a false name and the user name and password he had just stolen. He had used the VPN before and trusted it. It allowed him to send and receive encrypted data across a public network as if he was using one that was completely private. It would also allow him to get into the deep web when he needed to purchase some supplies. The signal would be bounced around the world. If anyone was able to trace his activity on the VPN, the poor man whose user name and password he had just poached would be a prime suspect.

Now Lee was set to engage in research to prepare his next move. He was long past being amazed at how technology made his job so easy. He just had to make sure he covered his tracks.

The newspaper article had told him that one of the president's planned rallies was going to be in Tampa. It was easy enough to find the venue. There were a limited number of locations that could hold such an event, so the search was straightforward. He narrowed down possible locations based on size, capability of physical security, and frankly, the opulence that this president would demand, and came up with a short list. He hacked into the schedules of the possible sites and was certain of the rally's location within minutes. It was a large convention center. His plans were falling nicely into

place. He was back in control. It wouldn't be long until his stature
back home would be regained.

But Lee realized he would need a degree of luck and ingenuity for
what was to come next. It all depended on the level of security on the
building's system management software. He loaded another piece of
software onto the laptop from his flash drive and asked it to search
for devices connected from the convention center to the internet. If
care had been taken to secure the building's information technology
infrastructure, his job was about to become infinitely more difficult.

As he scanned the screen, his eyes widened. He couldn't believe
what he was seeing. There were vulnerabilities staring him in the
face that he could easily exploit. This would be a straightforward
hack. There was the familiar tingle of excitement as he probed the
convention center's systems, finding more weaknesses. He guessed
the flaws would be shored up after his plan was executed. But that
didn't matter now.

He leaned back in his chair and lifting the cup to his lips, sipped
the now cold, even more disgusting coffee. He would have to eat
something soon to get rid of the taste. He leaned forward, nearly
missing the edge of the desk with the cup as his eyes penetrated the
screen and his mind raced.

This was what he was looking for! A flaw in the building's fire
detection system which would allow him to intercept the signal to
the monitoring company. By probing further in the convention center's system, he was able to determine the name of the company
responsible for servicing the building's fire detection system and the
type of equipment used. At the right time, he would create a bogus
malfunction in the system that would require immediate attention.
The monitoring company would not see the alert, but the system
management team at the convention center would. They would
want it fixed immediately, especially when the president would be
arriving in a few weeks for his rally.

The next step required more careful planning. Lee needed an ID
that would identify him as a repairman with a requisite skill set. And
he would need supplies. With a series of key strokes, he was into the
deep web again and communicating with his usual supplier. He had
no idea who or where the person was, but Lee knew he would get
what he wanted. It would be quality work and it would be delivered

expeditiously. The cost was outrageously expensive, but Lee was confident that he could rely on the reliability and discreetness of the individual and his network of conspirators. The contact assured Lee his needs would be met, so he wired full payment immediately through the VPN.

Lee's mind swirled as he rose from the desk and walked around the room. He rubbed his hands together as he walked. He was unusually nervous. There was so much at stake. He checked the frame of the suitcase for the hundredth time to reassure himself that the vials of chemicals were still there. He found the TV remote and flipped through the channels, but nothing held his attention. In the morning two days from now, he would establish the bogus malfunction in the convention center's fire alarm system.

And then, on the afternoon of the same day, Yang Lee, alias Willy Shen, would go in and fix it.

CHAPTER 40

Nathan and Marcie enjoyed the warmth on their faces and the sand in their toes as they walked barefoot along the beach. They had removed their shoes as soon as they reached the sand and carried them as they walked. It was a beautiful Florida early evening. The breeze off the ocean had chased the humidity away. The tall grass separating the beach from the condos rustled in the wind, the stalks hissing as they wrestled with each other. Footprints left behind by the lovers walking hand in hand were erased by the gentle tide soon after they passed by. They laughed at the antics of a sandpiper darting to the edge of the water to dig up a tiny invertebrate from the mud and then rushing away as the water lapped over the spot where the hapless morsel had been. Undeterred by the wave's action, the bird scuttled back and forth just ahead of them as they walked.

They strolled silently for a few minutes and put some distance between themselves and their condo. "What a beautiful evening," Nathan said as the setting sun dropped into the ocean, making way for the moon clearly anxious to make its rounds.

Marcie responded with, "Mmm, it's so peaceful." At that exact moment, a car horn blared from the front of the condo, followed by the crunch of metal and plastic and an angry shout. Two drivers must have wanted the same space at the same time. They both winced and laughed. Marcie added, "Or at least it was."

They walked in silence for a few more minutes until Nathan asked, "What did you do today?" They hadn't had a chance to talk as Nathan hadn't been able to extract himself from a conference call.

"Oh yes, I wanted to tell you. I spoke with Shoni on Facetime today." Marcie's face became animated as she talked about the African girl she befriended when she had visited Tanzania on vacation. It was also when she had met Nathan as he was in Tanzania at the same time working to solve a human trafficking scheme that ensnared Shoni and her friend, Irene. "She's excited about us coming to Tanzania for our honeymoon. She's doing really well. She's been accepted to take accounting at the University in Dar es Salaam. I'm so proud of her. She's pretty excited. She's come a long way since the human trafficking ring. Her future is so bright now. She told me to say hello to the handsomest man in the world."

Nathan smiled. "That's great news about the university. We were fortunate we could rescue Shoni." He turned sideways to look at Marcie, and added seriously, "A big part of the thanks goes to you, you know. You played such an important role. Besides that, you and I wouldn't have met if you hadn't come down to the police station to report your suspicions about the girls." Then he grinned. "Did she really say handsomest?"

"Yes, she did. But she also referred to you as the luckiest man in the world for meeting *me*, so don't let your head explode," Marcie shot back good-naturedly. "We also wouldn't have met if you hadn't been on assignment in Africa at the time. It's amazing how fate intervenes sometimes. Good ways and bad. Somehow, I had to put up with He Who Shall Not Be Named before I got to meet my Prince Charming. It was worth it. It's just that next time, I would prefer to skip the first part and go directly to the second."

Nathan's head shot around again to look at his fiancée. "What do you mean, *next time?*" He could see Marcie's spirit in the smile of the most beautiful woman he had ever seen. His pulse quickened at the sight of her silhouetted in the setting sun. I really am the luckiest man in the world, he thought. "Are you ready to head back?"

"Yes, it's starting to get chilly. Let's walk back on the street to be nosy and see what the crash was about."

They walked on a boardwalk between two restaurants until they got to the street and turned towards their condo. The juxtaposition was incredible. The condo buildings separated the serenity of the beach area from the bright lights and chaos of the street. Marcie and Nathan loved how they could opt for a quiet walk or drink on the beach or if the mood struck, choose instead a noisy bar or a romantic dinner at one of the fine restaurants along the street. Right now, flashing lights from emergency vehicles reflected off the windows of the surrounding establishments.

As they approached, a policeman talked to a man and took notes. A young woman in her late teens sat on a stretcher being tended to by a paramedic.

As they walked past, Nathan observed, "I have a feeling there's going to be a dad somewhere that's not going to be too happy. It looks like she was driving the Mustang and turned right in front of the guy in the SUV."

"You could tell all that in just a few seconds walking past?" Marcie questioned.

"It's the angle of the vehicles. She kept looking back at the Mustang, so I assume it was hers or her dad's. My money says that she has a difficult phone call to make to her parents after she stops flirting with the paramedic."

Once past the accident scene, Marcie said, "Anyway, I'm excited about going back to Africa for our honeymoon. It will be great to see Shoni and check out her old school there. It will be a great way to revive memories and celebrate our marriage. We'll be able to see some of the other friends we met there too. Maybe we should spend a week in Zanzibar."

Nathan concurred. "I think it's a great idea. Let's check out the accommodations you found when we go upstairs." They arrived at the condo and Marcie took her key from her pocket to retrieve the mail. The usual stack of flyers, brochures and junk mail were immediately ejected to a nearby recycling box. She sorted through the remaining envelopes until she came across one that stood out. "Whoa! What's this?"

Nathan looked over her shoulder as she slid her thumb under the seal of the envelope ready to rip it open. He admonished, "Whoa, careful you don't destroy that fancy envelope. It might be the only official thing we ever get from the White House." The envelope bore the presidential seal.

"Okay, let's wait until we get upstairs and use the letter opener."

Once inside their apartment, Marcie rummaged through the drawer in the desk in the office to find the little-used letter opener. She carefully slit the envelope and removed the gold embossed invitation. Her eyes widened as she looked at Nathan to ask the unspoken question. *What's this about?*

She read the script wording aloud. "President Hughes and the

First Lady request the pleasure of your company for dinner." She turned it over to see the details of the dinner, including the date and time. It was in three weeks.

Nathan shrugged. "My guess is that Craig and Annie had something to do with this. I didn't know the president planned on gracing Tampa with his presence. I guess it's not exactly a surprise that he would be doing political rallies in the first year of his presidency. He needs his ego stroked, I guess. Why don't you call Annie to find out what this is about and how we got an invitation."

Marcie carelessly tossed the envelope and its contents on the kitchen counter.

"Well, my love, I only have one question. Do we *have* to go?"

CHAPTER 41

Lee pulled the coveralls over his legs, shoved his arms through the top and yanked up the zipper. He buckled the tool belt and picked up the tool box. The name *Addison Fire Protection Services* was emblazoned across his back. He had stolen the coveralls, the tool box and a belt from a white van with the Addison logo on the side that was parked in the company's lot. The coveralls were nearly a perfect fit.

He had programmed the malfunction in the fire security system as planned and contacted the staff at the conference center to arrange a time to fix it. He knew they would be anxious to make certain everything was operational for the presidential visit, and they were more than happy to hear from him, satisfied that Addison Fire Protection Services was on top of it so promptly. He arranged to meet the security officials of the building at precisely 1 p.m.

Lee had parked the plain white van he'd rented for the day in front of the building so that the back portion remained visible to anyone looking from the security desk. It was highly unlikely someone would notice there was no logo on the van. The president's visit was still three weeks away, and there was no reason for anyone to be suspicious this far out. Lee was sure that if anyone did notice, they would simply see a white van that resembled those driven by the Addison company and assume it belonged to their fleet. He had learned long ago that people saw what they wanted or expected to see, not what was actually there.

He strode up the steps of the glass building at precisely the appointed time. A tall African American man in his forties stood at the front desk waiting for him. The man wore a green sports jacket bearing a nameplate on the lapel. Lee glanced at the name tag as he approached with his hand extended. "Good afternoon, Mr. Bellamy. I believe my office has called you about fixing a problem with your fire protection system."

"Amos Bellamy. Yes, they did. Thanks for alerting us to the problem and for coming so promptly. I'm the head of security here at the conference center. I'm happy your company is so quick to respond. That's good service. We have a special guest coming in a few weeks and we certainly wouldn't want anything to happen to him."

Lee searched into his pocket and pulled out the fake credentials. "I'm sure you're going to want to see these since you have an important visitor coming. We want to get everything in working order as soon as we can."

Bellamy glanced at the credentials and waved them off by indicating a sign-in book on the desk.

"I just need you to sign in and out and I'll accompany you to the ballroom, but I have a meeting to attend so I'll leave you to it. If you can't trust a security firm, who can you trust, right?" He paused before adding, "We're happy to have big shots here at the center, but we're happier to see them go, you know what I mean? We really have to be careful these days. Security has to be tight with all the stuff in the headlines that's happening around the country at big events. Concerts, clubs, sports events—seems like nobody's safe out in public, you know? If something were to happen here, our bottom line would take a huge hit. We especially need to stay on top of the fire protection system, that's for sure. Fires can be deadly, and we don't need that kind of publicity."

Bellamy initialed the guest book beside the signature of Willy Shen, the alias provided by Lee. He made a note of the time of arrival. A second guard sat at the desk, listening to the conversation taking place in front of him with a bored look on his face. Bellamy pointed Lee towards the ballroom and they started walking. Bellamy tugged on a lanyard attached to a magnetic key card hanging around his neck and then casually asked a question.

It could have been small talk, but to Lee it indicated that his mind was still on their unnamed special guest. "I saw in the news that the president signed a trade bill imposing extra tariffs on China. You look Asian. What do *you* think about that decision by Hughes?"

"I don't know," Lee answered. "I try to stay out of politics. They all seem to have good ideas until they get into office and then something happens to them."

"Yeah, I'll tell you what happens. They have to pay the piper. Do you think all those corporations and CEOs and big money people donate because they're concerned about the country? No! They want their own man in there, so they can benefit from sweetheart deals and favorable legislation later. That's why the leaders can't accomplish anything when they get in. They're too busy paying back the big money people that put them there. The president seems to be taking quite a bit of flack about the email his chief of staff's wife sent around about the Chinese tariffs. All that stuff about people taking over your computer. I don't know what the world's coming to."

Lee tensed but remained silent. He just shrugged and admired the ornate decor. The world outside was visible through the wall of glass forming one side of the corridor they were in. Ambient light gleamed behind oak wood panels on the other side and modern crystal glass pendant lights led their way towards the ballroom. The plush red carpet sunk beneath Lee's shoes with each step.

The man was still talking. "Well, my wife says I watch too much cable news, but I like to stay on top of things, ya know? I want to know if there's a nuke coming at me. They keep saying the Chinese are going to be upset about any trade tariffs. They'll probably start a trade war or something. Especially on electronics. Then there'll be hell to pay. We won't be able to afford to buy any more of our big screen TVs after that. That's the way I see it, anyway."

Lee was relieved they had arrived at the gigantic doors to the ballroom at the end of the hall. He really didn't need a political discussion right now. Besides, if this guy wanted to talk about politics, Lee could tell him a thing or two about how a closed country operates. The talkative manager might find out that somebody else always has it worse.

Lee waited patiently while Bellamy unlocked the door with the magnetic key card. The room was magnificent with Brazilian wood paneling and alcoves built into the walls. Lee removed his tablet from the toolbox and called up a screen that appeared to be a schematic of the room. Like everything else about this visit, it was fake, but it looked authentic enough to fool anyone who wasn't looking closely. He pretended to compare the schematic to the room while holding the tablet at an angle so that the security head couldn't see it closely. Meanwhile his eyes scanned the room, which was set up for a function. He judged enough seating for about 500 at the round tables. There was a large space between the tables and back wall, presumably to add more tables if need be. He noted where the escape routes were and where the head table was located. He had to assume the setup would be the same for the presidential visit. It didn't really matter. No one would be getting out alive when he was done.

After appearing to scrutinize the schematic, Yang Lee pointed to one section of the ceiling over the head table. He turned slowly to his host and pointed. "There's the problem. I'm going to need your motorized platform to get up there. And could you please shut off the water to the sprinkler system? The problem's with the sprinkler head up there. I see by the maintenance history that a couple of others haven't been inspected for a while. The glass bulbs should be replaced periodically just to make sure they continue to do the job. How would it be if I replace the older ones just to be sure?"

Bellamy looked surprised. "There's a glass bulb? I never did know how those things work. What's the bulb do?"

"You can't really see it up there. The builders did a great job of concealing it. I'll show you one." Lee took a sprinkler head out of his toolbox and held it up. The top was threaded to fit a water pipe connection and the bottom had the typical water deflector seen on sprinklers throughout the world. Lee pointed at the glass bulb separating the top and bottom. "It's pretty simple, really. The bulb acts as a valve. It's full of a glycerin-based liquid that expands when it gets hot. The color of the liquid tells us how hot the fire needs to be before it will burst. In this case, it's orange, which is conventional for this type of room. If there's a fire, it will heat up and break in a few seconds. Then the water that was held back sprays out at a high rate of pressure in a circular motion. Puts out the fire in seconds."

"Huh! Ingenious in its simplicity. Well, do what you have to do. I figured you'd need the platform, so we put one over there by the wall. There's a manual shut-off valve for the sprinkler system as well as the automated shut-off. Give me a couple of minutes to take care of it for you." By the time you have the platform over there, I'll have the water shut off. Then I'm going to go about my business. Bellamy turned to go, then stopped and delved into his pocket. "If you need me, here's my number." Bellamy handed Lee his business card. "Give me a call when you're done, and I'll sign you out."

Lee retrieved the motorized platform, stepped on it and pressed the button to raise its extension. He was quickly high enough to reach the sprinkler head designed to activate at any hint of excessive heat. He looked down at the unlit candles standing guard at each of the tables like Buckingham Palace guards. While they had protective covers around them, once lit they would serve his purpose.

He worked quickly and efficiently. He removed the perfectly good sprinkler head from the ceiling and replaced it with one of the ones he had brought with him. But his were different. He had replaced the glycerin-based product in the glass bulb with something far more dangerous, something he had been waiting a long time to use. It was the chemical he had brought with him in the suitcase, and now was the time. It contained a weaponized version of chlorosulfonic acid, colored to look identical to the glycerin-based liquid. Exposure to water, the copper piping and the metal of the sprinkler head would produce a violently-explosive hydrogen gas. Although not flammable on its own, when mixed with another chemical it would make simultaneous combustion a certainty. On release, it would also produce a dense toxic white vapor that would, at a minimum, create horrible irritation of the lungs and eyes. A direct hit would cause permanent blindness. And just a few short minutes of exposure would cause death.

If the explosion didn't do the job, the toxic fumes certainly would.

To be sure of his plan, Yang Lee had ordered the specially-constructed bulb from his contact on the deep web. It was larger and made of thinner glass that would break from increased water pressure. He would make sure that Bellamy turned the system back on slowly, so the pressure would not be increased enough to shatter the bulb. However, an alert to the automated system that he would personally trigger from his own computer would increase the pressure significantly, forcing excess water through the pipes. When this water broke the bulb and came in contact with the acid, the result would be an immediate and horrendous explosion, followed by a flash fire that would send flames and toxic gas into the room. The candles around the room would act as an ignition, adding to the conflagration as all the flammable items like table cloths and curtains turned the place into a hellish inferno. It would be immediate and deadly.

Lee reattached the sprinkler head. He replaced two others with his own and called Bellamy. Lee said he was nearly done and asked him to open the valve for the sprinkler system slowly so that he could check the system for leaks. It would be catastrophic for the bulb to break now with him still in the room. He could hear the water trickling through the pipes. He stayed on the phone with Bellamy as the security chief slowly increased the pressure back up to normal load. He let out a breath: the bulbs had held. Now all he had to do was wait until everyone was seated at the dinner and then press the button on his laptop to escalate the water pressure beyond capacity. There *would* be a fire all right, one of unthinkable magnitude, and the sprinkler system designed to put *out* fires would be the cause. The plan was perfect—and it would work.

Yang Lee returned the mechanical platform back to its original position against the wall and looked back up at his handiwork. The first death-dealing sprinkler was right above the head table where the President of the United States would be sitting.

As Lee left the building, he thought what a special evening it was going to be.

CHAPTER 42

The night of the dinner arrived, and Marcie looked resplendent in a blue off the shoulder floor-length gown. Nathan thought she was stunning and would easily be the most beautiful woman in attendance. It had taken some doing to get her to attend the formal dinner. Nathan's first attempt to convince her that people don't turn down invitations from the White House went nowhere. She had replied that her complete lack of interest in politics should qualify her to be the first.

It took Annie to convince her to attend. Annie wasn't anxious to go, either, especially after the email incident, but Craig was going to be in town for the event and he wanted her to accompany him. Annie and Craig decided to invite Marcie and Nathan to thank them, but more importantly, to be there for support. Perhaps what sealed the deal for Marcie, however, was when she was told that the major political speeches wouldn't happen until the day after the dinner when voters and supporters of the party were to be invited to a rally-style event.

The venue housing the dinner was a large convention center in downtown Tampa. Chandeliers, flowers and secret service agents were everywhere. Security was extremely tight. The surrounding streets had been closed off, manhole covers sealed, barricades erected, automatic weapon-carrying police officers stood at every street corner, helicopters overhead shone spotlights on every nook and cranny and bomb-sniffing dogs roamed the streets with their handlers. The area was basically on lockdown. As Nathan and Marcie drove through the various checkpoints, their credentials were repeatedly checked against the guest list and their car scanned for explosives. Nathan thought there was probably no safer place to be in the entire world right now.

He didn't know how wrong he could be

Nathan noticed a bulge in the jacket of the overly-large valet who took the keys from him to park the car. He knew when he noticed the bud in the man's ear that he was only serving as a valet for a day and would be reassuming his role on the security detail at the White House when the event was over.

As he and Marcie walked hand in hand towards the opulent ballroom, she whispered, "I want this for our wedding."

Nathan whispered back, "Okay, but I understand the secret service doesn't rent their agents out to just anybody."

As Marcie smiled at Nathan's comment, she and her husband-to-be simultaneously noticed Annie and a man waiting for them at the entrance to the ballroom. Nathan shook the man's hand and said, "You must be Craig."

Logan accepted the handshake. "I just want to thank you so much for everything you've done for us. It's difficult being so far away from home, especially with everything that's been going on. You two have been a rock for Annie, and we're both very grateful. I'm happy you accepted the invitation." He laughed heartily. "I don't know what your political persuasion is, but I can assure you, this is not an attempt to sway you. It's just a free meal as my way of thanking you. Hopefully I'll be able to introduce you to the president later."

Nathan squeezed Marcie's hand a little tighter before she could say anything. He wasn't sure what might come out of the mouth of his blunt wife-to-be. Then he noticed there was no need. She was busy complimenting Annie on her formal dress. Nathan observed that Annie looked better than when they'd seen her last. Her face had more color, her hair was done in soft elegant waves with a bun, and her makeup had been carefully applied. Nathan thought that underneath the facade, she still looked tired and maybe a little sad. He was sure that the email hacking weighed on her, along with everything else. He and Marcie knew Annie had nothing to do with the email, but most people in the room, ignorant of the facts, would have preferred to jump to conclusions at the time and blame her for what had happened. Optimistically, everything was behind the Logans now and they could start to move forward with their lives. Nathan sincerely hoped so.

Grim-looking secret service men took up posts around the

outskirts of the room. Craig and Annie led Nathan and Marcie past them, weaving between the tables and chairs to find their seats near the front of the room. Nathan recognized a few prominent politicians from seeing them on television. He immediately calculated a pecking order. Those with senior positions got to sit near the front and the lower the position, the less favorable the seating arrangement. He shook his head. Politics never sleep, not even for an evening. Everyone knew their place and, Nathan thought, most were probably plotting ways to improve it.

Nathan, Marcie, Craig and Annie joined two other couples at the table. Craig introduced them as Chief Legal Counsel Zyva Khan and her husband and Chairman of the Joint Chiefs of Staff General Jeremy Rawlings and his wife. They chatted about baseball and the weather and life in Florida, including the recent hurricanes. The political appointees and career politicians seemed to be quite comfortable talking about anything but politics. Waiters passed by with canapés, including eggplant, roasted figs with herb pesto and crab cannolis. A waiter carrying a tray of red and white wines stopped so Nathan could take one for himself and one for Marcie. An announcement that the president of the United States was arriving interrupted the group's easy conversation.

Everyone stood and clapped as President Hughes, the First Lady, the Governor and his wife and their invited guests came into the room. He watched as the president shook hands, slapped the men on the back and air kissed the women. Nathan glanced aside and noticed that even Marcie seemed to be caught up in the moment as she smiled and clapped along with everyone else.

They sat when the cheering died down. Marcie noticed everyone watching the president and first lady as they made their way around the room. She realized there was something about seeing someone for the first time that you'd only seen previously on television. They look different somehow, but they also seem special. The first lady looked even more beautiful in person.

Marcie picked up the program and scanned the list of head table guests. She didn't recognize any names except the president and his wife. The menu was fabulous. More canapés, stuffed pasta, butternut squash, roasted sherry duck and dessert. She nudged Nathan, held the menu open and whispered, "I want this at our reception."

He replied through the corner of his mouth, "We'll plan a bank robbery to pay for it." He looked around to make sure none of the secret service agents had heard him and were rushing over to take him down. Then he thought that might happen later after they listened to the recordings of the table conversations. Wow, he thought, does this crowd ever breed paranoia.

For her part, Marcie had decided to relax and accept the experience. She hated politics and everything it had done to Annie Logan. But this was, after all, a once-in-a lifetime experience and one that deserved to be enjoyed.

They stood as the president drew closer and Marcie saw her friend's jaw muscles tightening. Annie quickly picked up a glass of wine from the table and took a long gulp. A look of panic spread across her face as the president and his wife arrived at their table. Craig Logan introduced the president to his wife and Marcie thought a shadow passed across Annie's eyes. However, the president simply asked how she was doing and commented on how tough it must be to have a spouse out of town all the time. Then he commented that his old friend Craig was the perfect chief of staff. Marcie realized that in that moment, Annie Logan was the most important person in the room for the president. Of course, in a few seconds, Marcie Kane and Nathan Harris would be the two most important people in the room as they were introduced. Marcie thought it was a skill that politicians must be born with.

Logan mentioned to the president that it was Nathan and Marcie who had helped resolve the hacking issue and the world's most powerful man looked each in the eyes in turn and thanked them profusely, as if it was coming from the bottom of his heart. Marcie thought she could see right through him to the other side. The first lady was gracious, thanking them as well, and Marcie let the president's wife's sincerity wash over her, as if using it to cleanse herself.

After their brief conversation, the president moved on so that others could bask in his glow. Everyone at the table sat down to enjoy the canapés and wine. The waiters brought the paper-thin covered pasta and Marcie put some on her plate. She was determined to enjoy the company of her soon-to-be husband and their new friends.

She noticed Nathan fidgeting beside her. "What's wrong?"

Nathan whispered, "My phone's been vibrating non-stop for

the last ten minutes. After everyone turned away, I checked and it's Welchie. He knew we were going to be here. He wouldn't be calling unless it's important."

"Did he leave a message?"

"Yes, but I don't want to listen to it here." He glanced over his shoulder. "It looks like the president isn't going to be sitting down for dinner any time soon. I'm going out in the hall and find out what he wants."

She glanced around the table. The conversation had died down, and everyone sat quietly, seemingly waiting for someone else to say something. She whispered to Nathan, "Okay, I'll carry your end of the conversation while you're gone."

Nathan excused himself as Marcie sat back and used the napkin to wipe some canapé crumbs from the corner of her mouth. She smiled sweetly across the table at General Rawlings' wife. "Well," she said, "This is certainly going to be a special evening."

CHAPTER 43

Nathan walked quietly out to the hallway so as not to attract attention and immediately dialed James Welch. When Welch answered, he asked, "James, what is it? Marcie and I are sitting down to have dinner with the president right now, believe it or not."

"A private dinner with the president. Aren't you special?"

"Sure. It's just Marcie and me and oh, about 500 of Hughes' entourage and supporters. Actually, we were invited by the Logans. We're just keeping a low profile. So, what is it? You've been dialing me incessantly for the last few minutes. It must be important. Please don't tell me you've been pocket dialing."

"Nope, no pocket dialing," Welch confirmed. "But there's something I think you should know. The agency was tasked with checking out the venue before the president's arrival, but I think we missed something. I knew you and Marcie were going to be there, so you're in the best position to check it out. Obviously, we have other agents there, but I thought since you're there, you could do it quickly before involving our team or the secret service."

"James, you do realize this is the most highly guarded place on the planet right now, don't you?"

"Yes, I know, it's a fortress there now, but the convention center gave us full access to their computer system and I went back further in time to see if anything unusual might have happened. I found something that you should be aware of. Maintenance was done on the fire security system three weeks ago."

The words gripped Nathan's attention.

"So?"

"The convention center contracts the work out to a firm called Addison Fire Security Services. I checked with them to see what kind of work was done. They said they hadn't done any recently."

A shock wave spasmed through Nathan's system. "What do you mean? Are you sure? Is it just a computer glitch or did Addison forget to log it?"

"That's what the woman I spoke with said. She insisted that no work has been done on the fire system there for about two months and when they were there, it was a routine inspection. Everything worked fine. She also told me the monitoring system is showing green lights across the board. So that means that nothing's malfunctioning in the system."

"Okay, maybe they just lost the paperwork or something. It's probably nothing, but I'm going to talk to security here just to be sure. I'll get back to you if I find out anything. What date was the work supposedly done?"

After James Welch gave him the date, Nathan ended the conversation and hurried towards the front desk. Marcie came up behind him. "People are wondering where you disappeared to. Is everything all right? Was he just pocket dialing you?"

"Welch says he found something recorded in the automated log that someone was here working on the fire security system, but the company has no record of it. I'm going to check with the front desk to see if I can talk to the security people here."

Marcie walked in lockstep with her fiancé, although she had some difficulty keeping up with his long strides. Nathan was obviously more concerned than he let on. They arrived at the front desk and Nathan showed his identification. "Could I speak with the head of security, please?"

"Yes, sir, that would be Amos Bellamy. I'll get him for you. He won't be too far away on a night like tonight."

Bellamy arrived at the desk about five minutes later. Nathan flashed his credentials and pulled Bellamy aside out of earshot of the man at the front desk to quiz him about the fire detection system maintenance.

"Yes sir, there was a man here fixing the sprinkler system. He was from Addison Security. I'd never seen him before, but he had a white van and showed me his credentials. Here, I can show you his log-in information." He walked back to the desk and asked the attendant to pull out the log book. "We have an automated calendar of maintenance appointments, but this is one thing we do manually around here." He pointed to the scrawled signature and his own initials authorizing the man's entry.

"I see by the man's name that he might've been Asian. Was he?"

"Yes, he was, but his English was really good. He was probably raised here, I'm guessing."

Nathan's internal radar was picking up signals that he wasn't liking. "Is the fire detection system monitored here or just by the security company?"

"Both. We have a very sophisticated system. The doors to our common rooms are all automated so we can lock them all at once, and the heating and cooling systems and security cameras and systems are all monitored."

"Is it possible for me to look at the video from the security camera the day the maintenance man showed up? Also, could you show me the fire detection monitoring system? Marcie, this is sensitive and you probably need to go back inside the banquet hall, but why don't you wait with me for a few more minutes? Then you can go back to our table with my apologies. I'd just like to see what we have first."

Inwardly, Marcie was thrilled that she was going to be part of the action, but outwardly she remained calm.

Bellamy said, "I could show you the system on my phone, but let's go to the control room." He led them down the stairs to a door in the basement with an AUTHORIZED EMPLOYEES ONLY sign warning people to keep out. He unlocked the door to display a bank of computer monitors humming away, indicating that the heart of the building beat strongly. Bellamy walked over to one of the computers and pressed several keys that called up a screen with a schematic showing various common areas throughout the building. The steady green lights indicated that all was well with the smoke and fire detection systems.

Nathan asked, "What room did the Addison guy do the work in?"

Bellamy kept his eyes on the keyboard but said over his shoulder, "He replaced three sprinkler heads in the ballroom. He said one was malfunctioning and two were getting old. But look." He gestured at the screen monitoring the system. "Everything is great. If fire is detected, those sprinklers are going to soak everybody in that room." He chuckled to himself at the image and then added, "The lights would start flashing red and I would receive an alert on my phone if something goes wrong." He opened another file folder and scanned various dates, looking for the video of the man entering the hotel

Marcie turned to Nathan and said quietly. "I may be paranoid, but remember what Welch said about that virus that was used to attack the Iranian centrifuge system? The thing that stuck out in my mind the most was that the Iranians monitoring the system were tricked into thinking everything was working beautifully. The virus was somehow able to override the system to make everything look fine when it wasn't."

Nathan pursed his lips tightly together thoughtfully. Then he asked, "Yes, but what does that mean? That a fire will be started that will go undetected? Even if there was a fire and the sprinklers didn't activate, everyone should still be able to get out."

Bellamy found the video for the day in question and pointed at the screen. "There's the white van arriving. That's funny, there's no logo on the side. I recall distinctly other times when I've seen the van, that they have a logo. It stands out. It's a caricature of a guy putting out a huge fire single handedly with a garden hose. Could be that this one got in an accident and they repainted it. Just haven't had time to put the logo back on. Anyway, here's our guy getting out of the van. Too bad we can't see him better."

The man walked to the back of the van, put on his coveralls and retrieved his equipment. They were frustrated that his face never turned towards the camera. It reminded Nathan of the video of the man Hartman had met in Shanghai. The repairman carried himself similarly, as if he somehow knew he was being recorded on video and didn't want to be seen. Then, without warning, he caught his foot and stumbled on the top step as he headed into the building. For a very brief instant, a portion of his face was caught on camera. Would it be enough to identify him?

Quickly Nathan told Bellamy to freeze the image of the man onscreen, simultaneously reaching into his pocket for his phone. In seconds, he'd pulled up the sketch of the man they had seen on the Shanghai security cameras.

Marcie had been thinking hard while all this was going on. She hesitated, then spoke aloud. "I'm thinking outside the box here, Nathan, and you might think I'm crazy, but the guy in China likes to fool around with poisons, right? Is it possible he's actually here now—and that the sprinkler system will somehow be used as a delivery mechanism for one of his lethal concoctions?"

Nathan's head snapped around to look at Marcie. He stared at her for an instant, then looked back to compare the drawing and the frozen image on the screen. His eyes widened in alarm. He held the phone out so Bellamy could see it.

"Is this the man who fixed the sprinklers?"

Bellamy squinted at the phone. He shook his head slowly. "I'm not sure. That's not a great image. It could be. It's hard to tell. The man had a long, thin face like your picture. It's possible. But I can't be sure."

Nathan's mind raced back over everything they had uncovered in the last few minutes. He thought about the man replacing the sprinkler heads without any record of the visit at the company that supposedly sent him. He thought about the truck with no logo. He thought about the virus in Iran tricking the system. He thought about what Marcie had just said about the sprinkler heads acting as a possible delivery system. He thought about the president of the United States sitting in the very same room where the repair work had been done. And he compared the drawing again with the frozen video screen. It wasn't conclusive, but the pieces were adding up frighteningly fast. It was turning out to be more than just coincidence.

And he didn't believe in coincidences.

Oh my God, Nathan thought. *What if that man is here in the building right now armed with a device to set off the sprinkler system? A sprinkler system which he had contaminated with poison?* Nathan knew he couldn't take that chance.

He leaped into action. "We have to shut off the water pressure to those sprinklers! NOW!!! Can you do it from here?"

Beads of sweat had sprung to Bellamy's forehead. His fingers flew over the keyboard. He pressed "Enter."

Nothing happened.

He hit the key again.

Still nothing.

Again and again.

"What the . . . ?" he mumbled, banging the keys. "Something's wrong. The system is locked! I can't do anything. We'll have to shut it off manually. The override valve is in another room." He pushed himself away from the desk and his chair scraped across the concrete floor, the noise interrupting the hum in the room as if the heart of the convention center was going into cardiac arrest.

Nathan grabbed both of Marcie's arms. His voice was calm but emphatic. "Marcie, you have to go back to the ballroom. Talk to Craig Logan immediately. Tell him to get the secret service to move those people out of that room. HURRY!"

CHAPTER 44

Yang Lee sat in the airport in Tampa. His tablet lay on the chair beside him. Lee checked his watch. In just 30 more minutes, he would board the flight through Chicago that would take him home. In a few minutes, he would unleash the worst attack the U.S. had seen since 9/11.

He relaxed. He was about to regain his hard-earned reputation with the Chinese government and other organizations around the world that required his particular skill set. How dare they question his abilities. Soon enough they would know that it was Yang Lee who unleashed this event on America in retaliation for its unfair Chinese tariff. He would provide the proof when he got back. He would share details about the disaster that no one else could possibly know. Then they would truly understand what he was capable of.

It was nearly time. He leaned back in his seat with his legs extended in front of him. A mother muttered as she wound her way around him, dragging a suitcase with one hand and a young boy with the other. A large carry-on bag was draped over her shoulder, and Lee's legs hindered her progress as the travel-weary woman made her way to an open seat. Lee saw her shoot him a glaring look for not moving his legs, and the boy stared at him just before he put his head down and closed his eyes.

Lee imagined what it would be like in the ballroom. He had attended some formal functions in his lifetime and always hated them, but he knew how they worked. There would be time allotted for the president to shake everyone's hand before he sat down, and Lee had allowed time for that. Then there would be a few more minutes for everyone to get seated and start to enjoy the appetizers. By now, however, Lee calculated that they should have finished their hors d'oeuvres and the main course was about to be served.

He'd also factored into his plans the fact that he needed to get out of town before the manhunt started. All hell was going to break loose as soon as he pressed the keys on his tablet to set the disaster in motion. He knew that everybody in the government's alphabet soup of law enforcement agencies would be after him. It would be the biggest manhunt ever undertaken. His layover in Chicago was short. He would be half way home to China by the time they got the search organized and underway.

Lee ran his scenarios through his mind again like a video. Everything was perfect. The first boarding announcement had been made. The flight would be leaving soon.

It was time.

He picked up the tablet and with a few taps on the keyboard, he was into the convention center's central nervous system. He walked towards the pretty smiling attendant who was taking boarding passes. He offered his and she wished him a safe flight. He forced a smile and tucked the tablet under his arm as he walked down the ramp to the open door of the aircraft. He was greeted at the door by more smiling attendants who directed him to his seat. Laughter rose from the back of the plane as passengers tried and failed to avoid bumping each other while climbing into their cramped seats.

Everyone looks relaxed and happy, he thought. But that was about to change for 500 unfortunate guests inside the Tampa ballroom—and he would be the cause.

Lee stowed his carry-on bag under the seat as he sat down beside a window. He set the tablet on his lap. The WiFi signal from the airport was still strong.

He tapped the screen to nudge the device awake and the building's control system came up. Lee didn't hesitate. He tapped the screen again and he was into one of the building's security sub-systems. He hit Enter. Then he opened the screen that controlled the water pressure running to the sprinkler heads. He adjusted the pressure well beyond normal limits.

He hit Enter.

The next step was to ensure maximum damage and that no one would escape. He opened another subsystem, tapped on the screen and hit Enter one more time.

Finally, Yang Lee shut off the tablet and stored it in his carry-on as the cabin announcement came on telling everyone to put away their electronic devices.

He closed his eyes. It had all been so easy.

He was asleep before the airplane left the tarmac.

CHAPTER 45

Marcie ran down the hall to the doors of the ballroom. An imposing man with an ear bud stood sentry at the door. A chill ran through her as she approached. *She didn't have the invitation.* She had been with Nathan when they entered, and she had nothing to show that she was supposed to be able to get in. She didn't remember seeing this man at the door when they arrived. She ran breathlessly up to him, gasping for air.

"Please, you . . . HAVE . . . to . . . let me in! There's something . . . TERRIBLE . . . about to . . . happen! We HAVE to . . . get . . . everyone . . . OUT! NOW!" Panic was settling in and Marcie knew her words made no sense to the FBI agent guarding the door.

The agent stared at Marcie without moving a muscle. "Do you have an ID and your official invitation, ma'am? I will need to see them."

Marcie's breath was raspy. "Didn't you see me come out a few minutes ago? Remember? I came in earlier with my fiancé Nathan Harris? He used to be a full-time FBI agent like you—he's a consultant now and he's just found out there's a plot to kill the president here tonight! We have to evacuate this room! Now! The president's in danger! I *have* to get in there. Or you have to get these people out. Please!" Even to herself, Marcie knew she sounded like a crazy person babbling incoherently. She thought for a second, then added, "We're friends of the Logans. Craig and Annie Logan! He's the president's chief of staff. Go talk to Craig Logan—he's at a table right near the front! Tell him Nathan Harris said there's an emergency and he's got to get people OUT."

"I *know* who Craig Logan is, but you're sounding hysterical, ma'am. Maybe you should go to the lobby and sit down. I'll look into this. I can't let you in without an official invitation."

Marcie fished around frantically in her purse. "Here's my identification. Look! I'm Nathan Harris' fiancée. We came together. I don't have the invitation. Nathan has it. He got a call from James Welch. Do you know who he is? He's a computer expert at the FBI. We think there's going to be an assassination attempt on the president!" Her voice had reached a fever pitch. She tried to run around him, but he grabbed her arm and spun her back towards the hallway. She screamed, "LISTEN! This is a matter of life and death! Let me in, for Christ's sake!"

Just then the door opened, and Craig Logan came out. "Marcie? Hey, what's going on? Where's Nathan? We were worried about you two."

"Craig, oh thank God! The fire sprinklers have been tampered with! Nathan thinks it's the guy from China who killed Hartman, and now he's tampered with the entire sprinkler system here in the ballroom! You've got to get the president out before the system blows and fire breaks out. Nathan is trying to shut the sprinklers down, but he has to get to the valve. Please, Craig! Get everyone out. *Hurry*. Make an announcement!"

Logan hesitated, staring into Marcie's eyes. What he saw convinced him she was telling the truth. He ran back into the ballroom with Marcie on his heels. The FBI agent who had stopped Marcie pulled the door shut behind him. He had no sooner done it when Marcie heard a loud click. She whirled around and tried the door handle. It wouldn't budge. She pounded on the door and yelled, "OPEN THE DOOR. We have to get out."

The door rattled on its hinges as the FBI agent tried vainly to open it from the outside.

It was locked.

Marcie immediately grasped what was going on, and a shock wave shook her to her core. She recalled Amos Bellamy saying that someone had overridden the convention center's computer system. Now she realized that this probably included controlling the locking mechanism to all the common area doors. Everyone inside the ballroom was locked in a fire trap.

Which, in a matter of moments, was certain to become a death trap.

She ran towards Logan who was talking animatedly to a secret service agent. A buzz had started to rise around the room. All heads turned in their direction to see what the commotion was about. Lines appeared on concerned faces. Those close enough to hear what Logan and the agent were discussing had already turned a sickly pale and were rising from their seats. Marcie pulled her phone from her purse to call Nathan. She hit speed dial and listened as the phone rang and rang. Voice mail finally picked up the call. She could hear Nathan's voice cutting in and out. The signal wasn't good in the ballroom. There was interference from something. She knew Nathan would be preoccupied with shutting off the valve to the sprinklers. Marcie waited impatiently for his message to end before yelling, "Nathan, if you can hear me, we're locked in here. Override the locking mechanism. We can't get out!"

She heard Logan speaking to a different secret service agent as she arrived beside him. He was instructing Mike Tobin, the head of security from the White House, to get everyone out, starting with the president. She interrupted. "We can't *get* out! The doors are locked. Someone has taken control of the center's computer system. Can some of the agents break through the exit doors?" Marcie glanced up toward the ceiling and shuddered at what could be coming in a mere matter of moments. "I think we need to get everyone to the back of the room as far away from the sprinklers near the front as possible! It could be poison that will come from the sprinklers."

Tobin's face registered shock. "Poison? Are you sure?" He turned and began pouring the contents from half-full water glasses onto the cloth napkins lying around on all the tables. "If that's the case," he said over his shoulder, "we should wet down some cloths so people can put them over their faces."

Suddenly, the thought seemed to fade as he looked over toward the president and first lady. Tobin sprang into action, leaning to his right away from the table closest to him and speaking into a microphone on his wrist. Agents raced from their posts around the outside of the room to the president and first lady and the man in the lead whispered into the president's ear. Tobin ran to the front of the head table where he grabbed a microphone. His announcement for everyone to move to the back of the room in an orderly fashion resulted in chaos as people panicked, not knowing what to expect or where to turn.

Marcie waved at people and yelled at them to come towards her as she rushed to the back. Screams echoed as people realized a serious problem was developing. People were pushing and tripping over each other as they tried to get as close to the back of the room as possible. Some tried the exit doors to no avail. A flying wedge of agents plowed through the crowd, making room for the president and first lady at the very back. The agents formed a cordon around them with the crowd gathered in front of them, offering as much protection as possible.

Then it happened.

Three rapid violent explosions erupted from the ceiling, followed by orange flames licking and curling down at the front of the room, engulfing the head table where the president had been sitting only moments before. Tables overturned and skidded across the floor, scattering broken plates and wine glasses. A trolley with trays of canapés lifted in the air from the concussion before landing on its side. Flames consumed the entire front of the room. The decorative drapes hanging behind the head table caught fire, followed by the table cloths. An agent who had run to the kitchen to retrieve something to break down the door was hit by the explosion from one of the sprinklers as he returned. The impact sent him flying across the room and his back was engulfed in flames. The only thing preventing him from screaming was that he was unconscious before he hit the floor.

Another agent removed his jacket to douse the flames, but it was too late. When he turned the agent's body over, he was shocked to see that the man standing next to him only moments before was now charred beyond recognition. But it wasn't just fire that had done the damage. He had come in direct contact with the acid formed by the combination of Lee's concoction. Only sockets remained where his eyes had been.

Marcie reeled in horror. The flames danced on the water spewing from the ceiling at the front of the room. The ceiling that had concealed the sprinkler heads had been obliterated, replaced by a tangled metal support grid, insulation and shattered pipes. She thought her mind was playing tricks. This can't be happening. It ran counter to all logic and everything she had ever learned in science classes. Water puts fire out, her mind screamed. But it was as if the fire voraciously fattened itself on the water pouring from the ragged pipes that had been the lifeblood of the sprinklers. Anything flammable at the front of the room was now ablaze and dense white smoke filled the air where the explosions had occurred, obscuring where the head table had been.

The fire raged in front of them. Then as suddenly as it began, the water abruptly stopped shooting from the pipes and the flames seemed to be sucked back into the line. Maybe we're going to be okay, Marcie thought. Nathan and Bellamy must have shut off the valve providing water to the sprinkler heads. Agents holding the people back at the front of the crowd rushed forward to douse the flames. In the moments that everything had happened, they hadn't noticed it was water that was fueling the fire. One ran to the kitchen and brought back a pail of water that he dumped onto the blazing head table where some of the chemical had landed. Everything seemed to lift off the floor in macabre slow motion as another explosion rocked the room throwing him backwards.

"No," Marcie yelled. "The water is making the fire worse. Just douse anything that hasn't been touched by the chemicals." Her words were lost in the crowd of anxious, crying people. Fortunately, one of the politicians in the middle of the pack repeated what Marcie had said and others picked up the cry. The agents quickly caught on and started doing as they were told. They watered down everything that had not yet come in contact with the flames.

The agents started coughing and rubbing their eyes as they worked. A thick acrid cloud now hung in the room and was slowly starting to drift towards the large crowd of people huddled at the back.

She could hear above the cries and screams that people were pounding on the doors from the outside. The agents who had been pouring water from the kitchen on the tables and chairs were clutching at their throats and scratching at their eyes. Tobin yelled at people to cover their noses and mouths with anything they could find. Those closest to the back tables grabbed napkins and poured water from glasses and carafes on them to protect themselves. They were heaving, trying to draw a breath. Some had fallen already and the people at the front were pushing back into the crowd, crushing the people behind them, trying to get away from the advancing cloud of dense, white acid fumes. The sharp, penetrating odor worsened as the seconds ticked by.

Marcie, who was at the back of the crowd, not far from the president, could already smell it and her mucous membrane was becoming more and more irritated. Moreover, she could see the largest of the cloud mass inexorably drifting towards the group huddled together. She listened to the frantic pounding on the exit doors.

Her head was spinning and people around her coughed and struggled to breathe.

Time was running out for all of them.

She could only think of one thing.

Please, please get those doors open.

CHAPTER 46

Marcie pulled her dress up and ripped a piece off the bottom. Now was no time for modesty. She covered her nose and mouth with the ragged cloth. There had to be a way out. The people pounding on the outside of the exit doors must be making progress, but would it be too late? She crouched on the floor with her elbows extended, trying to avoid being stepped on by the crush of people. The odor was less intense near the floor. The agents surrounding the president and first lady were trying to calm them, but she saw from her vantage point as she looked up that the president's wife had her hand over her open mouth, her eyes wide in panic. She was hyperventilating, drawing more of the deadly fumes into her lungs.

Marcie tried to slow her own breathing to delay sucking in the thick white vapor and dense smoke as long as she could. She desperately wanted to talk to Nathan. If this was the way her life was going to end, she needed to tell him how much she loved him. The pounding on the doors became more frantic. *Didn't someone have an axe?* She took out her phone.

She leaned back against the wall to try to calm herself. *Wait, what was that?* The wall had budged ever so slightly. Was she hallucinating? Was it wishful thinking? She pressed back against it again and it moved again. Of course. The wall would be a mechanical divider. Ballrooms always have them! That's how hotels and convention centers reconfigure the rooms for the size of the event. The ballroom could probably hold an event of 5,000 people in a different configuration. The room they were in had been walled off to more intimately accommodate the 500 people invited to this event.

Marcie was starting to feel groggy and distant. She sluggishly hit her speed dial for Nathan. She shook her head to clear the spots in front of her eyes. The WiFi must be working now. She could hear the phone ringing. He picked up right away. His words spilled out in a torrent, but the signal was intermittent. The cries and moans around her nearly drowned out his fragmentary conversation. "Marcie . . . Hey, what's . . . on? . . . heard explosions . . . trying to reach you, but couldn't . . . through!" Is everyone okay?" Static roared in her ear. " . . . off the valve. What's happening?"

She struggled to get the words out. "There's no time for that now. Ask Bellamy where the switch is for the partition that separates the ballroom sections. Ask him if it's controlled the same way as the door you're trying to get through. Please hurry." She coughed harshly. Her lungs felt like they were being stabbed by porcupine quills.

Better reception. "Bellamy's right here working on the door. They're trying to get the hinges . . . There's another exit. Oh, they're also working on . . . a minute." His voice faded. There was muffled conversation in the background. "He says it's . . . of the door and it's operated separately." Then, much more clearly, she heard him say, "It's an electric door operated manually by a switch."

Marcie's breath was ragged.

She said weakly, "Where?"

" . . . right side of the door."

She could barely keep her eyes open. She gasped, "Okay . . . see you soon . . . love you."

If Nathan said anything else, it was lost as the phone tumbled from Marcie's weakened grasp. A mass of humanity lay between her and the switch. Some people were already unconscious. She shuddered. Maybe some were dead. Many were retching. Others took shallow, torturous breaths through the material they held to their faces.

Marcie took a deep breath through the torn piece of her dress as she struggled to her feet. The burning sensation in her lungs made her double over in pain. She held her breath as she staggered and stumbled towards the switch. It was slow going. She pushed some people aside and clawed her way over others. She recognized General Rawlings on the floor with his wife draped over him like a rag doll. Both were unconscious—or dead. She couldn't stop to help. Her lungs felt like they were on fire. Her eyes were slits as she tried to focus on the switch that faded in and out of view, obstructed by the image of people weaving in front of her like grain in a summer breeze.

The switch swam in and out of focus as she drew nearer. Her head was pounding. Each shallow breath racked her body with pain. She could taste the putrid air through the cloth of her dress, but she had to keep going. Keep breathing. Her mind was spinning out of control. Someone leaned against the wall directly in front of her, unmoving, his eyes closed, his head lolling to one side.

Marcie reached around him, groping sightlessly for the switch.

Her knees gave way.

Darkness closed in on her as she sensed herself falling into an abyss.

CHAPTER 47

Marcie's eyes fluttered open. She blinked rapidly, but the fog that had settled over her sight remained. She licked her lips, but they were dry and crusty. She needed a drink of water, desperately. Through the haze, she saw Nathan sitting in a chair watching her. Her breathing was labored, and it seemed like someone was planted firmly on her chest. The fresh air she breathed in through tubes in her nose was a welcome relief. The stark walls, humming machines and antiseptic odors immediately told her where she was.

Nathan rose quickly from his chair and sat beside her on the bedside. He took her hand and said quietly, "You're going to be okay. It's over now."

"I'm in the hospital? What's wrong with me?" Nausea forced a path partway up her throat. The raspy voice coming from her lips couldn't be hers. It sounded like the person speaking had been smoking a pack or two of cigarettes every day for her entire life.

Nathan leaned across her and grabbed a water glass from the table. He kissed her forehead before handing it to here. "Sweetheart, you're fine. There's nothing wrong that can't be fixed. The doctors say you'll be here overnight for observation. If they don't find anything, you can go home tomorrow. There's some inflammation in your lungs, but they're giving you medication to open the airways so you can start to breathe normally. Your eyesight will clear over time. You'll just have to bathe them periodically. They said the best treatment for chemical inhalation is pure oxygen into your system, and you're getting lots of that. You'll have some discomfort for a while, but you'll be as good as new soon."

Her words sounded distant and slow to her ears. "Did you catch him?" She struggled to find the word in her hazy mind. "Oh yeah . . . the Ghost?"

"No, there was no sign of him, other than the trap he set up. There's a huge manhunt going on but there aren't many clues. The good news is that you saved a lot of lives in there."

Marcie grimaced as she choked out the words. "*I* did? What did I do? All I remember is trying to get to that switch, but I didn't make it. I was so dizzy. There was someone blocking it. I couldn't get to it."

"You don't remember? You hit the switch that opened the ballroom partition, so everyone could escape! Craig Logan saw you. You were falling, but just as you did, you made a stab at the switch and you triggered it. He said the partition door started to move. Apparently, these doors only move a foot every 10 seconds, so it seemed painfully slow but as soon as the partition wall opened far enough, people started pulling others into the next room. It didn't take all that long to get everybody out, and then Logan closed the door to seal off the room you were in. That's how so many survived. When the Hazmat crew and the paramedics arrived, they broke the exit doors down and we opened the second partition, so we could move people into the next section farthest away from the fumes. Hazmat dealt with the chemicals and the paramedics took over and treated the injured, including you."

Marcie's eyes closed. Exhaustion consumed her. She murmured haltingly, "How many survived? Did the president and first lady . . . ? Her voice trailed off, afraid to utter the words.

"They're fine. They have similar injuries to yours, but I'm sure they're in a much nicer hospital room than this. Craig and Annie Logan are fine, too. Only minor breathing problems. But Marcie, four people didn't make it. They were all secret service agents. General Rawlings and his wife are the most badly injured. Right now, they're in stable but critical condition. Considering everything that happened, if it hadn't been for you realizing there might be another way out, more would've died for sure."

"I don't understand about the Rawlings," Marcie said feebly, feeling weak. "They were at the back of the room. I nearly tripped over them trying to get to the switch."

"Craig said the General ran to the front to try to help the agents and ingested too much of the vapor. Rawlings' wife ran after him to try to convince him there was nothing he could do, and she finally got him to go to the back of the room, but by then they had both taken a lot of fumes into their lungs. Marcie, please, don't worry, they'll be fine."

Marcie's eyes fluttered open momentarily and she wiped away a tear, trying not to touch the tubes in her nose. She said softly, "It's so sad. To think we were all talking only a few minutes before everything blew up. I feel so bad for those agents."

She closed her eyes for a few minutes, gripping Nathan's hand tightly. Soon, they quivered open again. Weak as she was, Marcie wanted answers.

"Nathan, the flames *accelerated* as the water came out. But water should put *out* fire." Her voice was barely audible. "We learned that in grade school, for God's sake, and it's common sense. What happened?"

"The experts at the FBI lab are still analyzing the compound that was used, but apparently there are some chemicals that react violently with water and metal to create a deadly explosion and toxic fumes. The compound itself may not be combustible, but it can set fire to everything flammable that it touches. I suspect that's what happened here. The combination of the chemical, the water and the metal in the pipes and sprinkler heads created the explosions."

"It seemed like the flames were shooting out of the pipes where the sprinkler head had been."

Nathan nodded slightly. "We'll have an answer soon enough. This guy is pretty smart, which makes him extremely dangerous. Maybe he combined it with something to accelerate it." Nathan leaned over to kiss her. "Anyway, sweetheart, you should get some sleep."

"I don't want you to leave."

"I'm not going anywhere. That chair is pretty comfortable, and besides, I like watching you sleep."

Marcie said drowsily, "I have one more question. How come it took you so long to break down the doors?"

"I know it must've seemed like an eternity when you were in there, but it was only minutes. The irony is that the doors are fireproof, so the ballroom can be a safe haven if there's a fire on the outside. They look like they're made of oak or something, but it's a veneer. They're really made from metal. The locking mechanism was to prevent anyone from forcing their way in. I think King Arthur might have used doors like that at one time to protect his castle. No one thought there might be a problem on the *inside* of the door. The hacker who took over the computer system blocked the system to control the door locks and shut off the air conditioner, so the fumes remained trapped in the ballroom. Maybe that's a blessing because everyone in the building could've died. We're just lucky the override to the water pressure system feeding the sprinkler heads is an old-fashioned valve that you have to turn by hand."

She looked at him, her eyes barely open. "What's the matter. You're frowning. Is there something you're not telling me?"

Nathan snorted and smiled. He couldn't keep anything from his wife-to-be. She saw through him every time. "I just wish I hadn't sent you back into that room. I feel guilty about not being there with you. I knew something was going to happen, but I hoped it wouldn't occur as quickly as it did, or that we could have prevented it from happening at all. I will always feel terrible about that. I wish things could've been different."

As Nathan talked, Marcie weakened, struggling now to keep her eyes open. She finally lost the battle and they closed. Her breathing deepened as the medication took over. He knew he would be telling the last part of his story again when she was fully awake. He got up from the bed and bent down to kiss her forehead. He whispered, "I love you, Marcie, and I'm glad you're okay."

He went back to his chair, listening to the quiet hum of the machines pumping air into her lungs and watching the healing medication drip into her system.

He sighed again and closed his eyes.

CHAPTER 48

Yang Lee sat in a chair in a hotel in Shanghai, his head bowed and his shoulders slumped. His lips formed a straight line behind the hands covering his face. He had failed. Somehow, inconceivably, his master plan had failed again. He had checked the news headlines on his cell phone the minute he got off the plane in Shanghai. His plan had worked as it should have—except for one thing. The president had somehow escaped! So had the first lady. Just four people died. *Four.* They were inconsequential, just secret service agents doing their jobs. The American media would tout them as heroes.

How could this happen? He had planned meticulously. It seemed from the breaking news stories that the detonation device had worked as it was supposed to. Had his timing been off? *What had gone wrong?*

The media was calling it a terrorist attack. Some news stories were speculating on whether it could have been a domestic terrorist cell. Or a lone wolf. Now he definitely wouldn't get any credit. His game plan was ruined, his strategy a colossal failure. There were even rumors in the media that China was involved, but the Chinese government vehemently denied it. More than one article even suggested that the president was so polarizing, there would be no end of suspects.

So now what, Lee wondered? If the explosion had worked like it was supposed to, his exploits would have been legendary, added to his unwritten resumé; and he would be more in demand than ever. But now if anyone found out he had failed, and brought suspicion on the Chinese government, his life in China was over. Ji Cheung, had ways of finding out everything and Lee would be linked to the failed events in Florida. Lee thought he should have killed the man in his office when he had the chance. He knew what Cheung was like. Lee didn't think for a moment that Cheung's methods were officially sanctioned by the government. He had his own ways of doing things and he wouldn't want Lee around anymore. It was too risky. Cheung's own reputation would be at stake and that would never do. Lee was even more disposable now, so he had to disappear. A sudden pain shot through his head as if a vise was closing on it.

At the very least, Cheung would get the word out that he had lost his edge. That he was making mistakes. Maybe he was. He would be a pariah in his own country. He would be marginalized by the people who had trusted him. He knew how it worked. It's all about what you have done lately and nothing he had lately done had worked. He would get small jobs maybe, but he did that type of work in his twenties. He was beyond that.

Maybe he could pull off something bigger to rebuild his reputation, but he would have to lay low for a while. Lee decided he would spend a few months in Thailand and take some time to think. He had plenty of money. He would spend a year deciding what his next move should be. Figuring out how he could rebuild his reputation. When he came back, his first priority would be to eliminate Cheung. That would be a pleasure. For now, he would leave his precious tools buried in the forest and retrieve them when he was ready.

But right now, his head pounded.

He decided to call the House of Pearls one last time.

CHAPTER 49

Nathan sat in the office of special agent Charles Walker, Nathan's boss and now the man in charge of investigating the attempted assassination of the president. As they waited for James Welch to arrive, Nathan's spirits lifted when he thought about Marcie's release from the hospital. The news was good. Her doctor confirmed there was no hint of pneumonia in her lungs from the infection. She was eager to leave the hospital, and if she'd been able to breathe normally, she would undoubtedly have skipped down the corridor to the exit. Nathan thought her relief and exhilaration at being released might have been enhanced by the strong prescription medications she had been ordered to take. Her breathing was improving, but her lungs needed to heal completely. Her eyesight was slowly clearing, but she still couldn't see without squinting, and she would need to wear sunglasses for awhile. At home, she would continue to need oxygen until everything was back to normal.

Nathan chuckled, aware of the biggest obstacle facing Marcie in her recovery. She had been ordered to rest quietly for a few days. That would be a challenge, but one that she grudgingly accepted. He resolved to himself to check up on her even more than he normally did.

Welch rushed into the office in a whirl. His attire was nearly the same as the first day Nathan had met him—baseball cap, golf shirt, slacks and running shoes. Only the brand name on the hat and the color of the shirt and slacks had changed. Red hair poured out the bottom and sides of his hat as it had the first day.

"Glad you could join us, Welchie," Walker said sarcastically.

"Sorry, I was just following up on another lead. Things are happening quickly. The media is going wild, of course, and there's all kinds of conspiracy theories being floated. Some of the coverage is even accurate, if you can believe that."

Nathan leaned forward with his elbows on the arm of the chair and his hands clasped as the special agent asked Welch to elaborate on the new lead.

"It seems like we've been one step behind this guy all the way along, but we think we have a name now. The guys in the computer lab in Kentucky have been doing some great work in tracing the hacking into Annie Logan's computer. They followed it back through the various servers and they put priority on it for obvious reasons. Without going into a lot of technical mumbo jumbo that no one wants to hear, there's a certain style to the Logan hack that's relatively uncommon. In fact, so far, it's only been seen once before."

Nathan and Walker listened expectantly as Welch continued. "The other time was the hack of the electronics firm in Canada. Our team followed up with the Royal Canadian Mounted Police and they mentioned an outstanding warrant that's on file for a Chinese guy whose name I can't pronounce, but it doesn't matter right now. They had a grainy picture of the guy, and it looked vaguely like the drawing we had from the apartment. Our guy Danny Chin in Shanghai showed it around to the tenants, and they thought it could be the same person. That was enough to follow up on.

"Now, here's where it gets interesting. When the Chinese Special Forces were going over the apartment in Shanghai, the place had been wiped completely clean. It was like the guy in the apartment didn't have any fingerprints. There were smudges, though, so it's not like he wore gloves. Unless the person had a cleaner in there wiping down everything, their best guess was that he had his prints surgically removed or perhaps skin grafted on at some time. That's serious stuff. If that's true, then our guy does some heavy-duty criminal activity for a living. Oh, and they did find another thing that they followed up on. There was a toothpick lodged behind a garbage can. They thought it could've been possible that our ghost tossed it in the garbage and missed."

Harris and Walker sat quietly as the story unfolded, but Nathan could feel an all-too-familiar buzz running through him. They were closing in! It was a feeling he always got when the pieces started to come together. It was a combination of excitement and caution, but the scales always tipped more heavily to the side of exhilaration. He anticipated what was coming next. "Were they able to find any DNA on the toothpick?"

"They did indeed, my friend. The agents in China were able to trace the DNA on the toothpick to the United Kingdom. It seems that the owner of the toothpick, or at least the person who stuck it in his mouth, graduated with degrees in computer engineering and chemical engineering from Cambridge. Sounds like someone who could hack into a computer and rig a water sprinkler so that it would go off like fireworks on the Fourth of July, don't you think? When our agents talked to the professors at Cambridge who had contact with him, they said he was a loner who didn't associate with anyone. They also said his IQ was through the roof. When they saw the pictures, they confirmed that they thought he was the same man. They provided his college photograph."

Walker asked, "Do we know if this genius traveled to the U.S. recently?"

"We don't know that for sure yet, but I suggest we put as many resources on it as we can muster. A Customs agent at the airport in Chicago thinks he may have cleared the man when he saw the photo supplied by Cambridge University that we circulated and compared it to the drawing we had. He said the guy was distinctive because he wore a snazzy hat. If we can make that link, we can start extradition proceedings when we find him and bring him here to the States to crucify his ass."

Nathan had been lost in thought while the discussion had been taking place. He expressed his nagging concern. "Had he committed a crime in the U.K.? I mean, how come his DNA was on file there?"

"Well, it seems our boy liked the occasional drink when he attended university. According to some of his former classmates, that's the only way he could bring himself to socialize. He had a little too much one night and got arrested for drunk driving and refusing to take a breathalyzer. That's what's known as a "recordable offense" in the U.K. and he had to serve a few days in the tank, so they required him to open his mouth for the swab. If we can find him, the genius is going to be brought down by a toothpick and a few too many drinks." Welch chuckled to himself. "Funny, isn't it?"

Charles Walker said, "Let's put everyone we have available on finding out if he was in the U.S. during the time of the attempted assassination. I'll talk to Danny Chin in China and get him to make sure the Chinese Special Forces are working on locating this guy. The Chinese government has agreed to let us send agents to China to assist in the search. Believe it or not, they're bending over backwards to help us find the perp. Apparently, they want to negotiate with our government to resolve the trade dispute and they think that by cooperating, it may help their case in Washington. I told them that was above my pay grade.

"Now, Nathan, we've got this, so I think you should go home and take care of that soon-to-be wife of yours. According to the invitation I got, you have a wedding pretty soon in your future."

Nathan rose from his chair and thanked Walker. The special agent in charge was right. He did want to go home. As he pushed his chair to get up to leave, he said to Welch, "Great job, James. Hopefully this can all be tied together, and the Ghost can be brought to justice."

Welch shook Nathan's hand and as he did so, he added, "There's one last bit of information. Remember I said that the person in the RCMP's file had a name that was unpronounceable? It could be a pseudonym. The people who knew him at Cambridge were able to put a name to the picture, and the man we're looking for now has a much easier name to pronounce."

He had the agents' undivided attention.

"His name is Yang Lee."

CHAPTER 50

Lee had showered, put on the hotel bath robe and sat at the desk speaking into his cell phone. He was making arrangements with an airline to leave for Thailand in the morning. He would travel under a different pseudonym and buy whatever he needed when he got there. It was essential that he disappear as quickly as possible. While he showered, he had run through the scenarios in his head. He couldn't figure out any flaws in his plan unless it was the van. Maybe the hotel security manager was sharper than he had given him credit for and had figured out that there was a problem since the van had no logo. But why would the manager have left him alone in the ballroom if that was the case?

His headache had increased in intensity. He squinted and rubbed his forehead as he waited for the airline agent to come back on the phone with a confirmation. The escort from the House of Pearls should be arriving at any moment. He shook his head. The more he thought, the worse his head throbbed. He knew the FBI was good at what they did, and they must've discovered something. If they traced him to China, the local authorities would be working at finding him, too.

"C'mon," he said impatiently to the music playing on the phone. He wanted to hurl the phone against the wall and smash it into a million pieces. *Why do they make us suffer through this annoying music? Is it supposed to be soothing? It's driving me* CRAZY. Finally, the agent came back on the line with a cheery, "Okay, we have you booked onto a flight leaving tomorrow at 7 a.m. as requested."

A light tap at the door interrupted the conversation. He got up from his chair as he finalized arrangements for the flight. A look through the peephole confirmed it was a woman on the other side of the door in a short, tight dress accentuating her slim figure. She was not tall and wore a large floppy hat that hid her features, but the House of Pearls had never disappointed him. The mystery added to the excitement. The pounding in his head was subsiding already.

He opened the door with his free hand as he held the phone firmly to his ear with the other. He couldn't see her face clearly, but the woman appeared to be stunning. Blond curls peeked out from beneath her hat. Dyed or a wig? It didn't matter. She carried a small clutch purse and her arms were covered in long white gloves. The combination of the gloves, hat and her coyness gave her an air of mystery that excited him.

As she brushed past him and entered the room, she looked up briefly. A feeling of familiarity shot through him with the fleeting glimpse of her face. Lee's head cocked to one side as he looked at her, but she cast her head down again shyly as he impatiently dealt with the clerk on the phone. He closed and locked the door. *I like this*. This is a great act, he thought. *She's pretending to be shy and mysterious. This is really going to be special.* He said into the phone, "Are we done? Is the reservation set? I have things to do."

The woman gestured in the direction of the bathroom and he signaled with his free hand for her to go ahead while he tried to conclude with the annoying airline agent on the phone. He watched her hips sway as she walked. Her short skirt exposed plenty of thigh. He couldn't wait. He clicked off the light on the desk and the room fell into darkness. Any thoughts of mistakes he might have made were gone. This was the only time he felt comfortable around people. There was no relationship involved. No emotion. It was anonymous. There were no requirements of him. He didn't even have to talk. He clicked the key on the phone to disconnect, set it on the bedside table and climbed on the bed to wait. He sat upright on the pillow. He tried to rub the remnants of the headache above his left eye away, but it didn't work. Oh well, that's what this woman is here for. She was in for a rough time. His pent-up frustration would be taken out on her.

The bathroom door opened, and she emerged, framed in the faint glow of the light she had left on. He expected her to be naked, or at least nearly so, but she came out fully clothed. She even wore the hat and gloves. She held a small hand towel in her left hand. Her right hand was closed in a fist.

Lee thought it odd she wore the gloves and hat, but it must be part of the mystery act she had going on. Why the towel? Maybe she was going to pull everything off in a slow, exotic striptease.

She walked slowly towards the bed, pulling a chair from the desk with her as she went. She set the chair beside the bed, sat down and crossed her legs. She laid the towel on the arm of the chair and peeked from under the hat at Lee, her face betraying no emotion.

Lee leaned forward, breathing deeply in anticipation.

She slowly removed the hat, turning her face aside as she did so.

Lee's headache was forgotten. He licked his lips, which had become dry as he hadn't realized he was breathing through his mouth.

Then she did a strange thing. She removed the wig and shook her dark hair out. She looked directly at Lee.

The open door of the bathroom afforded just enough light. He slumped back against the pillow as a high voltage shock wave charged up his spine.

It can't be. My eyes must be deceiving me.

He didn't realize he was holding his breath. He exhaled slowly, trying to slow his suddenly accelerated heartbeat.

"YOU? But I thought . . . "

Lian Lu cut him off. "You thought I was dead? You were badly mistaken, Yang Lee. I'm very much alive and I've been waiting a long time for this."

Lee's stomach churned, and he winced as the throb in his head resurfaced with a vengeance. His face revealed a contradiction of shock and suspicion. He couldn't quite believe what he was seeing, but he was starting to realize he must have made still another careless mistake. He thought back to the night in Lu's hotel room. He had been commissioned to kill her and he had spread enough poison on her keyboard to bring down an elephant.

Lu continued. "I've spent days and nights watching your every move. I knew you used the services of the House of Pearls. I paid them a lot of money to double their profits the next time you called so that I could replace whoever they would've sent. I thought of following you to the United States, but that would've been too complicated. I know you made an attempt on the president's life." She laughed very softly. "It looks like you failed at that, too."

Lee put his hand to his head. A vein pulsed. He had to think. He didn't know what Lu planned to do, but he had to get close enough to get his hands around her throat. He had never actually killed anyone with his hands before, but he knew he could. He had fought the military man in Cheung's office and come out the victor because the element of surprise had been on his side. The man never thought Lee would fight back. He had the same thing going for him with Lian Lu. He would catch her by surprise and he would make sure he did the job this time. He edged closer to the edge of the bed. He just needed the right moment.

Lu sat unmoving on the chair. Her voice was monotone, as if she read from a script. Her hands remained by her sides. "I had a reason for meeting you and being with you. You thought I actually liked you, but someone very dear to me asked me to watch you. He always told me to keep my enemies close. He told me to be very careful, that you were a dangerous man. That's why I got closer to you. While you were trying to seduce me, I was also seducing you to get to know you better and determine your weaknesses. To understand you. I knew there were people who wanted me dead, and it just happened to be you they asked to do it. I saw right through you, Mr. Lee. You are emotionless, unable to feel anything. I knew it was all an act you were performing for me. Then you tried to kill me in my room. It's amazing what they can do with electronics these days as you of all people should know. That's what saved me."

Lee could feel the heat rising up his neck. This woman had the audacity to sit in a chair in his room and ridicule him. But he wanted her to become more comfortable. He shifted slightly as he spoke. "I guess I was careless, but why would I try to kill you? I enjoyed our time together."

"There are lots of people who want me dead and any one of them could've hired you. I'd like to know but I doubt that you're going to tell me. I could torture you, I suppose, but I don't have time for that." Her lips turned up for the first time, curling slightly in a sneer. "I have defended some members of the Triad, but that may have upset other gangs enough that they would want to get rid of me. It could've been some of them who hired you. I'm not well liked for supporting the continued autonomy of Hong Kong. There'll always be someone, because of the work I do and my beliefs. But as for you trying to kill me, the charger plugged into the wall by the desk in the room had a tiny camera in it. After you left, I downloaded the video to my phone and there you were, spreading poison on my keyboard. Very clever, but not clever enough." She goaded more. "Probably would've worked if I hadn't been one step ahead of you. You failed again, Yang Lee. Needless to say, that laptop has been safely destroyed."

She stopped for a moment, then turned straight toward him. Speaking the words flatly and slowly as if for emphasis, Lian Lu taunted him one last time. "You know your biggest mistake, Lee? You let self-importance get in the way of work. You lost track of your goal. You were good at what you did, but you let ego get in the way."

Lee's temples pounded. Each time she mocked him, it was a dart to the heart. He tried not to betray his rage. He didn't want her getting to him. "Are you going to turn me in?" He propped one leg on the bed to give him leverage. He wanted her to relax enough that he could launch himself off the bed, get his hands around her throat, and squeeze the life out of her. This time, there would be no mistake. His muscles were coiled like a sprinter in the starting blocks.

"That depends on you. Are you going to admit to your crimes? Trying to kill the president of the United States? Trying to murder me?"

Now!

He launched himself off the bed and straight at her. He intended to knock her off her chair and strangle her, but she was ready. At the same instant he jumped off the bed, she leapt to her feet from the chair. Too late, Lee realized what she was doing. She had been goading him into making a move and she was prepared to act when he did. She had no intention of turning him in. She grabbed the towel with her left hand and put it to her face. She had quickly turned away from Lee's advancing body that had been launched like a missile. She pointed something at Lee that she had been holding in her closed fist. It was a small container that looked like eyeglass cleaner. With the strike of a snake, she squirted its contents directly into his face.

The effect was immediate. Lee's momentum carried him to the floor with a dull thud that probably startled the people below. He quickly straightened to his knees, clutching at his eyes. He somehow stood upright and staggered around the room, knocking over a lamp before falling to the floor again. Lu frowned slightly, concerned about the noise. "Don't worry, it will be quick, Lee. It's a nerve agent. Paralysis will come soon and then you will die. I believe you know how it works. From what I understand, you have used something similar on others. Now you will know what it feels like to be facing nearly instant death."

She walked to the bathroom to retrieve the floppy hat and put the wig back on. She wrapped the spritzer bottle in the cloth and put it in her purse, and after carefully washing her hands and wiping down the sink, she returned and bent over Lee as the promised paralysis set in. She stared into his blistered face and damaged eyes.

"I hope you can still hear me. I have to leave now, Yang Lee, but I go knowing you won't hurt anyone else."

She pulled the floppy hat down over her eyes. She walked around the bed and retrieved Lee's cell phone. She would dispose of it later.

She unlocked the door and turned the knob to exit into the night.

CHAPTER 51

Nathan and Marcie were just sitting down to dinner when the secure landline in the office rang. He had been away from the FBI for a few days to stay with Marcie while she recuperated. With the wedding just days away, as he suspected, his biggest challenge was preventing her from doing too much. They'd taken time to watch movies, enjoy their balcony overlooking the ocean and listen to some music, mostly of Marcie's choosing.

Nathan had managed to put most of his work out of his mind, although his thoughts still drifted back to the man known as Yang Lee. He knew that the FBI, in conjunction with other agencies and the Chinese, were diligently and relentlessly hunting the man down and hopefully, it was only a matter of time. He hoped that Lee couldn't do any more damage before they found him. The man was evil, dangerous and from everything the Chinese police had turned up, a complete sociopath, which made him doubly lethal. But he would be hard to track, since his motives seemed unpredictable and his desire for revenge was strong.

Nathan thought about just ignoring the ringing phone, but Marcie motioned with her chin for him to go and pick up the call. He recognized the number as belonging to James Welch. He picked up the phone to answer.

"Welchie, how are you?"

"Fine, thanks. I forgot to mention I got your invitation to the wedding. Thanks for thinking of me, but I'm golfing that day, so I can't make it."

"Golfing?? *Golfing*? You golf every day of the week! I thought you didn't go on Saturdays. Sounds like a feeble excuse to me."

"Yeah, actually, it is. I'm just kidding. Of course I'll be attending. I'm even going to send the RSVP today. Thanks for inviting me. I hope the food's good."

Nathan laughed. "Nice. I'm happy you're coming. Listen, can I call you back? We're just about to have dinner."

"Okay, sure. I was about to tell you how the Yang Lee case ended, but that can wait."

Nathan gripped the phone, riveted by what he was hearing. "What? *Ended*? Are you sure? What do you mean *ended*? Did we catch him? Can I put you on speaker so Marcie can hear this, too?" Nathan's heart was racing in anticipation and excitement.

"Marcie can hear it," Welch answered. "I'm sure she won't be blabbing to the newspapers about it. Charles Walker is tied up, but he asked me to give you a call to bring you up to speed. A lot's happened since you've been off the case just hanging around at home."

Nathan called to Marcie to come into the office and tapped the speaker button. Welch's voice echoed around the room. "Marcie, how are you doing? You must be excited about the wedding."

"I'm feeling much better, thanks James. Yes, we're definitely looking forward to the wedding."

"Great, I'm looking forward to being there. By the way, General Rawlings and his wife are both coming along well." Before either Marcie or Nathan had a chance to respond, the computer expert continued. "Now, you're both going to be interested in this. First, the man who tampered with the water sprinkler system in the convention center was definitely Yang Lee." Nathan and Marcie could hear him rustling through notes. "As you know, we got pictures of him from his university days from the school he went to. Homeland Security circulated them to the customs staff at all the airports and a few came forward to identify him from their surveillance video. He was traveling under an alias as Ches Wong. His flight came through Washington from Shanghai and on the way back, it went through Chicago. The dates line up perfectly with the assassination attempt.

"The trail went cold for a few days in the U.S. We don't know where he stayed, but it picks up again, as you know, on the security cameras at the convention center. The head of security there is beating himself up for not being more diligent. I guess when people start trying to lay blame, the guy could be in some trouble, but I'm not sure I wouldn't have reacted the same way he did. Lee showed his credentials, it was three weeks until the presidential visit and everything seemed legit. I think I would vouch for the poor guy."

Nathan said, "I would too." He was conscientious—and very upset when everything happened. He was a professional, though. Once we knew what was going on, he immediately took me to the shut off valve for the water to the sprinkler system and took care of it. Without that, it would've been much worse. By the way, why didn't you tell me this when you found out?"

"You've got a lovely injured fiancée to look after, and a wedding to attend. You need to focus, man." Welch laughed. "Besides, this is all recent news."

"Okay, let's hear the rest of it. Then what? Did they catch him?"

Nathan shook his head slightly in exasperation and made a rolling sign with his hand to Marcie, quietly urging the man on the phone to get to the point. Welch continued his story, maddeningly drawing it out. "In a manner of speaking. The homicide division in one of the districts in Shanghai got a call from a hotel manager about a dead body that a maid stumbled across when she went in to clean the room. Besides being dead, the person wasn't in great shape. He had blisters all over his face and his eyes were burned. Sound familiar?"

Marcie shuddered at the reminder of the people trapped in the room and especially the agents who had been hit directly by the chemical.

"They did an official autopsy, and it appeared the man suffocated from some toxic chemical. According to our guy Danny Chin, who was overseeing everything, it would've been a horrible death.

"Oh, and they discovered an interesting little compartment in the lining of his suitcase near the frame. It would be perfect for smuggling small things, like say, containers of chemicals.

"The other thing they discovered is that the man had skin grafts on his fingertips, which would effectively wipe out any possibility of leaving prints. From the marks on his feet, it looks like that's where the skin came from. Remember, the investigators in China thought that the man who was apparently in that apartment where they found all the computers might not have had any fingerprints?"

Nathan couldn't wait. "Was it Lee?"

"You bet," chortled Welch on the other end. "It definitely was Lee. The DNA from the body matches the person who went to Cambridge and the toothpick in the apartment they raided."

"But that only proves he was in the apartment and that he's got an education."

"No, my perceptive friend. You will recall that the supposed repair guy who was going to repair the sprinkler system stumbled up the steps on his way into the convention center. Our computer forensics team were able to get enough from the screen capture of the image to run facial recognition on his jaw line. The convention center also has a camera in the ballroom. Besides, Bellamy was pretty sure it was him from the photos we had. The video clearly shows Lee replacing the sprinkler heads.

"The security cameras in Shanghai tracked Lee going out of town the day before he boarded the plane. He carried a box into the forest when the cameras lost him. Then he returned from the forest without the box. Danny said the special forces were going in with tracking dogs to try to find out what he was carrying. Could be interesting. He must've buried it somewhere he thought no one would ever find it. Also, they've found an apartment with a pseudonym on the lease. It appears to be where he lived. They're checking the DNA. He had a nice penthouse suite there."

A thin smile grew across Nathan's face and he winked at Marcie. "Wow, that's great work. I guess it's beyond a doubt then. But who killed him? Are there any leads? Or did he poison himself somehow?"

"The all-seeing security camera at the hotel has video of a woman in a floppy hat and wearing long white gloves entering and leaving the room. Danny said she could've been a high-class lady of the evening by the way she was dressed. She left the room about fifteen minutes after she arrived. There were no fingerprints in the room. I mean none. I guess she left her gloves on the whole time she was in there. Then they thought they could maybe glean some information from his cell phone. Like maybe he had a date or something. But guess what!? No cell phone. Nada.

"There are about 700 million women in China, some of whom might've had a reason to dispatch Mr. Lee and others who might've been paid to do it. The local police will make an effort to find the woman, but I'm not convinced they'll put much manpower on it. I'm getting the sense the Chinese government and police force are treating it like the woman did everyone a public service."

Nathan asked, "You remember what started this, right? Our

beloved president decided to sign that executive order without any dialogue with the Chinese. Maybe this will convince him to use a more diplomatic approach and get experts on his team involved next time. Otherwise, we could be fighting a few more of these fires—literally."

Welch shrugged on his end of the conversation. "Apparently, President Hughes wants to negotiate with the Chinese now, but they're not so keen. Oh, something else, our CIA friends tell us some Vice President of something or other named Cheung was booted from the Politburo. That's pretty rare, and the timing is quite the coincidence. I know how you like coincidences. Anyway, I leave the politics to the geniuses in Washington. Our job is to clean up the mess that the geniuses create. Oh, and to vote at the next opportunity."

Nathan took a deep breath. "That's for sure. Well, at least we don't have to worry about Mr. Yang Lee anymore. Thank you for letting me know, James."

"No problem, my friend. Count this as my wedding present."

CHAPTER 52

The dazzling early morning sun in Shanghai broke through the clouds as a business magazine writer wrapped up an interview in the office of the new CEO and owner of Hu Electronics. The reporter stared thoughtfully at the gorgeous executive as she closed the blind. A cellular phone sat on the desk with the voice recording app open to capture the interview.

"I just have a couple of more questions," he said as she sat down. The intensity of her eyes bore into him like a welder's torch. *I have to stay professional*, he thought as he checked his notes.

"Now that America has imposed their huge tariffs on electronics, what will you do to make sure your company survives?"

"We've already started negotiating with new trading partners. We know that this president's term will not last forever and a new one will come in with more moderate ideas. Until then, we will go elsewhere. When America wishes to reopen trade negotiations, we will be on much firmer ground because we will have established new and different trading relations. The Americans will find negotiations will not be so easy. My grandfather did a wonderful job of placing the company strategically so that it could overcome any obstacles thrown in front of it."

"Will you continue your crusade to keep Hong Kong free from going back under the rule of China now that you've assumed ownership of Hu Electronics?"

"Of course. It's important that Hong Kong retain its democratic rights. I will continue to pressure the Chinese government. I've relocated to Shanghai, but my heart will always be with a democratic Hong Kong."

"What about your legal career? Will you have time to continue it as well as assume the role of CEO here?"

The woman smiled thoughtfully. "My legal career is on hold for now. We'll see what happens in the future."

"One final question. Are you aware of anything new with regards to the death of your grandfather, Bai Hu? Was the cause of death ever determined? Our readers would be interested in knowing."

The woman hesitated for a very long moment before answering. Then, "The police decided my grandfather died of a heart attack while smoking one of his favorite cigars. That's not to imply there was a connection, of course. He was merely enjoying one of his guilty pleasures when it happened. I'm sure he died happy. He lived a long and successful life and built a prosperous business from nothing. I'm here because of him and everything he taught me."

Her mind drifted as she thought of the nerve agent she had acquired from the member of the Triad whose acquittal she had won, and what it had done to Yang Lee. She only prayed her grandfather had not suffered the way Lee had.

She was brought back to the present by one last question from the reporter.

"Just for the record, could you please spell your name?"

"Certainly. My name is spelled L-i-a-n L-u.

〈〈〈 〉〉〉

On the opposite side of the world, a dazzling sun beat down on Tampa from a cloudless sky. It was a gorgeous day, the frosting on the cake for the beaming couple. The wedding day had finally arrived and the ceremony itself was quickly over. Marcie was stunning in a simple floor-length sleeveless white dress. After the ceremony, friends and family clapped as the newly married couple walked hand-in-hand through a flower laden archway into the reception area. They laughingly stopped and posed for the official photographer, while cell phones poked into the air to capture personal photos.

They received ecstatic hugs, congratulatory kisses and warm handshakes from their friends and family who wouldn't have missed being there for them on their special day.

There was great excitement among the women who had gathered at the party at Sami's house in what now seemed like ages ago. So much had transpired since that time. They temporarily abandoned their spouses so they could have a picture taken with the bride.

Marcie sat with Sami Seaforth and Carole Brouse on either side. Linda Mitchell, Annie Logan and Claire Hanright stood behind. They beamed at the camera at first, and then they all made exaggerated faces for the next shot. As the women went back to their husbands, Annie stopped Marcie by throwing her arms around her in a hug that nearly crushed her ribs.

When she let go, Annie said, "Marcie, I just wanted to thank you again for everything you did for me. If you hadn't been there, I don't know what I would've done, and I'm so happy for you and Nathan. You deserve a long and happy life together."

"Thank you, Annie. We just did what anyone would do under the circumstances." Marcie looked into Annie's eyes and noticed how clear they were. Her makeup was applied perfectly and the bright yellow dress she wore shimmered in the glow of the ballroom lights, enhancing her new radiant image. She looked healthier than Marcie had ever seen her, and she told her. "You look great, Annie. I'm happy for you, too."

A flush crept across Annie's cheeks. She said, "You don't need to hear this now, but I'm excited that I haven't had a drink for quite a while. I've been going regularly for counseling and it's helping so much. A big part of it is having Craig home. He comes to the meetings with me. He's been so supportive."

"Well, I don't suppose the president was too happy when Craig told him to shove his job, but I'm glad he did. Things seem to be working out perfectly for the two of you."

"They are, Marcie. Craig had told me he had a surprise for me and it was that he wanted me to move to Washington. It turned out even better now that he's back here. He said he made up his mind after a meeting with the president. He realized he was vulnerable and couldn't support the president's policies." A hearty laugh punctuated her next statement. "I don't know who's going to control the president now, but Craig is so much more relaxed. He's back to his old self. Now, you have lots of people to see. We'll have you over for a barbecue when you get back from Africa."

Marcie embraced Annie and said, "Sounds like a plan, my friend. Dance up a storm tonight. I know I will."

ABOUT THE AUTHOR

Barry Finlay is the award-winning author of the inspirational travel adventure, *Kilimanjaro and Beyond – A Life-Changing Journey* (with his son Chris), Amazon bestselling travel memoir, *I Guess We Missed The Boat* and two award-winning thrillers, *The Vanishing Wife* and *A Perilous Question*. Barry was featured in the 2012-13 Authors Show's edition of "50 Great Writers You Should Be Reading." He is a recipient of the Queen Elizabeth Diamond Jubilee medal for his fundraising efforts to help kids in Tanzania, Africa. Barry lives with his wife Evelyn in Ottawa, Canada.

Contact Barry Finlay:

Author Website: **www.barry-finlay.com**

Fundraising website: **www.keeponclimbing.com**

Facebook Page: **https://www.facebook.com/AuthorBarryFinlay**

Twitter: **https://twitter.com/Karver2**

Thank you for reading *Remote Access*.
If you like what you read, please consider leaving a review at your favorite online book retailer.

Note to Book Clubs: A study guide is available for *Remote Access* at **www.barry-finlay.com**.

www.ingramcontent.com/pod-product-compliance
Lightning Source LLC
Chambersburg PA
CBHW031230120726
47905CB00002B/541